MICHAEL BRAY'S

FUNHOUSE

Cover by Stu Smith at Graviton Creations
www.gravitoncreations.tumblr.com

Edited by Sylvia Kerslake
www.writaz.com
&
Garrett Cook
www.chainsawnoir.wordpress.com

MR GHOUL'S QUAINT LITTLE GHOST TRAIN

The funfair had appeared overnight, and without warning. Potter's Field had gone from an empty expanse of green, to a dizzying kaleidoscope of colour, as rides were erected and stalls set up. Alfie Jones stared out of the window with twelve year old enthusiasm at the construction and thought that perhaps this particular Saturday wouldn't be quite as boring as he had anticipated. He ran downstairs to the kitchen.

"Can we go to the funfair today?" He asked as he sat down and took a sip of his orange juice.

"Funfair?" Alfie's dad said as he peered over his paper.

"Didn't you see it?" Said Alfie's mother as she put the bowl down in front of Alfie.

"I can't say I did."

"They're set up on Potter's Field dad," Alfie said excitedly. "Can we go?"

Alfie's mother and father shared a look, and then his mother gave the good news.

"I don't see why not. Eat your breakfast and get dressed, and we'll go over and take a look."

"Yes!" Alfie said and began to shovel his cereal into his mouth, spilling milk onto his chin.

"Slow down, you'll make yourself sick."

"Sorry," Alfie said, doing as he was told to ensure he stayed in his parent's good books.

"Would it be okay if I asked Tommy if he wanted to come?"

"Why not, that boy spends as much time here as in his own home anyway." Alfie's father said as he winked at his son.

"Thanks, dad."

"Don't get too excited yet, make sure Tommy asks his mother if he has permission first."

"I will."

Alfie ate the rest of his breakfast as fast as he dared without risking getting into trouble, then dressed and waited for his mother and father to hurry up and get ready. Tommy's mother had said it was okay for him to go, and he arrived around thirty minutes later.

He and Alfie had been friends for three years. Tommy was 14 and already tall for his age. He stood awkwardly and waited for Alfie and his parents to get ready, and then the four of them headed off to the fair.

They were early, but the funfair was already filling up with curious people. The air was thick with the smell of hotdogs and burgers. The foursome stood at the entrance, looking at the array of rides and stalls.

"Can Tommy and I go and explore?"

"Go ahead, but be careful. And don't leave the fairground without us." Alfie's father said.

"Thanks, dad."

The two boys walked away, looking at the rides and soon disappeared into the growing crowd.

Alfie's mother linked arms with her husband and rested her head on his shoulder.

"Well Dean, it looks like it's just you and me."

"Yeah, it does." He replied. He was looking around him at the stalls and rides.

"What's wrong?"

"I don't know, something seems odd about this place."

"Funfairs are odd by design honey, that's why kids love them."

"No, I don't mean that, I… I don't know."

"Are you okay?" She asked him as a mother carrying a screaming toddler walked past them.

"I'm fine Sally, really. I think I just have an issue with places like this that's all. I always found them creepy."

She grinned at him and dragged him by the arm.

"Come on, I'll let you win me a prize or two then you might come around."

He grinned and dismissed whatever discomfort was there. They walked, arm in arm. The stalls were old, decorated in garish reds and blues, with dancing strip lights around the edges. There was a test your strength machine, a towering red structure with a bell on top. The couple watched as an overweight man in baggy shorts tried his luck, but came nowhere close to making the bell ring.

"Wow, I haven't seen one of those things in years," Dean said as he watched someone else try their luck.

"Most places aren't as traditional as this. They have arcades and thrill rides. This seems more of an old school funfair."

Dean nodded. His wife had hit the nail right on the head. Although it was two thousand and thirteen, this place looked like it had arrived straight out of the fifties. He looked around at the other families, who seemed to be having fun regardless. He convinced himself he was being stupid, and that, in fact, it stood to reason that if the funfair was family run, it would still have its original fittings and rides. The pair walked on, and Dean tried as best he could to relax.

For the next half hour, they ate ice cream, talked and admired the old rides and attractions. Dean had won a huge, fluffy toy rabbit on the hook-a-duck for Sally, and had already forgotten his discomfort. They had snaked their way around the attractions and were about to try their luck on the duck shooting stall when the two boys raced towards them.

"Dad, Dad!" Alfie yelled as he dived around the families who were in his path.

A surge of panic raced through Dean, and he forgot all about fairground rides and turned to his son.

"What is it? What's wrong?" He asked.

A cloud of uncertainty passed over his son's face.

"Nothing, I just wanted to ask if we could go on the ghost train."

Dean relaxed, and hoped that nobody had noticed his overreaction, although a quick glance towards Sally told him otherwise.

"Of course." He said, trying to relax. "Go right ahead."

"We can't the man in charge said it's too scary for kids. Adults have to go with them."

"He was probably pulling your leg, Alfie," Sally said as she tucked the toy rabbit under her arm. "It's just to get you worked up enough to want to go on."

"No, he's serious. He said it's the best and scariest ghost train in the world. You should see it."

"Okay. Relax." Dean said, trying to show that his earlier discomfort had gone, even if it hadn't. "Let's go over and take a look at this world's scariest ghost train."

"Thanks, Dad," Alfie said, and then led the way.

The ghost train was at the very back of the Funfair and was quite spectacular. It was fronted with ornate gold angelic figures with demonic faces scowling at the customers from above. The structure itself was large and adorned with large red flashing letters which read. *Mr Ghoul's Terror Train*. The train seemed to be a three car affair, and the entrance to the ride itself was a ghastly clown face with purple hair and one pupil missing. It was quite disturbing, and it appeared that the train entered the ride through the clown's open mouth, which was part grin, part laugh, part scream. As the group approached, they were greeted by a tall, thin man dressed in full ringmaster outfit. His eyes were wide and ringed with dark makeup, and his white hair stood to attention as he interacted with the people as they passed.

"Good day folks." He said as the four came to a halt. "I'm Mr Ghoul, and this is the world's most terrifying experience. See your worst fears come to life, experience your most private terrors up close and personal. Only here, on Mr Ghoul's horror train!" He threw his arm behind him, as he flashed a wide-eyed grin.

"How much is it?" Dean asked flatly, taking an unconscious step back from the colorful host.

"Oh, no charge sir." The grinning host said. "It's just a case of holding your nerve long enough to say yes!"

"Okay. Then I say yes. Go ahead, boys."

The boys started to go forward when Mr Ghoul stopped them. "Oh no! Not alone, it's too terrifying without an adult."

"Come on," Dean said under his breath. "Give me a break here. Let the kids on the ride. I'm sure a few plastic dummies and glow in the dark sheets won't give them too many restless nights."

Mr Ghoul's smile faltered, and Dean thought he saw a flicker of rage bubbling below the surface.

"I'm sorry mister, all children must be accompanied by at least one adult."

"Fine." Dean snapped. "I'll go with them."

They set off towards the train, and Mr Ghoul again held up a restraining arm.

"Ahh, I don't think you understand sir. Mr Ghoul requires each child to be accompanied by an adult." As he said it he slid his eyes towards Dean's wife. "Nice rabbit." He said with a wink.

"Look, just forget it." Dean snapped, and was about to walk away when Tommy spoke up.

"It's okay, Mr. Jones, I don't mind waiting out here."

"Tommy, come on!" Alfie whined, but Dean saw in the boy's face that he was spooked, and didn't want to embarrass him anymore.

"Alfie, if he doesn't want to, he doesn't have to. Come on, I'll go on with you."

Alfie glared at his friend, who in turn shifted and looked at the ground.

"So, it's just the two of you then?" Mr Ghoul said with his usual wide grin.

"Yeah, just us," Alfie said, shooting his friend another pained look at his apparent betrayal.

"Okay then." Mr Ghoul said, clapping his hands together. "Please sign the disclaimer, and then proceed to the first train car."

"Disclaimer?" Dean said with a snort, finding the entire process, and the larger than life, Mr Ghoul, ever more irritating. Unperturbed, Mr Ghoul pulled a rolled sheet of paper out of his jacket and handed it to Dean along with a pen.

"The disclaimer states that you are entering the ride of your own free will and that Mr Ghoul and all known subsidiaries are not responsible for anything that happens to you whilst on the train. Please sign and initial on the bottom for yourself, and on behalf of the child."

Dean shook his head, scrawled his initials and handed the paper back.

"There. Good enough?"

Mr Ghoul checked the document, rolled it up and slipped it back into his pocket.

"Go ahead and board the train, sir." Mr Ghoul said, standing aside and showing Dean and Alfie to the train.

Alfie climbed in the small wooden car first, and Dean somehow fitted in beside him, his legs coming up to near his chin. As he sat and waited, Dean noted that it wasn't a train at all and that the other cars behind them were separate and unattached. Ahead were twin black double doors which were set under the ghastly clown face which would set them on their way as soon as the ride began.

Dean looked across to his son, who was waiting with nervous anticipation. Dean hoped that he wouldn't have built his hopes up too much following the overblown performance of Mr Ghoul, as he was sure that once they were underway, only disappointment would follow. Another couple climbed into the car behind them, and a short time later, Mr Ghoul walked to the front train and grinned at Dean as he lowered the safety bar across them and clicked it into place.

"Enjoy the ride, folks." He said, flashing a grin.

Ghoul moved to the car behind and repeated the process, then walked to the control panel by the doors.

"Here we go folks, prepare to be horrified!"

He pushed the start button, and the train jerked forward and began to move towards the grinning, one eyed clown above the entrance. Dean flashed a quick glance to his wife, and couldn't believe how beautiful she looked as she stood with Tommy waving in the morning sun. He had a sudden urge to get off the train, sure that if he didn't, he would never see them again, but he knew it was stupid and was instead about to wave back as the car bumped through the doors and enveloped Dean and Alfie in darkness.

It was exactly as Dean expected. Cheesy music accompanied the rickety train as it moved past cheap, plastic models of vampires and demons, which moved pneumatically when they neared. They rounded a rendition of the Frankenstein monster, complete with flashing lights and jerky robotic arm movements, and then came to a path with two doors. The pre-recorded voice of Mr Ghoul echoed around the dark confines of the ghost train.

"And now, we move to the personal horror section of our ride. Be afraid, be very, very afraid!"

Dean shook his head, trying to place which movie Ghoul had lifted the 'be afraid' line from as they bumped through another set of doors and came to a halt.

"And here, on our left, we see young Tina Robinson." Ghoul's voice boomed over the speaker system.

Dean froze at the name; sure it was a coincidence until he saw it. The darkness to the left had illuminated to show a bedroom scene. Now the animatronics had been replaced with live actors, although actors wasn't the word. Dean was looking at a younger version of himself, and the girl sitting on the bed was indeed the Tina Robinson he knew, the girl he hadn't seen since high school. His stomach rolled and he gripped the handrail tightly, unable to tear his eyes from the scene.

It was a bedroom; Tina's bedroom, accurate down to the smallest detail. Tina sat on the bottom of the bed, nervous and afraid. The younger version of Dean swaggered towards her, and he heard the impossible – an exact transcript of the conversation that they had had that day. It was impossible, he knew that, but nevertheless it was playing out in front of him. Her saying that she didn't want to, him pressuring her and telling her if she didn't, one of her friends would.

Dean flicked his eyes to his son, who was staring open-mouthed. He knew, of course, he had seen photographs of his father when he was younger, and he too knew that they were in a very unique ghost train indeed.

Ghoul's voice blasted over the speaker system, causing Dean to utter a short yelp.

"Tina said no, but Dean knew best, so he forced the issue."

As if on cue, his younger self slapped Tina across the face and started to force himself on her.

"He got his way, even though she didn't want to. Then guess what happened?"

The scene faded to darkness and Ghouls voice was continued

in a whisper.

"Poor Tina got knocked up, but Dean didn't want a kid, so he threw her down the stairs and she lost it."

A screaming, blood covered foetus suddenly appeared inches from Dean's face as he peered into the darkness, accompanied by Ghoul's cackling shout.

"Say hi, Daddy!"

Dean screamed, and tried to get free of the car, but the bar was locked tight against his legs. The grotesque image faded, and the car moved on as Dean stared into the darkness.

"Dad! What's going on?" Alfie asked, his voice sounding both hollow and afraid in the darkness. Dean had no answer and waited as the train delved further into the black.

"Next up, on your right." Came Mr Ghoul's voice "Is another of Dean's sordid little secrets. This one takes place back in the summer of nineteen eighty two, when, after a drug fuelled night out, things took a bad, bad turn."

As before, the scene illuminated beside the car, which came to a halt. Dean glanced over his shoulder, but the other cars had gone in a different direction, and they were alone.

The scene was a dark alleyway. Rain fell from grey skies, and apart from the murky light from the overhead street lamps, it was bathed in shadow. Dean watched as he — a younger version as before — staggered down the alleyway, drinking a beer straight from the can.

His modern day equivalent couldn't help but watch. Whatever this was, it was more than just a simple ride. Whatever he was watching wasn't a set, or actors dressed up in costume. He was looking into a window from the past. He could feel the wind on his skin, accompanied by the occasional splatter of rain. He could smell the earthy stench of urine and rotten food seeping out of the alleyway. And because he knew what was coming, he understood that he couldn't let his son see it.

"Look away Alfie, cover your eyes."

Alfie stared at his father in the gloom and then looked past him to the scene unfolding behind him.

"I want to see it." He whispered.

Dean pulled the boy close to him. Covering his eyes with one hand and pressing the other against his ear.

Pain jabbed into his spine from the seat, causing him to scream and release his grip on his son. He tried to lean forwards, but the restraining bar held him firmly in place. He screamed and squirmed as his son looked on.

"No Dean. The boy must see. He must know the truth." Mr Ghoul's chastising voice said as the pain subsided.

"Please, he doesn't need to see, it was a mistake, I..." He trailed off, and then looked at Alfie.

"Just remember it's not real. Can you do that son?"

Alfie nodded, but Dean could see well enough that it was just a token gesture. His eyes were focused on the alleyway behind his father. He wanted to see, he wanted to know what was going to happen. Knowing that he couldn't stop it, Dean turned back and watched.

His younger self staggered down the alley, his white shirt open to the chest. He was soaked to the bone but seemed not to have noticed, as he was singing loudly to himself.

There was an old hobo sitting in a doorway, trying to protect himself from the downpour. He didn't look up at the younger, drunk Dean. Instead, he pushed himself further into the dark recess. Dean passed him, flashed him a glance and then stopped, turning towards the cowering hobo.

"What's your name old man?" He slurred.

The hobo didn't respond. He lowered his gaze and pulled his filthy blanket further up his body.

"Hey, I'm talking to you."

Still, he didn't speak. Dean took a last drink from the can and tossed it aside.

"You think you are too good to talk to me, eh old man?"

The hobo shook his head, still refusing to make eye contact. Dean laughed, then took a two-step run up, and kicked the old man in the face. The sound was sickening and crisp, and Alfie let out a sharp gasp as his younger father fell on the defenseless old man and began to punch and kick him, laughing all the while.

"Dad, stop it," Alfie screamed. But Dean couldn't answer; he was watching himself beat a defenseless old man for no sane reason. The scene faded, and again they were sitting in darkness.

Mr Ghoul's voice was now chastising, and Dean could imagine the sneer on his face.

"The poor old homeless man didn't do anything, and yet, you Dean, took it upon yourself to beat him… to death."

"That's wrong, he didn't die, besides, I didn't mean it!" Dean was sobbing, and could feel the burning eyes of his son on him in the darkness.

"Oh, no, he didn't die right away. He suffered. He cowered there, broken, bleeding and afraid, left in the cold and rain. He lasted a few hours, and then the bleeding on his brain killed him."

"No, it's a lie..."

The man appeared in front of the ghost train, illuminated by a single spotlight. His face was bleeding and misshaped, and his eyes were shadowy opaque pools. He grinned, showing his broken teeth.

"Why did you kill me?" He whispered.

"I didn't mean to, it was an accident, please, you have to believe me."

"Murderer." The old man spat, and then the light faded away, leaving Dean and Alfie in the dark. Dean was breathing in shallow gasps, his eyes darting as he looked into the darkness for whatever came next.

The train clicked to life, and they moved forwards, pushing through another set of double doors and into a long, thin room. People lined both sides, all of them standing in silence and staring at the ghost train as it moved forwards. Dean stared at them, shaking his head as the train moved on.

"Who are they?" Alfie asked, staring at his fathers' haunted face in profile. Dean stammered, but before he could find a response, Mr Ghoul answered on his behalf.

"These, young Alfie, are the people that your father has wronged in his life. People who he stepped on or kicked aside to give you and your mother the perfect little bubble that you live in. Women he had affairs with whilst your mother was pregnant with you. Former friends, who he scammed, cheated and manipulated for his own personal gain."

Dean looked at them, and they looked back, the silence in the corridor broken by the steady *clack clack* of the train car as it rolled forwards.

The car came to a halt at another set of double doors.

"Time to get off the train now." Mr Ghoul's voice echoed

through the room.

Dean grabbed at the restraining bar, as Mr Ghoul's laughter echoed through the room.

"Not so fast. Not yet. Just the boy for now."

Alfie's restraining bar lifted. He looked at his father, then hopped out of the train, standing on the platform with the people from his father's past.

"Let me out, you hear me let me out," Dean yelled, shaking at the bar and trying to squirm his way free. "Alfie, go get help, tell your mother to call the police..."

He stopped speaking, watching as Mr Ghoul pushed his way through the crowd. He stood beside Alfie and folded his arms as he shook his head.

"And so ends our ride." He said, smiling at Dean.

"What happens now?" Dean asked, his voice trembling.

"That depends."

"On what?"

Mr Ghoul smiled and turned to Alfie.

"You have seen, and you understand. Now, you must choose."

"Choose what?" Alfie said, taking a cautious step away from Mr Ghoul.

"His fate."

"I don't understand."

"Either he goes free, or he is punished for his deeds."

"Punished how?"

Mr Ghoul nodded towards the large black double doors.

"You understand this isn't just a ghost train, don't you Alfie?" Mr Ghoul said.

"Son, don't listen to him, make him set me free please..."

Ghoul snapped his head towards Dean and pointed at him, the veins bulging out of his neck as he screamed. "You keep your damn mouth shut until I tell you to talk."

Dean recoiled, and tried to push himself back into the seat, as Ghoul turned back towards Alfie, and smiled, his voice now back to its normal register.

"As I was saying, this isn't an ordinary ghost train. We were waiting for your father to come because he needs to be punished."

"Waiting for him?"

"Oh yes. We have waited for a very, very long time."
"What will happen to him?"
"Only what he deserves."
"Will you kill him?"
Ghoul grinned and shook his head. "No. Death is too good for some people. We will teach him to live the right way."
"But I won't see him again, will I?" Alfie said, a single tear tumbling down his cheek and rolling off his chin.
"Don't waste those." Mr Ghoul said as he handed Alfie a tissue. "Save them for somebody who is worth crying for."
Alfie took the tissue and wiped his eyes. He looked at his father, then back to Mr Ghoul.
"You said I had to choose."
"Yes. You see, we can't just take him. It's in the disclaimer." Ghoul patted his jacket pocket. "If you choose to forgive him, then the two of you will walk out of here right now and that will be the end of it."
"Okay."
"But, be sure that you genuinely do forgive him, because if you don't, one day, it will be your turn to ride the ghost train."
"And what was the other choice?"
"You walk out of here, alone right now and leave him here. Let us do our job. And we will see that he is punished, and better still, can't hurt anyone ever again."
"But he's my dad; he's not a bad man."
Ghoul nodded, then leaned close and whispered in Alfie's ear.
"Tell that to the homeless guy."
Alfie swallowed, and then looked at the double doors.
"What's through there?"
"Nothing for young eyes like yours, Alfie."
Alfie nodded, and then looked at his father.
"I'm sorry dad, but you need to pay for what you did. You always told me that people need to be responsible. And I think you need to do the same."
"Alfie please help me I..."
Dean's protests were silenced by a glare from Mr Ghoul, who then turned towards Alfie.
"You are a good boy, Alfie, and you did the right thing. Now go home, and live a good life. Don't make me have to come and

see you in the future. Okay?"

Alfie nodded furiously, as his father started to pull at the restraining bar.

"Good. Now go, back to your mother. Live well, and know that you did the right thing."

"I want to see, I need to see what's behind the door first," Alfie said, forcing himself to look Ghoul in the eye.

Ghoul sighed and shook his head.

"No, you don't. What lies behind there isn't for the eyes of the innocent. Go now, and let us do what needs to be done."

Alfie looked at his father, their eyes locking.

"Bye, dad," Alfie said, and then turned towards the exit door, which was behind Mr Ghoul. He heard the click clack of the train as it started to move, and as the doors opened, and despite the warnings, he couldn't help but turn around and take a look."

Sally and Tommy were waiting outside the ghost train, watching a colourful clown craft balloon dogs for a group of toddlers when they heard the scream. Sally knew straight away that it was her son, and turned towards the sound, dropping her ice cream at the sight of him as he pushed his way out of the ghost train's exit.

He charged towards her, eyes wide and frightened, skin ashen. She saw that he had wet himself, the front of his jeans now a growing shade of darker blue. He had gone onto the ghost train a young, brown haired boy, and come off a shambling, white haired, shrieking thing. He slammed into her, clutching her so hard that she could barely breathe. She lowered him to the floor and tried to silence his pained screams.

"I saw." He said between ragged gasps of breath. "He said not to, but I saw…"

"Where's your father Alfie? Where is he?" Sally screamed, grabbing him by the arms.

"Oh, he's gone. Gone and won't be coming back." He whispered, then began to cackle and whoop and twitch as Sally, in turn, began to scream for help.

The funfair disappeared as quickly as it had appeared. The following morning, all that remained was an open field littered with rubbish.

Alfie spent the next three months in the hospital, and now sat in his bed, drooling onto his pajamas and staring at the wall. He hadn't spoken since that day at the fairground, and the doctors said there was a good chance he would never speak again.

Although he couldn't tell them, he was just waiting. Waiting for his turn. Because he had seen what was behind the doors, and they had seen him. He drew breath, and turned towards the door to his hospital room to the sound that was drawing closer, his heart increasing in tempo, but it was just a nurse pushing a trolley full of medicine. She walked past the door without even looking in. He watched the door for a few seconds and then turned his attention back to the wall, where he continued to wait for that tell-tale *clack clack* sound of Mr Ghoul's ghost train to come and get him and take him to his father.

99.9 AM

The day Doyle first tuned into the pirate radio station was a Tuesday. He was working at fixing up an old hi-fi system with a twin tape deck and old school turntable with the intention of selling it on to a vintage collector.

Now that it had received some much needed TLC, the unit seemed to be in pretty good shape. He plugged it in and powered it up, smiling as the red and green graphic equaliser flashed up to advise him that he had selected the tape deck. He pushed the button to cycle through and watched as the display responded to his commands. Tape. Aux. Tuner.

He cycled through again and came to rest on the tuner. Today's radios came with a seek function, but this unit had a dial that you had to turn, to physically tune in the station that you wanted to listen to. He wished technology hadn't taken such a strong grip on the world, and turned the dial to find one of the local stations, so that when he took the unit to the shop to sell, he would be able to show that it worked.

He tuned in, 78.5FM, the local pop music station. Some god awful rapper was mumbling over a horrible, monotonous beat. It may have been what passed for good music, but it wasn't something he wanted to listen to, so he moved on. Next up was a religious broadcast, with a doom and gloom preacher begging for donations to keep their church alive. He quickly skimmed along, right to the end of the FM band.

Shaking his head, he flicked the switch from FM to AM and began to work his way back down. There was a news show that sounded as if it were being broadcast from the deepest, darkest hole they could find, and he moved on.

The station at 99.9 AM he didn't recognise. The signal was good, though, crisp and loud, and the DJ had a nice, smooth tone to his voice. He sounded familiar somehow, but Doyle wasn't sure why. Maybe he had once been a DJ on national radio and had now ended up on an AM station that probably had a listenership in the low hundreds, if that. Doyle paused, listening to the DJ and trying to place his voice.

This is DJ D on 99.9AM, the underground voice of Oakwell. The time is a little after nine o clock, and now, as promised, here is the brand new track from Kurt Cobain, called, I'm Sorry I Missed the End. Check it out, people.

Doyle listened to the acoustic tones of the guitar and the unmistakable, scratching vocals of the former Nirvana frontman as he sung inventive lyrics about the anarchy of the 2001 World Trade Centre attacks in New York.

Even as he listened, he knew it was impossible, because Cobain had committed suicide in 1994. Doyle felt a rush of fear and adrenaline race through him, and he turned up the volume. The more he listened, the more convinced he was that this was the real Cobain, which in turn made him see how impossible it was. And yet, the lyrics referenced events that took place seven years after his death. For two hours he sat perched at his workbench, listening to music from dead artists, past, present and future that had never been recorded. The show went off the air at two a.m., and Doyle sat there, staring at the hi-fi system like it were an object from the future rather than a relic of the past. He thought Terry might know more about it, and although he wanted to, it was too late to call him. Instead, he showered, and lay down, and despite the questions racing around his head, was soon asleep.

Terry Simms was a genius. Not in the literal sense, but there was a brilliance about him with regards to all things electronic. He had known Doyle for twelve years, and although on paper they were an unlikely pairing, they were great friends. Doyle stood and chewed his nails as Terry inspected the innards of the hi-fi, its wires and circuit boards snaking out onto the desk.

He had been reluctant to let Terry open it at all, and it was only because of his supreme knowledge and skill that he allowed him to poke around inside the unit. Doyle stood in silence and watched as his friend systematically put the hi-fi's guts back inside the casing and screwed it closed. Terry lifted his magnifying lens and perched it onto his sandy mop of hair, then turned to his friend.

"It's fine. Actually, it's in good order. There was a little dust on a few of the resistors, but I cleaned that away for you."

"So nothing in there that's out of place?"

"Like what?"

"I don't know, custom parts or something?"

Terry shook his head. "Oh no. This is all original. Late 80's, early 90's at best. It's a nice unit. Why? What's wrong? You having issues with it?"

"Not really! Well actually yeah I am."

Terry grinned and sipped his coffee. "Well? Which is it? You either are or you aren't."

Doyle hesitated. He trusted Terry but didn't think that just telling him would be enough. He wanted to show him, and more importantly, have someone else there with him to verify his own sanity.

"Look, there is something, but I think I ought to show you. Can you come back over later?"

"Why can't you show me now?"

"I can't, it has to be later."

He knew it sounded odd, but he also knew the pirate radio station aired between ten pm and two am, the DJ had said as much, several times during his broadcast.

"Okay, I suppose I can come by later. What time?"

"Say, nine thirty?"

"Yeah, okay, no problem. I'll be here."

"Thanks, I appreciate it."

Terry left, and Doyle spent the rest of the day trying to keep busy, when in reality, he had nothing to do but wait until Terry came back. He cooked but couldn't eat, lay down on the sofa but couldn't sleep, and tried to read but couldn't focus on the words. In the end, he switched on the TV and watched it without seeing, watching the time tick ever slowly towards the evening. Terry arrived a little after nine fifteen, and Doyle had to force himself not to race for the door and pull it open. He invited his friend into the house, and the two sat and made small talk in the sitting room. Now that he was there, Doyle was reluctant to tell Terry about the bizarre radio station and its content, but time had seemingly tired of dragging on and was now racing towards ten pm and the start of the show.

"Okay," Doyle said, perching on the edge of his seat and wringing his hands. "The reason I asked you to come is because I wanted to get your opinion on something that's pretty crazy."

"Yeah? Like what?"

"That hi-fi I had you look at for me, I was testing it out and found something."

"Okay!" Terry said, flashing an amused smile. Doyle knew that his friend wasn't taking him seriously, and instead of explaining further, he stood.

"It's easier to show you. Come on through to the workshop."

Doyle led the way into the workshop, which was, in reality, the spare bedroom that was now so full of electronic gizmos in various states of repair, that it resembled a workshop. Doyle sat on the bench in front of the hi-fi, as Terry perched on the edge of the bed. Doyle checked his watch and was filled with a giddy excitement. It was two minutes to ten.

He switched on the hi-fi, and watched the display illuminate, then he selected the radio, the room filling with a static hiss.

"So?" Terry asked. "What's happening?"

"Just wait. Okay?"

They waited. Time had now reverted to its slow crawl as the seconds went by. Doyle waited, and on some level was sure that he had imagined it all, and the station would not come on air. He ignored the amused stare of his friend, and instead concentrated all of his efforts on the hi-fi.

Ten o clock.

Doyle's mouth was dry, and his heart was beating a little too quickly as he waited.

"What are we waiting for?" Terry asked, half amused and half concerned at his friend's behavior.

"Give it a second."

Terry smiled. "Okay, whatever you say, but I wish you..."

Hello, hello, hello. It's ten pm on Wednesday evening, and that means it's time for the DJ D show, here from now until midnight.

We have a lot coming up tonight, including some new tracks by some old favorites. But first, some sad news for the community.

Long-time Oakwell resident, Hal Johnson, died today aged sixty four as a result of a heart attack. Mr Johnson owned the store on Main Street, and will be sadly missed by everyone in the community. But now, let's get back to the music; here is Jim Morrison with his new single, only the way I go.

"What the…"

Terry paused mid-sentence, and Doyle saw him go through the same processes that he had the night before. The two friends sat there in silence and listened to the thirty seven years dead Jim Morrison sing his brand new song. They listened to the broadcast from beginning to end. They heard new material from a veritable who's who of musical history. New songs from Lennon, Elvis, Joplin, and even a particularly rousing guitar based duet between Jimi Hendrix and Dimebag Darrell, who had been shot and killed on stage back in 2004. When the show ended, and the airwaves were once again filled with static, the two friends shared a look which said more than words ever could, because they both knew that they had experienced something impossible.

"So, what do we do now?" Doyle asked.

Terry licked his lips and cleared his throat. "I think I have an idea."

Terry had promised to come back the following day and had left Doyle to try and see if he could find any reference or listings related to the radio station or the DJ. His searches had drawn a blank, and as his frustration reached boiling point, which his sleepless night hadn't helped, he heard Terry's familiar knock on the door.

He knew as soon as he saw his pale faced friend that something was wrong. He had a bag with him but also had a vacant expression which Doyle had never seen before.

"What's wrong?"

"You got anything to drink?" Terry said, answering the question with one of his own.

"Beer?"

"Anything stronger?"

"Yeah, there's scotch in the kitchen."

Terry nodded and shuffled into the apartment. Doyle was concerned. He knew that Terry didn't drink, and hadn't touched a drop of booze since the day his divorce came through. Doyle counted back the years to when it was and was shocked to realise that it was more than four years ago. He followed into the kitchen, where Terry sat at the table. He had found the bottle, and was pouring a glass as Doyle sat opposite.

"Want one?" Terry asked as he finished pouring a large glassful.

"No, no thanks."

Terry nodded, screwed the lid back on the bottle and took a long drink, draining the glass. He set it down and looked across the table at Doyle.

"He wasn't dead."

"Who?"

"Mr Johnson. From the store."

Doyle felt his stomach somersault and considered joining his friend in a mid-morning tipple.

"You sure?"

Terry laughed, the sound sharp and only an octave away from shrill. "I spoke to him, he served me." He shook his head and finished off the rest of his drink.

"Surely this is a good thing; I mean maybe it's all a hoax," Doyle said hopefully.

Terry looked at him his eyes haunted and vacant.

"You don't get it, he *wasn't* dead. But I'm pretty sure he is now."

"What do you mean? Come on, spit it out, Terry! What happened?"

"As I said, he served me in the store. He was making small talk, just doing his attentive storekeeper part, and it happened. He grabbed at his arm and fell to the floor."

"Jesus!" Doyle said, finally deciding to pour himself another drink. He topped up Terry's glass as well as filling one of his own.

"There were only a few people in the store, and we tried to

save him, but we couldn't. He died right there on the floor."

Doyle said nothing. His brain was too busy coping with the situation. Terry continued.

"How could he know? The DJ on the radio. How could he know a full day before it happened?"

"Probably the same reason that they play music that shouldn't exist from artists that are long dead."

"You think it's supernatural?" Terry asked, finally making eye contact with his friend.

"Well, you know I'm a skeptic to things like this, but what the hell else could it be?"

"Look, all I know is that I have been trying to think of a plausible explanation for this, but so far I'm coming up empty."

"So," Doyle said as he sipped the bitter liquid. "What do we do now?"

Terry picked up the bag and emptied the contents on the table. Doyle looked over the collection of wires, resistors, circuit boards and chips, and raised an eyebrow at Terry.

"I think I can hook up a device to trace the signal. Find out where it's broadcasting from."

"Is that something we even want to know?"

"Aren't you curious?"

"Of course I am, but I'm not ashamed to say I'm also pretty scared by the situation."

"Then let's just go one step at a time, see if we can get a fix on this broadcast, then decide from there what we want to do. Okay?"

Doyle nodded, and stood, pacing about the kitchen.

"Okay, build the unit and we can tune in tonight and see if we can get a fix on the place."

When it was completed, the unit looked like a small sat nav, with a series of dials on the front. It was just a few minutes to ten o clock, and Doyle and Terry were apprehensive.

"As soon as he starts to broadcast, this unit should be able to pinpoint the source of the transmission," Terry said.

Doyle nodded, impressed and nervous in equal measure.

"Then what?"

Terry sighed and rubbed his temples. "I don't know, I haven't thought that far ahead."

"Maybe we shouldn't do this."

"Why not? I don't see what harm it can do."

"Do we really know that? I mean this is far from an ordinary situation, Terry."

"Then why bring me in on it? You wanted my help to find answers, didn't you?"

"I did — I *do*. I just don't want us to get in over our heads that's all."

Terry was about to respond when the static cleared, and the broadcast began. He picked up the unit and looked at Doyle.

"Well?" He asked.

Doyle licked his lips and tried to still the gnawing in his stomach.

"Okay, go ahead and do it."

Terry nodded, and turned on the device, as the DJ went into his motormouth routine.

Just one day to the weekend late night listeners and we are going to get you in the party spirit tonight. We have an exclusive interview with the legend, the megastar. Michael Jackson is here in the studio tonight to talk about the circumstances of his death, and we also have worldwide exclusives from Tupac Shakur and the one, the only, the godfather of soul, James Brown. But first, some breaking news. Word has just reached DJ D, that the world famous rapper, Big T, has been shot and killed in a drive by shooting outside his Los Angeles home.

"Check the news, and the internet," Terry said.

"On it." Doyle shot back as he powered up his laptop.

Big T's album, It's All About T, went triple platinum just last year, and his fans are said to be devastated. His family has asked to be left alone to grieve in private. This one goes out to all the Big T fans, here is global number one smash hit, It Ain't Over 'til the Phat lady sings. Check it out.

"Anything?" Terry asked as he tweaked the controls on the device.

"Nothing, not a damn thing," Doyle responded as he cycled through the local news sites. "I'll go check the TV, see if the news channels have anything."

Doyle stood and left the room, as Terry continued to tweak the device to the backdrop of Big T's colourful rap.

Doyle came back into the room. "Nothing on the news, or the internet. The guy isn't dead."

"Not yet," Terry said softly, as Doyle sat on the bed.

"Is it working yet?"

"Almost. The signal is bouncing all over the damn place. Give me a minute to fix it."

That was Big T with, It Ain't Over 'til the Phat Lady Sings, played in tribute to the man himself, who was shot and killed in what looks to be a gang related attack. Rest in peace T. Next up, we have our interview with the one, the only Michael Jackson, but first, check out the sultry tones of the beautiful Selina, with, All I Want is You, right here with DJ D, on 99.9 AM.

"Got it. Terry said, flashing a grin. "He's broadcasting around three miles from here. My guess is from a motorhome or something."

Doyle nodded, staring at the device in Terry's hands.

"So, what's the plan?" Terry pushed.

"What do you think?"

"I say we drive out there and take a look."

"That sounds pretty risky."

"We drive, we look, and we come back. No leaving the car, no hero stuff."

"I don't know Terry; I have a really, really bad feeling about this."

"Me too, but aren't you curious?"

"Not enough to risk my life."

"Come on, what risk is there? We drive out and look. That's all."

"Why are you so determined to do this?"

"I just am." Terry snapped.

"But why?"

"Because for the first time since Katie left me, I feel like I have something to get excited about."

Doyle nodded, regretting making Terry bring up the past.

"Okay." He said, folding the laptop away and clapping Terry on the shoulder.

"Let's go take a look."

Doyle drove whilst Terry gave directions from the passenger seat. He didn't expect to find 99.9AM broadcasting from the car radio, but there it was, as it had been on the vintage hi fi in the house. They drove in silence each listening to the unearthly broadcast and trying to come to terms with it. Occasionally, Terry would give an instruction as to which direction to go. They left the suburban comforts of green lawns and quaint white houses and headed towards the outskirts of the city. Doyle noticed that the closer they got the clearer the broadcast became.

"Stop here," Terry said.

Doyle obliged, pulling the car over to the shoulder and staring out of the window. To their left was a run-down old service station, its pumps having long since stopped supplying gas. Doyle felt his stomach somersault at the thought of going into there and discovering whatever might be lurking in the dark.

"Hey, relax," Terry said, jabbing his thumb over his shoulder. "The signal is coming from over there."

Doyle looked past Terry, and even though at first glance it was less sinister, he felt even more uncomfortable at the thought of walking out into the wilderness.

The road fell away at a shallow angle to a non-descript landscape of sand and scrub punctuated by occasional outcrops of rock. Terry cupped his hands against the glass, looking for a light, or some evidence of the broadcast, but Doyle knew he wouldn't see anything. He knew in his gut that there was nothing out there.

"I can't see anything." Terry said, taking a second to re-check the readouts on the signal tracker.

"Me either." Doyle added.

"I think we should go take a look, just to the edge of the road."

"No, Terry, we agreed. This isn't a game."

Terry turned in his seat, and Doyle saw the excitement and curiosity in his eyes.

"Come on, we came out here, we can't see enough from the car. Let's just look. Hell, leave the engine running if it makes you feel better."

"Don't you think we should maybe call the police?"

"And say what? That a ghost pirate radio show is playing new and unheard hits from beyond the grave? Good luck with that one."

"Look, maybe you are right. But what can we do?"

"We don't need to do anything," Terry said with a wry smile. "Just take a look."

"Ah, the hell with it." Doyle sighed "I should know better than to try and talk you out of something you have set your mind to."

Terry grinned. "It will be fine. We get out, take a quick look, and then get back in the car. You must be curious, I sure as hell am."

"Point made. Let's just get this over with." Doyle said sharply.

They climbed out of the car, and now out in the open, it all seemed so much more real. The day had been a hot one, and even though it was now fully dark, residual heat still drifted off the asphalt. They looked out over the barren landscape, looking for any evidence of anything other than wilderness. A light, warm breeze pulled along the floor, dragging the loose, dry sand with it.

"I don't like this," Doyle whispered, but Terry didn't answer, he was staring at his tracker, brow furrowed in concentration as he made minute adjustments to the dials.

"This makes no sense; we should be able to see something. He must be broadcasting from somewhere."

"How far off is the signal?"

"According to the readout, thirty feet straight ahead." Terry looked over his shoulder as he said it, and Doyle now saw fear in place of his earlier curiosity.

"Come on Terry; let's get the hell out of here."

"Wait, it could be behind that outcrop." He said, pointing to a large shadow draped formation.

"You really want to go down there to check?"

“Just a quick look to see if it’s there, and that’s all.”

Doyle wanted to protest, but Terry was already walking down the embankment.

“Terry, just leave it, this is stupid.”

“Wait there if you want.” He said as he ran the last few steps down to level ground. I’ll go take a look and come right back.”

Doyle hesitated, he wanted no part of it now, and the more obsessive Terry got over the situation, the more he wished he had kept it to himself. Doyle watched as his friend walked towards the outcrop. He noted with more than a little envy that Terry seemed to carry none of Doyle’s own apprehension or fear. He reached the outcrop and disappeared out of sight behind it.

Doyle waited. He knew it had only been half a minute at most, but it felt as if an age had passed until Terry poked his head back around the edge of the rock.

“Hey, come on down here and take a look, this is… unusual to say the least.”

Despite his apprehension, he was also curious, and before he could think about it, he was carefully baby-stepping down the embankment and walking towards his friend and the huge rock formation. He covered the ground quickly and stood next to his friend.

“Take a look,” Terry said with a grin.

Doyle did.

There was nothing there.

Doyle looked at the expanse of empty land and then turned to his friend.

“I don’t get it, what are you trying to show me?”

Terry pointed straight ahead.

“There.”

Doyle looked.

Rock, grass, sand. The warm summer breeze sent more sand rolling lightly across the surface with a soft *ssssssssssssssss*

“I don’t see anything.”

“Exactly.”

“Come on, stop with the riddles. Spit it out.”

Terry grinned, his face taking on a ghastly appearance in the shadowy half-light.

"Warm night tonight isn't it?" Terry said.

"What the hell does that have to do with anything?"

"Trust me."

"I do, it's just a freaky enough situation as it is, without you talking in riddles and getting all cryptic," Doyle said, unable to mask his annoyance.

"I'm sorry, it's just... this is incredible. Okay, the less cryptic version. Tonight is a warm night. Right?"

"Yeah, it's been hot every night for weeks. But you already know that."

Terry nodded. "I do. Now walk with me."

"Why?"

"I can't tell you, I need to verify my findings."

Doyle sighed and shrugged his shoulders.

"Whatever you say, we have already done more than I bargained for anyhow. Let's go."

The pair started to walk, and Doyle was aware that Terry was watching him, waiting for some reaction or other. He had gone only seven paces when he felt it. The sticky warmth of the day was replaced by an icy cold.

"What the hell?" Doyle said, taking a few backwards steps. Again, he was in the residual heat of the summer night.

"Did you feel it?" Terry asked. "The change in temperature?"

"Yeah, yeah I did." Doyle said, staring at the ground in front of him. He reached an arm out, and he felt the shift from warm to cold.

"What the hell is this?"

"This," Terry replied, "is where our broadcast originates from."

"But there's nothing here," Doyle said, still moving his arm from cold to warm air and back again.

"I don't know what it is, although I have my suspicions. All I know is that this could be one of the greatest discoveries that man has ever made."

Doyle pulled his arm away, flicking a glance to his friend. "Do you think it's paranormal? You know, spiritual?"

Terry shrugged and grinned, pushing his glasses up his face.

"I don't know, maybe. It could be an interdimensional thing. There are a lot of questions that need answers Doyle, but for now, we need to keep quiet. We need to think about what to do."

"So you don't think it's dangerous?"

"No," Terry said, shaking his head. "I think whatever it is, is residual. It's like crossed wires on a telephone. We shouldn't be able to hear it, and I doubt it's aware of us."

"How do you know?"

"Well, we're standing right in the spot where the broadcast is coming from; I would think they might have noticed."

Doyle pulled his arm back out of the cold space, and glanced towards the dark shape of the car up by the road.

"What now?" He asked.

"Now, we need to do some research. And think about what happens next. This could be big Doyle, really, really big."

"What do you mean?"

"I mean, it answers questions. Which questions are to be determined, but my best-educated guess is that it will either prove the existence of alternate dimensions running parallel to our own or that after death, life goes on. Either way, it's pretty heavy."

"No shit," Doyle said quietly, staring into the blank space that was both everything and nothing at the same time.

"I think we have seen all we can here, let's get out of here, and talk about what to do."

"You don't have to tell me twice, this place gives me the creeps."

"Relax," Terry said as the pair walked back to the car. "There is nothing here to be scared of, it's just science. There is no such thing as ghosts; the living are the ones you should be worried about."

"Aren't you full of joy tonight?" Doyle said as they clambered back up the embankment.

They climbed back in the car, and for all of Doyle's fears, it already seemed unreal. They sat and listened to the broadcast. They were playing some more Big T, although the one in the world that Terry and Doyle inhabited was still very much alive and kicking. How long he stayed that way, remained to be seen. Doyle was about to gun the engine when the song faded and the smooth voice of the DJ filled the car.

Some more Big T for you there with his chart topping classic, 'everythin' ain't what it seems.' Before we go on, a couple of shout outs, to you, our listeners. First up, to Kelly and Alice tuning in during the nightshift at Penny's. Keep it up girls, and keep listening to DJ D. also, shout outs to Ken, Andrew, Simon and Dexter who are out to celebrate Ken's birthday. Enjoy it boys, and don't do anything that DJ D wouldn't do, which leaves pretty much everything on the table. And lastly, a personal shout out from me, to Doyle and Terry, who I know are listening tonight. All I can say, boys is don't underestimate the things you don't understand. Coming up, the debut solo single by former Sex pistols bassist Sid Vicious. First I—

Doyle turned off the radio and turned towards Terry. He was no longer smiling.

Big T – the one that inhabited Terry and Doyle's world was killed early the following morning. The world's press went into overdrive, to Terry and Doyle, it was already old news.

"Thirteen hours, give or take," Terry said as he sipped his umpteenth cup of coffee.

"What is?" Doyle asked, rubbing his stubble fluffed cheeks.

"The time. Between it happening in their world and ours."

Doyle nodded, and they sat in silence, watching the news of the Rapper's death. Neither had slept and although they had sat up all night discussing options, the reality was, that they were no further along than the night before. They had almost come to blows about how to proceed, the combination of stress, the unreality of the situation and their differing opinions making a potent fuel for their aggression. Doyle had wanted to ignore it, take their veiled warning for what it was and forget all about it, but Terry had wanted to explore further, and continue in his quest for answers. There was now a tense, if not awkward peace between them. Terry stood and stretched.

"I'm going to go home, grab a few hours' sleep."

"Good idea, I might do the same."

Terry nodded. "I'll come back later, and we can try to come to some kind of compromise on what to do."

"Sounds like a plan."

Terry hesitated and then left. Doyle put his feet up and lay on the couch. He didn't expect sleep to come, he was too jittery, his brain too active. He closed his eyes anyway, as it helped with the coming headache.

He was asleep within minutes.

Terry came back just after nine pm. He was excited and anxious, and sat at the kitchen table, opening the notepad he had brought with him and grinning at Doyle.

"I went back out there." He said, eyes glittering in excitement.

"What the hell, I thought we were supposed to talk about this?"

"I know, I know, but just listen. I went out there and took some measurements."

Doyle's anger dissipated, and he sat at the table.

"Go on."

Terry spun the notebook around so Doyle could see his scrawled notes.

"The cold area is still there. It's around ten feet square. It's about seven degrees cooler than the normal air temperature. There is definitely something there."

"Yeah, but that still doesn't help us with what to do about it."

"I had a thought about that too," Terry said.

"Go on."

"How about this? Let me take a few more measurements, record some video, hell even record the broadcast tonight. First thing tomorrow, we report it, anonymously of course, then sit back and let the publicity build. As soon as it's common knowledge, we can present our evidence as the first to find it."

It wasn't ideal, but it was more of a compromise than Doyle had expected.

"One more night, then that's it."

"Perfect. I brought my recording equipment. Let me set it up, make sure it's receiving the broadcast, then we can head out there."

"Fine," Doyle said standing up and going to one of the

cupboards in the kitchen. "But just in case, I'm taking this."

He came back and set the handgun on the table.

"What the hell are you doing with a gun?" Terry said, glaring at the weapon.

"I got it for home protection, but I figured if nothing else, it will make me feel better to have it."

"I don't see why you would need it, but whatever. Just be careful you don't get spooked and start shooting the damn thing into the night."

"I won't. I'm just being cautious."

"Some might say irrational."

"Some might say we shouldn't be messing with something we don't understand." Doyle shot back.

Terry nodded and scooped up his notepad.

"I'm going to go set the recording equipment up; then we can make a move. Okay?"

"Fine. I'll be ready." Doyle said, as that horrible dull ache in his belly started to appear.

They were underway by ten fifteen. As before, they had the station tuned into the car stereo. Big T, he who had been shot and killed earlier that day in Doyle and Terry's world and the evening before wherever DJ D was broadcasting from, was a guest on the show and was conducting his first live interview.

Terry looked excited; Doyle was horrified but kept his expression neutral. They arrived, and parked the car. As they had agreed, they wound down the windows and turned up the radio, so they could hear the broadcast as they investigated. The conditions were the same as the night before, hot and dry and as they walked down the embankment, the feeling of dread in Doyle's stomach increased as he looked both ways down the expanse of the tarmac where the car was parked. There was no sign of any traffic, which increased the sense of isolation. Terry marched on, rounding the corner and taking out his notepad and digital thermometer, taking readings of the air. Doyle stood and waited, half watching for anything strange, half listening to the broadcast. He wondered why Terry wasn't afraid, or at least concerned with the enormity of the situation. It wasn't exactly a normal everyday occurrence, and yet he had taken it all in his stride. He watched his friend, crouched in the dirt taking his readings, and the thought crossed his mind that perhaps, this was all a big joke, and Terry was in on it.

The broadcast was interrupted mid-song, which got Doyle's attention.

We interrupt this broadcast to bring you, our fans, news. We are sad to report that one of our loyal listeners, Doyle Reynolds, aged just thirty seven, passed away today.

Cold rolled down Doyle's spine, as he turned towards the car.

It seems he got too close to something he didn't understand, and he paid the price with his life. Rest in peace Doyle, this one goes out to you.

The Door's track 'The End' filled the airwaves, and Doyle turned towards Terry.

"Holy shit, did you hear...?"

Terry was gone.

Doyle glared into the darkness, and without thinking about it pulled out the gun from his jacket and flicked off the safety.

"Hey, come on, this isn't funny. Stop screwing around."

He walked towards the cold spot, his eyes wide as he tried to see where his friend might be hiding. Confusion, anger, and fear raced through him as he stared into the dark. He couldn't move, rooted to the spot by fear. The song finished, and once again, DJ D filled the airwaves.

That was Mr. Mojo Risin' himself, Jim Morrison, who will be joining us live next week to perform a few of his classics and maybe a new song or two. Next up is...

Doyle pushed it aside, trying to ignore it and will himself to move. He took a single step, such a small thing feeling like a huge achievement.

"Damn it, Terry where the hell are you?" He screamed into the night, listening to the sound of his voice echo.

You know where he is.

The voice in his head startled him, as it had been dormant for a long time. He knew it was a bad sign that he was hearing it again, and so tried to ignore it. But it wouldn't be silent.

Don't think you can ignore me. I'm here to help.

"Go away." He whispered.

You know why I'm here. You know what's happening to you, don't you?

"I won't listen to you, you aren't real."

None of this is real. That's the point. Whispered the voice in his head.

Doyle stared at the cold spot, then at the car. The broadcast was silent, the air filled with the static hiss of dead air.

"I don't understand," Doyle whispered, letting his gun arm fall to his side.

You are sick again. Remember? Like before.

He could remember snatches. A hospital bed. Medication. Therapy.

"I'm okay now, they said so...."

You never heard of a relapse?

"Terry, I need help buddy," Doyle shouted into the night, trying to ignore the voice emanating from the centre of his brain.

Terry isn't here.

"He is. I know he is."

Terry's dead. Remember?

"It's not true, he's here," Doyle screamed, falling to his knees.

No, he's dead. Dead because of you.

"It wasn't my fault," Doyle whispered.

It was your fault. You were the one who fucked his wife, remember?

"It wasn't like that, we were in love…"

And when he found out, he went apeshit. Come on, help me out here. This is all buried somewhere in this head of yours.

"I can't remember, it's not true."

You remember, you just had it all repressed by the shrinks. You lost it, buddy. Lost it big time.

"But why?"

Because he killed her. Terry killed his wife because of you, then he came out here, and killed himself.

"But the radio, the broadcast…"

It's in here, just like I am. The radio station, Terry helping you out, all a fantasy, all a failed attempt by this brain of yours to untangle the cables in here and put itself right.

"No, it can't be."

Really, let's take a look at it. What was Terry's wife called?

"She was called Dianne."

But that wasn't what he called her was it? Can you remember?

"Dee, everyone called her Dee."

As in DJ D. coincidence? I doubt it. And the playlist, all dead artists, true, but also your own personal favourites.

"They played new songs, songs that shouldn't exist."

They didn't. They played songs you wish had been created. It was never real. You told yourself it broadcasted from here because you know this is where Terry came to end it all after you fucked his life up.

"I don't remember…" he wailed, openly crying.

You are broken, Doyle. I think you are going to be spending the rest of your life in the hospital, the best place for you, really.

"I won't do it, I won't go back there." He shouted, pounding his fist on the ground.

You don't have a choice, a man who can't separate reality and fantasy isn't safe to roam the streets. I'm sorry it had to be me who told you, but somebody had to.

"No, I refuse to go back there. Not again."

He put the gun in his mouth and pulled the trigger. His world exploded into a haze of white light and pain as the side of his face sheared away. He lay there on the ground, his blood soaking into the sand as his ears rang. He waited for death and was relieved when his vision faded.

Six years had passed since that day in the desert. The bullet had exited through Doyle's cheek, taking with it most of his lower jaw. The surgery to repair the damage had gone as well as could be expected, but his once handsome features were gone, his ravaged face held together with screws and plates. He had been admitted to Penry Hospital following his recovery, and there he had stayed since. His routine was mundane, pills in the morning, electro shock therapy twice a week. He had a room with a view of the gardens and part of the large wall preventing patients from leaving. It was a simple life.

The voice in his head had been silent since the night he had shot himself, but he knew it was still in there, repressed by the electro-shock therapy for now, but there nonetheless.

The doctors told him he was making progress, and he wished it were true, but at night, when he was lying in the dark, strapped to his bed by the wrists and ankles, he would sometimes hear DJ D's show, and smiled as it played one of his favourite songs.

Doyle closed his eyes and slept.

THE EYE

Timmy was desperate. He had known it for the last half hour, but he couldn't tear himself away from the fantasy land of magic and monsters that was unfolding on the carpet of his bedroom floor. For a while, crossing his legs had worked, but now even that was doing nothing to fend off the sharp ache in his belly. He set down the toys and hopped to his feet, leaving the Beast Lord Ragnock and his companions in situ as he hurried towards the bathroom. He charged down the hallway as his mother's disinterested voice, automatically activated by the sound of his feet padding on the carpet drifted to him from downstairs.

"Timmy, slow down."

Timmy didn't answer. He hit the brakes and slid to a halt outside the bathroom, went inside and slammed the door behind him.

The bathroom was quiet and cool. Its floors were black-and-white tiles, and the porcelain bath and sink gleamed under the artificial overhead light, which hummed steadily. None of that mattered to Timmy, however, because the ache in his belly told him he needed to go *now*, or there would be an accident, and he didn't want that.

He had just turned nine years old and hadn't had an accident for a long, long time. However, sometimes, like today, Timmy got so involved with his toys that he simply forgot to go. He hurried toward to the toilet and lifted the lid, and then paused, letting out a short, surprised gasp.

There was an eye in the water.

It looked like a toy, a joke left for him to find, but unlike the fake vampire's teeth or plastic dog mess that Timmy's dad used to buy him from the joke shop, this was definitely real. He was aware of just how afraid he was, but was even more aware of the sharp ache in his stomach, and so he stood there, hopping from foot to foot as he tried to figure out what to do. The eye in the water blinked, and Timmy gasped.

Its eyelid had teeth. They were thin and sharp, like tiny yellow needles which protruded forwards as the eye blinked, sending tiny bubbles to the surface of the scented water. Timmy continued to hop from foot to foot, and clutched his belly, trying to ignore the aching need to empty his bladder. The eye watched him, its glassy black pupil betraying no hint of emotion. Timmy opened his mouth, intending to call for his mother, as he was sure she would know what to do, but he remembered that Sam was with her tonight, and he snapped his mouth closed.

No.

He couldn't call out, not with Sam in the house. However, his decision didn't solve his problem, as he still needed to go, and go badly. The eye offered another sharp-toothed blink, sending more ripples through the water. Timmy moaned softly and looked around the room, assessing his other options. He considered the option of trying to do his business anyway, and pretend the eye wasn't even there, but as he looked at it and those sharp, needle like teeth, he had a vision of it bursting up out of the water, wrapping its stalk like body around his neck and biting him with those horrible teeth. He knew it would happen that way, he just *knew* it. But knowing still didn't help him, and as another cramp gnawed at his stomach, he knew he had to make a decision. He looked around the room, and his eyes landed upon the bath, but he immediately dismissed the idea. He was too afraid of the consequences if he were caught going in there. For as much as hoped his mother might understand his desperation—especially if she saw the eyeball in the toilet — Sam most certainly would not. He had moved in not long after Timmy's dad moved out, and although he pretended to be nice enough — especially when Timmy's mother was around — the reality was that he was a horrible, nasty man with a violent temper.

He would often shout at Timmy (especially if he had been drinking), and say horrible things about Timmy's dad. He wanted to tell his mother about it, about how frightened he was, but all she cared about was Sam, and whenever he would try to explain, she would just tell him to be nice and not cause any problems. He did as he was asked, because despite everything, he loved his mother, but he couldn't deny that he wanted his dad to come back home more than anything, and for the three of them to be happy again without Sam hanging around the place and making life hard.

He cast his gaze back to the toilet bowl, and still the eye watched, waited, and blinked. With his stomach sending him another sharp warning that he would need to empty his bladder soon before he made a mess, he looked around and an idea came to him. He hurried across the room, grabbed the tube of toothpaste, and approached the toilet.

Carefully screwing the cap off, he squeezed the tube over the bowl and watched as a long, white slug poured out of the nozzle. He snagged it off between his finger and thumb and watched as it fell into the water. The eye twisted and snapped at the minty paste, shredding it with its eyelid teeth, and then, perhaps realising that it wasn't to its taste, ceased its attack and settled back to watching Timmy, ignoring the small lumps that settled around it. Timmy glared at the floating, bulbous eyeball and considered what to do next. He pulled off a few sheets of toilet paper, screwed them up into a ball, and threw it in. Again, the eyeball lunged, snapped, and devoured the paper, tearing it into shreds, and as with the toothpaste, it seemed to give up almost immediately and returned its glassy gaze to Timmy.

He shook his head at his own stupidity, and realised that he was, of course, being silly. Monsters — even floating eyeballs — didn't eat toothpaste or rolled-up toilet paper. They preferred meat, flesh and blood. An idea came to him, and without hesitation, he rolled up his trouser leg and frowned at the sticking plaster on his knee. He had fallen off his bike a day earlier when he was racing Joey Appleseed down at the park, and had cut his knee. It didn't hurt anymore, but he was sure there would still be a little blood underneath. Remembering the advice of his father, he grabbed the edges of the band-aid and tore it off in a short, quick, and thankfully painless motion. The underside was as he hoped. It was spotted with dry blood. With more curiosity than fear, he held it over the toilet bowl. Timmy thought that perhaps the eye could smell the blood (although he couldn't see anything resembling a nose) because it began to thrash in the water, banging its thick body against the sides of the porcelain. As Timmy watched, it began to move, stretching out of the water towards the sticking plaster, its eyelid pushing forwards and out as the eye retreated. It was now a mouth with an eyeball inside, and underneath it, Timmy could see a deep, dark throat. Terrified, he dropped the band-aid and watched as it fell into the water. The eye lurched and snapped, devouring it, and sending small droplets of water arcing on to the floor.

Taking its bloody prize with it, the eye submerged again. Timmy hoped it would go away, perhaps slink off back down the drains, and go bother somebody else, but it sat there in the water, pulsing, watching, and waiting.

There was a short, sharp bang on the door, and Timmy's bladder almost let go. The eye rolled towards the sound, and its fanged lid narrowed slightly.

"Hey come on kid, hurry up in there, I need to take a piss," came Sam's muffled, voice. Timmy grimaced as he heard his mother chastise Sam for swearing, even though Timmy had already heard worse. Joe Raspin in his class at school would always swear, and even sometimes used the F- Word.

"Just a minute," Timmy said, surprised at how calmly the words came as he continued to stare at the eye. As he watched, it rolled its single black pupil towards him, and there was a moment of understanding.

Timmy heard Sam muttering on the other side of the door before he banged on it again.

"Come on! how long does it take damn it?"

Timmy ignored him. He was watching the eye.

It blinked once and then retreated. Timmy could only hold on until it was just out of sight before he took care of what he needed to do. The relief was immediate, and he kept his eyes firmly fixed on the water, praying that the eye would stay away. He finished and flushed, wondering why he never thought of that in the first place. He watched the water swirl and rise, draining slowly as if there was something just out of sight blocking the flow. And of course, there was.

Timmy washed his hands and glanced at the toilet. The water was clear and blue and yet, as he watched, small bubbles rippled out from under the U-bend. Timmy nodded. He and the eye understood each other. Timmy opened the door and glanced up at the towering form of Sam, dressed in his red plaid shirt and grubby baseball cap, which, as always was pushed to the top of his sweaty head.

"It's about god damn time. Move it kid!" Sam said, dragging Timmy aside by the arm and slamming the door behind him.

Normally, such a thing would frighten Timmy, but not today. He walked down the hallway to his bedroom and sat on the carpet. He didn't return to his toys, as the game that he had been so involved with now seemed unimportant. Instead, he sat cross-legged and watched the bathroom door at the opposite end of the hall.

For a long time, there was no noise, then Timmy thought he heard a gasp and a deep, *bloop* followed by a splash of water on tiles.

Timmy's mother's voice floated up from downstairs.

"Sam, are you almost done? Survivor is coming on."

Timmy looked at the door and tilted his head.

No.

He was sure that Sam wouldn't be watching any more episodes of Survivor, or spending more nights drunk and hitting his mother or being cruel. He thought Sam would be in a different, darker place. Timmy smiled and closed his bedroom door.

SCARECROWS

Spyder was drunk, and pushed the cherry red convertible up past seventy, cheering and whooping as he sat with one elbow hanging out of the window. His mother had died earlier that day, and Spyder's answer had been not to spend the day with his family in their mourning, but to go out and get shit faced. It was all a front of course, but for Spyder (or Dwayne to his family or anyone outside of his school) it was the reaction that people would have expected.

It was a hot, sticky July day, and the Red missile which was piloted by the grieving teen tore across the blacktop, the miles of empty country roads perfect for their endeavours. They thundered past Oakwell Forest, veering at speed around the occasional traffic on the road, and through the industrial area where Dwayne's father had worked at the lumber mill before he was laid off.

"Hey, maybe you should slow down."

Spyder glanced to the passenger seat, and his friend Randy squirmed a little. Perhaps he saw a little of the hurt in Dwayne's eyes, or maybe he was just scared. Either way he didn't elaborate and by way of reply, increased his speed, pushing the car even harder.

In the back, Kenny whooped and cheered, and almost as drunk as their driver, either didn't acknowledge or didn't care about the potential danger of the situation.

"Yeah, Spyder, come on man, redline this thing!" Whooped the acne ravaged Kenny, who flicked a grin missing both of its front teeth at Randy, who was glaring at him from the front.

"What's with you?" Kenny asked, the venom in his voice hard to miss. Randy wasn't afraid of Kenny, or anyone else for that matter. He was a wrestler, and one of the best in the school. Undefeated, he had the luxury of a high school life untroubled by the constant tests to see who the alpha male was. It was him, and nobody disputed it. He would never admit it, but he was, however, just a little bit afraid of Dwayne.

He wasn't a physical threat, Randy was sure that if things ever came to blows he could quite easily overpower him, but something in his personality, just little things like the way he would get a look in his eye that made you wonder just what the hell he was capable of. It was moments like that which caused him caution, and why he didn't quite want to commit to taking control of this particular situation. And even as his eyes flicked from his friend — his prominent cheekbones and strong jaw framed by the moonlight as he stared at the road ahead — to the speedometer, which was close to the 90mph redline that Kenny seemed so desperate to reach, he tried to think of a way to diffuse the situation.

Dwayne took a long drink of the beer that had been nestled on the front seat between his legs, and Randy saw that, for a few seconds, both of Dwayne's hands were off the wheel, and the car began to drift into the opposite lane.

"Hey, hey man, the wheel," Randy warned, reaching out to steady the vehicle, but Dwayne didn't take too kindly to the intrusion and pushed his friend's hands away.

"Leave it alone, I got it." Slurred Dwayne, as he took control of the vehicle.

"Hey man, stop being such a pussy," Kenny added as he drained his bottle and tossed it over his head, where it smashed some way behind the speeding car.

"Jesus Kenny, you could have hit someone with that thing," Randy said, glaring for the second time in quick succession at their back seat passenger. Normally it would be enough, but Kenny had been made brave by alcohol, and he sneered at Randy, and then glanced at Dwayne.

"Hey Spyder, why the hell did we bring this guy with us?"

"Whaddya mean?"

"This guy, he's dragging me down with all his warnings and rules."

"Randy is a decent guy, I want him here."

"Whatever man, I just wish he would relax."

Dwayne glanced at Randy, who was watching him carefully. Dwayne broke into a grin, and Randy saw it again, that little glimmer of something sinister hiding within, that every now and again, came to the surface to check the lay of the land before it went back to wherever it came from.

They were out on the outskirts of town now, the lands here were rolling fields of green farmland, accentuated by the smell of cow shit, which lingered in the air all year round. The huge Oakwell Forest loomed ahead of them, a black ocean of treetops stretching for miles. Suddenly, and without warning, Dwayne slammed on the brakes, the car fishtailing as it struggled to stop, leaving great dark lines on the asphalt.

"What is it, what's going on?" Kenny mumbled as the car came to a halt and Dwayne switched off the engine. Kenny's question was ignored. Dwayne was staring out the window, and Randy watched him carefully, wondering why he was getting that nervous feeling in his stomach that he usually got right before a big wrestling match.

"What's up man?" Randy asked, looking out of the window to try and see what had been so important as to stop and stare. He could see nothing but the road, shrinking away into a thin vein which draped over the horizon. Without the throaty growl of the engine, there was a thick silence, broken only by the monotonous sound of the crickets as they sang to each other. Randy flicked his eyes towards Kenny, and now he too looked a little more apprehensive as he sat perched in the middle of the back seat.

"Dwayne, what is it, what's wrong?" Randy asked again. Dwayne didn't answer.

They sat in silence, listening to the crickets and looking up into the sky at the stars. Without warning, Dwayne turned and looked at Randy, the small smile transforming into a grin, which Randy thought belonged to the hidden thing that lived somewhere deep inside his friend.

"You guys ever hear of Jorell Samsonite?"

"Who?" Kenny asked as he let out a boozy burp.

"Jorell Samsonite," Repeated Dwayne.

"I have heard the name, not sure who he is, though," Randy said, watching his friend and liking what he saw less and less by the minute.

"He's a farmer, lives out here on the edge of town," Dwayne said, reverting to that wistful smile. "They say he's a recluse, a hermit. He hasn't left his house since his wife died back in 57', lives off the land and all that shit."

"What about him?" Randy asked, unsure if it was a question he wanted answered. Dwayne continued.

"Word is he's crazy. You should see his house, all boarded up and broken, and that's not even the best part." Dwayne grinned, and in the dull glow of the moonlight, he looked just a little bit crazy. "He grows all his own food, he has these scarecrows. Only, he doesn't just have one like any normal person. This guy has dozens of them."

"Bullshit," Kenny said as he opened another beer and took a long drink.

"No, it's true. A buddy of mine drove out there and saw it for himself. He said the old guy gets really defensive, screams and shouts at anyone who goes anywhere near the house."

"Guy sounds like a loon," Kenny said, then sat back in his seat and took another drink of his beer.

"People say he talks to them," Dwayne went on, "they say he stands out in his garden for hours and chats to the damn scarecrows like they were people."

"What does that have to do with us?" Kenny asked, and although he wasn't the brightest bulb or the sharpest tool, Randy thought that the question was the right one, and its answer would define how things were going to proceed. Dwayne licked his lips and then flashed a wide grin over his shoulder.

"I wanna go see for myself what the old fuck is up to."

"It's a waste of time," Randy said, not sure why he was so against the idea.

"Hell, count me in," Kenny grunted. "better than doin' nothing anyway."

Dwayne nodded, and turned towards Randy.

"What about you, man?"

Randy wanted to say no, but peer pressure counted for a lot, and as he looked Dwayne in the eye, he could still see a little bit of that instability that made him nervous lurking there. And besides, he figured anything that would get him out of the driver's seat for long enough to sober up, could only be a good thing.

"Sure, whatever. Count me in too."

Dwayne grinned. "Alright then, let's go."

He gunned the engine, and streaked away, the car struggling to find purchase with the asphalt.

As Dwayne and Kenny cackled and laughed, Randy wondered why he was half hoping they would crash before they arrived.

The Samsonite farm was at the end of a narrow dirt road which snaked across the outer edge of Oakwell Forest. The red convertible bucked and shook as Dwayne teased it down the road. Despite his intake of alcohol, Dwayne expertly controlled the vehicle, and just before the road curved out of sight, he pulled over, and switched off the engine.

"Why are we stopping?" Kenny asked.

"We can't just drive up there you idiot, he'll see us coming. We need to get out and walk now."

"I hate walking! Is it far?"

Dwayne shook his head, and Randy tensed up, unsure how it was going to play out. Eventually, Dwayne broke into a grin.

"Come on, the walk will do your fat ass the world of good."

"Hey, it's not my fault," Kenny whined.

"It never is for you lard-asses. Come on."

Dwayne got out of the car, and Randy and Kenny followed.

The heat of the day was still lingering, and the sky was a breathtaking blanket of stars. The wind gently nudged the trees, and the three boys stood at the front of the car, waiting until Dwayne lit his cigarette.

"You girls ready?" He said as he took a long drag. "Then let's go." He added without waiting.

They walked down the edge of the dirt path, and Randy was a little uncomfortable at the total isolation. Not a single car had passed them, and he wasn't surprised. There was nothing out here but acres and acres of green, and although there were a few farmhouses scattered around, they were spread far from each other.

Dwayne was in front, Randy keeping pace and Kenny was a little way behind, red faced and breathing heavily as he followed. Randy jogged ahead and pulled level with Dwayne.

"How are you holding up?"

"I'm fine."
"You sure man?"
"I said I'm fine."
"I was just thinking that you might want to be with your family..."
"Drop it Randy. I know what's best for me."
Randy didn't say anything else, and they walked in silence, broken only by Kenny's grumbles. They had walked about a quarter of a mile, and as the road curved uphill and left, they could just make out the yellow glow from the Samsonite Farm.
"Well, at least he's home." Kenny gasped as he leaned into the hill.
"He's always home, you dumbass, he's a recluse remember?"
"Oh yeah."
"So," Randy said, "what's the plan when we get there?"
"I don't know yet, I just wanna see the scarecrows. See if it's true about how many he has."
"Then what?"
"Then nothing."
Randy nodded, not sure why he was still feeling so uncomfortable.
They walked on.
Even before they got close to the house, they could see the scarecrows. Knowing how rumours and the ever knowledgeable '*they*' exaggerated things, Randy expected to see a few scarecrows, ten, maybe twenty tops, but as they neared, he could see that on this occasion '*they*' were bang on the money.
There must have been more than a hundred of them, silhouetted in black against the moonlit sky. They were haphazardly placed and surrounded the house. Some, Randy saw, were the size of a full grown adult, others were smaller, and planted in-between their larger counterparts.
The hovel like house sat in the centre of the strange display, a thin wisp of smoke drifting from the chimney.
"Holy shit, would you look at that?" Kenny said as he tried to catch his breath.
Dwayne didn't say anything, and surveyed the landscape of scarecrows. Randy could see well enough, and it was with some dismay that he noticed that little occasional glimmer of whatever

lived inside his grieving friend, was now more evident than ever.

"What do you think the old fuck does all day in there?" Kenny whispered.

"Who knows, the place is out here in the middle of nowhere, he could do anything he wants and get away with it," Dwayne replied as he took a swig of the beer he had brought with him. "You don't have much to say about it." He added, glancing at Randy.

Randy shrugged, trying to feign disinterest despite the gnawing horror in his guts.

"What is there to say, it's a bunch of scarecrows. The guy is probably senile, or well on his way."

"I say we go take a closer look," Dwayne said, flashing a slick, predatory smile.

"I don't know," Kenny mumbled, and Randy could see the uncertainty in his eyes. "I mean, why bother? We have seen what we came here to see."

"I'm with Kenny. Come on, let's get out of here."

"No. you pussies can go wait by the car if you want to, I'm going to take a closer look."

"At what?" Randy snapped "What do you expect to see down there?"

"Well, I don't know until I get over there do I?"

"Look, let's just go home. Call it a night, okay?"

"Yeah, maybe Randy's right, Spyder. Let's go home." Kenny said, eyeing the scarecrows.

"I don't wanna go home!" He hissed.

Dwayne's lip trembled and he turned away so that his friends couldn't see it.

"I can't go home. Not yet." He repeated.

Randy thought he understood. Dwayne wanted to grieve for his mother, but perhaps he didn't know how, or just wasn't ready to accept it yet, and so would do whatever he could to delay having to make that decision.

Randy looked at the house, then to Dwayne.

"Okay." He said. "Let's go and take a quick look, then we get out of here. Agreed?"

"Yeah, exactly," Dwayne said, still not quite free of the tremble in his voice.

"Okay, then let's go, but keep it quiet. This guy has been here alone for a long time, and he might get easily spooked."

"You afraid, Randy?" Kenny sneered.

"No, all I'm saying is we should be careful."

"Why?" Kenny pressed.

"He probably has a gun," Dwayne said, then turned and flashed his alligator smile. "And I doubt he would think too long and hard about shooting at us."

"Oh!" Was all Kenny could muster, and the trio were silent for a while.

"So, how do you want to do this?" Randy asked.

Dwayne licked his lips.

"The scarecrows will give us cover; we just walk straight up to the house. If we see or hear anything, try to blend in."

Randy didn't like it, but he also had a duty to do whatever he could to help his friend through the process of grieving, and so he decided to push away his own uncertainty and get this little voyeuristic mission over with as quickly as possible.

"Well." He said with a sigh. "No point standing around and waiting. Let's get on with it."

They walked towards the house, weaving around the scarecrows as they neared. Randy saw that some were older than others, the tired plaid shirts they wore were rotten and hanging off the straw sack bodies. He drew a deep breath, and his senses were filled with the scent of moist earth, straw and rot.

"Is anyone else freaked out by these things?" Kenny whispered.

Randy was, but he wasn't about to admit it, and so remained silent, and Kenny's question remained unanswered.

They were close now and crouched behind the last row of scarecrows, beyond which were the farmers crops and then finally the house.

"That's weird," Dwayne said as he looked at Randy with a wide grin.

"What is?"

"Look at his crops," Dwayne said, finishing his beer and tossing the can over his shoulder.

Randy did. They looked remarkable. Rows of well-kept tomato plants and potatoes. Behind that, rows of cabbages and beets, then by the side of the house a modest size cornfield.

"It all looks normal to me. What are you seeing?" Randy asked.

"My uncle has a farm," Dwayne whispered. "He had crops like this too, but this whole setup is wrong."

"What do you mean?"

"Come on Randy, think about it. Why would a farmer have a scarecrow?"

"To protect his crops from birds I guess."

"Exactly, now look again."

Randy did and was still unsure what he was looking for. He was about to say as much when it hit him.

"You see it now, right?" Dwayne pressed, and flashed another sick grin.

He did see it. He looked over his shoulder, then back at the crops, and questions began to fill his mind.

The crops were the only place where there were no scarecrows. They were open and exposed, and as Randy looked around him he thought he understood.

"The scarecrows aren't protecting the crops." He said as he looked at Dwayne. "They are protecting the house."

"What the hell would they be protecting the house from?" Kenny asked, now desperate to leave.

"I don't know Kenny, giant birds? Shut up and let me think." Dwayne hissed.

Kenny mumbled and lowered his head, as Randy and Dwayne stared at the house.

"What do you think?" Randy asked.

"I think we go take a closer look."

"I'm not so sure, I have a bad feeling here."

"Look, this is just a crazy old man who doesn't know what he's doing. Nothing more." Dwayne said with more than a hint of bravado.

"Then why are you so determined to look into the house?"

Dwayne was about to reply when he saw a flash of silver in his peripheral vision. The object landed on the dirt between him and Randy, and the two of them looked at it, and then in unison, whipped their heads around to look behind them.

"What?" Kenny said shrugging his shoulders, but he was

ignored. They were looking past Kenny, into the tangle of sticks, straw and old clothes which swayed and creaked in the breeze. Kenny joined them in staring into the dense mass of scarecrows.

The air was still, a thick silence hanging heavy as the trio glared into the darkness from where they crouched.

"You saw me toss that, right, Randy?" Dwayne said, his voice now stripped of bravado.

Randy nodded. He had seen Dwayne throw it over his shoulder when they first arrived here at the edge of the crops. And now, someone had tossed it back.

"Yeah, I saw it."

"Will someone tell me what's going on?" Kenny asked, his voice a little too high and his eyes a little too wide.

"Someone's out there," Dwayne said, flashing that sly grin that reminded Randy of the cat from Alice in Wonderland.

"Shut up man, that's not funny," Kenny whispered, then he saw that neither of his friends was laughing, and the three of them stared into the dark.

"I think we should get out of here," Randy whispered.

"Yeah, me too." Dwayne agreed. "You ready Kenny?"

Kenny didn't answer; instead, he stared into the scarecrows.

"What's wrong? Dwayne hissed.

"They are moving out there."

"Who, the people that are screwing with us?"

"No. The scarecrows."

Dwayne started to laugh, but something in Kenny's eyes made him stop, and he too stared. They watched and waited.

"This is bullshit," Dwayne said, and he scooped up the can and for the second time tossed it deep into the forest of scarecrows. They waited for it to come back, but there was nothing out there but that same heavy silence.

"That's it, I'm done," Randy said, standing and brushing the dirt from his knees. "I'm leaving."

"Yeah, me too," Kenny added.

Randy was expecting to have to convince Dwayne and was surprised when he too stood and zipped up his jacket with shaking hands.

"I'm with you; let's get the hell out of here."

They moved quickly, crouched over as they crisscrossed their way around the maze of scarecrows. It was hard to see which way they had come and combined with their panic, disorientation set in.

"Which way?" Kenny said, closer than ever to losing it completely.

"Keep going straight, we'll be out soon enough."

"It shouldn't be taking this long." He shot back. "Screw this."

Kenny stood, and there framed by the moonlight, both Dwayne and Randy saw it all.

One of the scarecrows moved. It turned its head – a cloth bag stuffed with straw and adorned with a rough hand drawn face. At the same time, it swung towards Kenny, the wooden frame which held its arms at its side hitting him full in the face.

Kenny yelped as the wood smashed into his nose, staggering him backwards. The scarecrows behind him swung aside to accommodate him and then closed behind him.

Kenny was gone.

"What the fuck was that?" Dwayne croaked as the scarecrows began to sway and move as if rocked by the wind. The way ahead was closed, lost in the movements of the scarecrows.

"Come on, back the way we came," Randy yelled as he turned and ran back towards the warm yellow glow from the windows of the house.

"What about Kenny?" Dwayne said as he followed.

Randy didn't answer. If it were a movie, they would surely go back and retrieve their portly friend, but here in real life, Randy didn't care enough about Kenny to risk his own skin. His concern was getting free of the scarecrows.

"Hey!" Randy screamed. "Hey, you in the house, open up!"

The pair burst free of the scarecrows, and charged over the crops, giving the cabbages and carrots underfoot little regard. They arrived at the house, and Randy pounded on the door.

"Hey, open up!" He yelled.

"Jesus, look at this," Dwayne said quietly.

Randy turned and pressed his back to the door and looked at the scarecrows.

When they had arrived, they were all facing out away from the house, but now as the two boys stood with their backs to the farmhouse door, the scarecrows were facing inwards. They were like sentinels, watching with eyes that were as unreal as the heads they were drawn on. Any sense of a path through them was gone. The house was surrounded. As they waited, the door swung open, and Randy fell backwards, landing in a heap on the floor of the farmhouse.

"Hey, what the hell..."

Dwayne's protests were cut short by the double barreled shotgun which was pointing at his face.

He looked beyond it to its owner and raised his hands.

"Get the hell in here, boy, and pick your damn friend up off the floor."

Dwayne did as he was told, and the farmer ushered them in, the gun still trained on them.

"Take a seat." He said as he closed and locked the door.

Jorell Samsonite looked almost exactly like Randy had envisioned him. He was old and wiry, and peered at them with mistrustful eyes from a face hidden by his dirty white beard and knotted unkempt hair. Jorell glared at the two intruders, who were pale faced and sitting at the kitchen table in silence.

The farmhouse was minimal, and obviously designed for the single life. Jorell glared at the two intruders, licking his lips as he swayed from side to side.

"What are you doing here? Why did you come?" Asked the manic old man.

"Hey, take it easy," Randy said. "We had no choice. Your scarecrows…"

"Stopped you, didn't they?" Jorell cackled. "Stopped you from leaving."

"Look pal." Dwayne said, "I don't know what the hell kinda game you think you are playing here..."

Jorell lowered the gun and began to cry. He sat on the wooden chair by the door and put his head in his hands.

"You don't get it, do you?" The old man said. "None of this is me. This isn't my fault."

"Look, Mr Samsonite, if we could use your phone, we'll be out of here and leave you in peace," Randy said, keeping a close eye on the shotgun.

"No phone, haven't had one for years." The old man muttered

"You can't just keep us here," Dwayne said, his eyes flicking for a split second to the shotgun held in the old man's hands.

"You don't get it, do you, son?" Jorell repeated, flashing his toothless grin. "You're free to go whenever you like as far as I'm concerned. But them." He said pointing to the closed door. "They won't allow it. They'll make you stay."

"You could call em' off." Dwayne said, rubbing the back of his neck. "Call em' off and let us go, we won't tell anyone what you're doing out here."

The old man grinned and shook his head.

"You really don't get it, do you, sonny?"

"What do you mean?" Dwayne asked.

"You're trapped here too, aren't you Mr Samsonite?" Randy said quietly.

The old man looked at him and then lowered his gaze.

"Yes, yes I am." He said, exhaling and relaxing his grip on the gun.

"What do you mean? What are you saying?"

Dwayne was close to losing it, and Randy didn't like to think what might happen if he did. The old man must have seen it too because he stood and walked to the fridge and pulled out a jug of cloudy moonshine and grabbed three glasses from the cupboard.

"Relax, son, you're safe enough here in the house. Drink?"

"What is it?" Randy asked.

"Moonshine. Brew it myself here on the farm. Not bad stuff if I say so myself."

"I'll take one," Dwayne said.

Jorell poured them both a drink, then returned to his chair, propped the shotgun against the wall and lowered himself down with a sigh. They sat in silence in the grimy kitchen, and without warning, Jorell began to speak.

"Thirty seven years ago, I came here to this farm. I was a young man, and back then I thought the world was at my fingertips. My father had bought it and put it in my name. He wanted me to learn the family business. To earn my way in the world. That first year was a tough one, and the learning curve for those intending to live off the land is a high one. I enjoyed it though and got to be competent. I grew everything I need right outside my own door, Fruits and vegetables. Out back, I have a coop with chickens and a few cows for milk and cheese. I have my very own little food chain."

The old man smiled and began to pick the thick dirt from under his overgrown fingernails.

"Two years went by, and I was doing fine. My wife was with our child, and I loved my job. First time I thought something might be wrong was the summer of '57. I was out front there, ploughing the earth. I had this idea to grow wheat and thought it was just about the perfect place. I was out there digging, and the sun was fierce on my back. That's when it happened."

"What happened Mr Samsonite?"

"Well, sonny, I don't rightly know for sure. All I know is that there was something in the dirt. Something foul and evil and forgotten, and I was unlucky enough to find it. I don't know what it was, and I ain't about to speculate, but whatever it was, I had a desire, a compulsion to protect it. Built my first scarecrow out there later that week. Called it George after my father.

My wife asked me what the hell I intended to frighten away from an empty field, and I told her to leave me to my work.

Well, it turns out whatever was in the dirt was a powerful thing, and I took to going out there as often as I could. I would sit all day at that damn scarecrows feet, and these ideas of what I had to do came to me. That week I built two more crows, planted em' right out there next to George. By now of course, my wife was startin' to think I needed to see a doctor, and so I took fists to her and put her in her place."

Randy and Dwayne shared a quick glance, and Jorell smiled. "You boys don't have to judge me; I have punished myself enough for that and more over the years. I don't want to get distracted if I can help it."

Randy and Dwayne nodded, and the old man licked his lips and continued.

"So, it went on like that for weeks. I didn't sleep, I barely ate. All I did was sit out there in that damn field and soak up whatever was down in the dirt, and do as it told me. By that winter, the field that was intended for my wheat held just short of sixty five crows. A little after Christmas of that year, I came back to the house to find a doctor waiting for me, wanting to examine me. Well, I chased him out of the door and told him not to come back. My wife threatened to leave me if I didn't explain, so I dragged her out there to the field, and showed her."

His smile faded, and he swallowed as he recalled the memory.

"Crows took her that night. Part of me knew it was gonna happen, and yet I dragged her up there anyway. There was a lot of blood, and I knew they liked that, they liked the blood soaking through the dirt. Later, where that blood had flowed, smaller crows started to push through the dirt. You probably saw some of the juveniles when you snuck in."

Randy nodded, and the old man shrugged his narrow shoulders.

"Well, that's how they grow. Come up fully shaped like that. Don't ask me how or why, because I don't know. They just did. You gotta remember, I was just a young fella back then and scared of what would happen to me if I told the police. Without my wife to keep me in check, things got worse. I stopped looking after the farm; I stopped even really spending time in the house. I would either be sitting there, cross-legged in the dirt, or I'd be building crows and planting them. By June of '59, I had planted over three hundred of them all around the perimeter of the house. Another hundred and a half had sprouted out of the ground of their own accord. I think even then, on some level, I knew what they were doing, and what they were making me do, but I was scared, and so I did as I was told. Took me a further year to fence myself in, by then I was lost anyway. I was a slave to whatever it is that lives in the dirt out there. They forced me to get off my ass and make the farm self-sustaining. They…"

The old man grimaced, and ran a dirty hand through his hair.

"They feed on things, living things. I lost count of how many corpses I found out there in the fields. Always drained of blood, always at the feet of one of the crows. At first, I used to burn the corpses, then they told me it was safe to eat them, and being a man who likes meat as much as anyone, I did. Mice, rabbits, foxes, badgers. Anything that the crows killed and drained, I finished off. We helped each other."

"Why didn't you try to leave?" Randy asked as he sipped his drink.

“I did try, once. It was back in '63. I don’t know what triggered it, but I decided one day that I had had enough, and that I would leave the crows and whatever lived down in the dirt to its own devices. I set out from here and made for the main road, the same one I suspect you came from. I didn’t make it even half way through the field before they stopped me. Blocked me in, stopped me in my tracks. Seems they needed me after all, to tend to them when they were blown over in winter, or one of the straw bags that I used for the heads and bodies split and needed to be repaired, or if they needed fresh clothes when the others had rotted off them. And of course, to dispose of the corpses. They told me then that I wouldn’t be allowed to leave, and even though I cried and begged and screamed, they didn’t listen.”

“What happened then?” Dwayne asked.

The old man sighed and shrugged his shoulders.

“Then, I did as I was told. Fast forward thirty something years and here we are today with you kids breaking down my door to get in.”

The old man grinned and stood, wincing as his knee joints popped.

“You kids just made the biggest mistake of your lives.” He said as he shuffled out of the room, leaving Dwayne and Randy alone.

The following morning was overcast, and a light drizzle fell. Jorell had made breakfast (which both Randy and Dwayne were grateful to see, contained no meat) of porridge and jam, and then told them they could have the run of the house apart from his personal rooms, which were on the top floor.

The two friends sat opposite each other at the kitchen table, neither having slept. Randy glanced out of the window at the vast ocean of scarecrows, which had thankfully returned to facing away from the house.

“How’d you sleep?” Randy asked as he rubbed his stubble fluffed cheeks.

“I didn’t. You?”

Randy shook his head, and the two were silent. They could see

Jorell out in the fields, walking amongst the scarecrows and making sure they were tidy and in good order.

"So, any ideas?"

"No, I'm still struggling to come to terms with this," Randy said as he drummed his fingers on the table top.

"I think I have an idea if you want to hear it."

Randy looked at Dwayne, expecting to see the hidden craziness, but he saw only his friend, and for that he was glad.

"What you got?"

Dwayne reached into his pocket and set his lighter on the table.

"We can burn our way out."

Randy looked out of the window, and the driving rain which showed no sign of slowing down.

"It's too wet, nothing will burn."

"No, I know that. So we wait until it dries out."

"You wanna wait here?"

"No, I don't want to, I just don't see any other choice."

"Maybe the old man's story was a way to keep us here," Randy muttered.

"What about Kenny?" Dwayne shot back.

Randy was silent. He had forgotten about Kenny and felt ashamed for it. Kenny was always more Dwayne's friend than his, and Randy only knew him by association, but he acknowledged that even so, it gave him no right to have forgotten about him so completely.

"We can't help him now. We have to look out for ourselves."

"That's exactly what I'm doing," Dwayne said. "It just might take a little time."

"We can't stay here."

"I don't like it either, and I sure as hell don't intend on trying to walk my way through those things again."

That was enough to bring silence back to the table, and for a time they sat there.

"When were you thinking of doing it?" Randy said, nodding towards the lighter.

"A few days. The weather report says it should brighten up tomorrow, so allowing for a couple of days for the bastards to really dry out, I'd say four days. Five tops."

"We don't even know this guy, I mean, surely he would have thought of this idea, why is he still here?"

"Come on Randy, you heard his story. He's frightened, and I guess now he's just too old to do anything about it."

"I suppose we have no choice, do we, assuming he even lets us stay."

"I don't see how he has a choice."

"Can I ask you something, Dwayne?"

"Shoot."

"His story… do you believe him?"

"I don't know," Dwayne said slowly. "All I *do* know is that those things out there were moving, and that's enough for me to not want to be out there."

"That's good enough for me," Randy replied. "Let's see if the old man will put us up for a few nights."

"He will. He's too old and weak to stop us."

"Should we tell him about our plan?"

"No, absolutely not, under any circumstances." Dwayne snapped, and there, just for a split second, Randy saw the dark thing that lived inside his friend.

"Why not? What harm can it do?"

"You ever heard of something called Stockholm Syndrome, Randy?"

"No, I can't say I have."

"Back in the early '70's, '73 I think, it was, two guys robbed a bank in Stockholm. Things got a little crazy, so they take the bank workers hostage, and hold them in the vault for six days. Anyways, things came to a head, and the police talked the two guys into surrendering and freeing the hostages. The funny thing is, the people who had been held captive, sympathised with the guys who had held them there and tried to stop them from being sent to jail."

"Why would they do that?"

"Who knows, they say the hostages formed a bond with their captors and a relationship built between them. My point is, this old man has been here for so long doing the will of these damn scarecrows, that I don't think he would leave now, even if he could, which means that he could be dangerous if he gets wind of what we plan to do."

"So what do we do until then?" Randy asked as he watched the old man fuss around the scarecrows through the kitchen window.

"Play nice, offer to help him out around the farm. God knows, the place could use it." Dwayne said, looking around the dilapidated kitchen.

"Okay, but I want us out of here as soon as we can do it safely."

"You don't need to convince me of anything. As soon as those damn scarecrows are dry enough to burn a path through; we're getting the hell out of here."

Randy tossed the twin armful of carrots into the wheelbarrow and wiped a dirty forearm across his brow.

Jorell had been happy for them to stay and had put them to work on the farm. For the last three days, Dwayne had worked on the inside, tidying the house as Randy picked and tended to the crops.

Despite the weather reports, the rain had continued in spotty showers, and the dry periods that did come were few. Frustration was starting to set in, and Randy glared at the ocean of wooden effigies which stood between him and freedom.

The old man spent most of his days out in the fields. Randy watched him as he walked among the scarecrows, adjusting their clothes, talking to them and repairing any damage. It was obvious to see that he was quite mad, but both he and Dwayne chose to ignore it, as it made the wait to make their escape easier to bear. It was then, as he was watching Jorell in the distance, that he saw a second figure standing in the field speaking to him.

It was Dwayne.

Randy watched from afar and wondered why the situation tugged at his guts and made him feel as if he were being left out of whatever conversation they were having. Randy looked on, and a few minutes later, Dwayne began to head towards the house. Randy walked to meet him, unsure why he was so angry.

"What was that about?" He asked as Dwayne neared.

"What?"

"You and the old man."

"I don't know what you mean."

"Why were you over there in the field? I thought that would be the last place you would go, considering what happened to Kenny."

Dwayne looked at the ground, then at his friend.

"It's nothing to worry about; the old man just wanted help planting one of his scarecrows, that's all."

"And you did it?" Randy spat. "I thought we were trying to get out of here, not build up the defences."

"Jesus Randy, it was one damn scarecrow and nowhere near the route where we will be leaving. Just relax. I know what I'm doing."

"I just don't think we should be going out there in those fields, especially after the old man's story."

"Okay, take it easy, if I had known you would start acting like my mother I..."

He trailed off, and looked at the dirt, then continued. "Just relax that's all. I know what I'm doing. Okay?"

Dwayne didn't wait for an answer and went back to the house.

Randy watched him go and then turned to the field of scarecrows. They were still facing away from him, and he couldn't see the old man, but he couldn't shake the feeling that they were watching him, and that, on some level, he now stood alone.

The rest of the day passed without incident, and their routine was as normal. Randy worked outside, bringing the crops back into some kind of order whilst Dwayne worked on tidying the house. The light of the day began to fade, and as Randy stood and stretched, trying to ignore the agony in his back, he smiled, because even though the day had been overcast, it hadn't rained, and so they were a little closer to their escape.

The three of them ate in silence at the kitchen table that night. The old man came back after sundown and didn't say a word to either of them. He finished his meal, and then went upstairs, leaving Dwayne and Randy to tidy away the dishes.

"How does tomorrow look?" Randy whispered.

"Possible, although it might be worth waiting another day just to be sure. We really need those damn things to burn."

Randy glanced over at Dwayne and saw that his friend was distracted. He seemed to have the weight of the world on his shoulders, which, under the circumstances was understandable.

"You sleeping alright?" Randy asked.

"Not really, I can't seem to settle."

"Tell me about it. Its knowing that those damn things are out there."

"Just a couple more days, then we are out of here. Just try to keep it together until then."

The next morning, Randy woke to blazing sunshine. He looked out of the window and could barely contain his excitement. There wasn't a single cloud in the sky. He dressed and went downstairs; hoping to speak to Dwayne about their improved chances of leaving, but found the house empty. He opened the door and stepped out, enjoying the warmth of the sun on his face as he glared at the scarecrows, looking forward to finally putting them to the torch.

His smile faded when he saw Dwayne and the old man. They were in the field amongst the scarecrows again, only, this time, Dwayne was sitting cross legged watching the old man as he spoke and gesticulated, Randy wanted to go over and find out what the pair were talking about, but the thought of being near the scarecrows terrified him, and he didn't want to go near them until it was time to leave. A slight breeze ruffled his hair and brought with it a snatch of laughter. He hoped it was from the old man but he couldn't be sure. He went back into the house and closed the door, then crossed to the kitchen table and sat down hard. He looked out of the window, and the beautiful day that he had greeted with such joy, now seemed to be mocking him.

The morning came and went. Randy worked the vegetable patch, which was now almost presentable. Dwayne and the old man stayed over in the field with the scarecrows. Although he tried to concentrate on his work, Randy couldn't help but repeatedly look to see what his friend and the old man were doing.

A little after mid-day, Dwayne walked towards the house. His hands were filthy, as were the knees of his jeans. Although he had intended to be calm, Randy grabbed Dwayne by the shirt collars as he approached.

"What the hell's going on?" He spat.

"Hey, take it easy."

"What were you doing over there? We agreed it's dangerous."

"The old guy asked me to help him. What could I say?"

Randy released his grip, and Dwayne smoothed down his shirt.

"What else could I do?" Dwayne repeated. "Refuse?"

"Yes, you could have refused, hell you *should* have refused."

"And then what happens? Say the old man decides to kick us out of the house, did you consider that?"

"No, I suppose I didn't," Randy said as his anger faded. "I just… I don't think we should be going over there that's all."

"Don't worry. The old man isn't so bad when you get to know him."

"I don't want to get to know him, I want to go home."

"If this heat holds up, we should be good to go tomorrow."

"I hope so. The longer we stay here; I worry that we'll never get to leave."

"Don't worry, as long as we stay calm and stick to the plan, everything will be fine."

"I just can't shake this feeling that's all, that something bad is going to happen to us."

"This is a messed up situation, that's for sure, but we need to stick together. Just trust me."

Randy nodded and looked over Dwayne's shoulder at the ocean of scarecrows. There was no sign of the old man, but Randy supposed he could be anywhere, hiding in plain sight amongst his creations.

"I'm just stressed. That's all." Randy said with a sigh.

"We both are." Dwayne agreed. "Just let me worry about getting us out of this mess. After all, I got us into it."

Randy nodded again and cast another wary eye towards the scarecrows. Dwayne looked over his shoulder.

"I better get back; the old guy will wonder where I am. Told him I needed a drink of water."

"What is it that he has you doing out there?"

"I... I'm not supposed to say."

"What happened to trust? Come on, Dwayne, you can't keep things from me, especially when it comes to this place."

"Please, just drop it. Okay?"

"Tell me." He hissed, fighting the urge to manhandle his friend again.

"I buried Kenny." Dwayne said, his eyes wide and frightened.

"He made me bury Kenny out there with the scarecrows."

The words were enough to stop Randy in his tracks. All he could do was stare at his friend and wait for his mind to make some rational sense of the situation. Dwayne swallowed, and then lowered his voice.

"You should have seen him Randy. He was all… fucked up, and the old man said if we didn't bury him the crows would be angry. I didn't want to man, but we were right there in the middle of them, and let me tell you, it feels like they are watching you all the damn time. Not just looking at you but through you. I had no choice."

"And when were you going to tell me about this?"

"I don't know, later maybe. Just as soon as I had come to terms with it myself. You don't know how difficult it was Randy, you really don't."

"You could have refused."

Dwayne smiled, and for the first time since they had arrived, Randy saw a flash of that darkness appear in his eyes.

"No, it doesn't work like that man. You might think so, but you are safe down here by the house. Out there!" He jabbed a dirty thumb over his shoulder. "It's... *different*. The atmosphere is different. And that old man, he talks and, damn, it makes sense."

"Sounds like excuses to me."

"Fuck you, man," Dwayne said, still wearing that same horrible smile. "You don't know anything about it, you don't understand."

"I think I'm starting to. I think it's all starting to make sense."

"Don't you tell me my business. Back at school, you might be a big hotshot wrestler, and Mr Popularity, but out here, you're no better than me."

"What the hell are you talking about? I never said I was better than anybody."

"Bullshit, you know what I'm talking about. Here comes Randy, everyone loves him, everyone wants to be his friend, well that's fine, but here and now, someone has to do the dirty jobs that nobody else wants to, and because I'll do anything to save our ass, it's up to me to do it, so don't you dare preach to me and try to come across like some clean cut, never-do-anything-wrong asshole, because I won't stand for it."

Dwayne was glaring at Randy, his fists balled at his sides. Randy didn't want to fight, and the ferocity of his friend's outburst hurt him more than he would have ever expected.

"Something's changed, you aren't the same," Randy whispered, backing away from Dwayne and trying to diffuse the aggression. It seemed to work, as Dwayne relaxed, and ran a dirty hand through his hair.

"Look, we can talk later when we've both calmed down, but right now, I have to get back to work."

Randy didn't have an answer for that, and Dwayne didn't wait for one. Instead, he turned and jogged towards the field. Randy watched him go, and still couldn't shake the feeling that the scarecrows were watching. He imagined they were smiling.

Randy spent the rest of the day alone. Dwayne and the old man had stayed out in the fields, and even after sundown hadn't returned. Not wanting to speak to either of them anyway, Randy went to bed early, but the combination of paranoia and isolation meant that sleep took a long time to come. He heard them come in just after midnight, and a little later, the house was silent. He tossed and turned for a further hour, and then realising that sleep wasn't going to come to him anytime soon, got out of bed and went downstairs.

He put a pan of water on to boil, hoping that a cup of tea (the old man had stockpiled bags of the stuff in the cellar) would help him to relax enough to get a few hours rest.

He saw the dancing torch beam through the kitchen window as he was rinsing his cup. He stared into the field, watching the zig-zagging blade of light as it moved around in the darkness. In an instant, all thoughts of drinking tea were forgotten.

He hoped that it was the old man who was out there, and somehow ignored his instincts which told him otherwise. Quietly he walked to the door, knowing that just outside would be his answer.

The old man had a thing about dirty floors, and insisted on shoes and boots being left outside the house. As Randy opened the door, he hoped to see Dwayne's boots next to his own trainers, and the old man's missing. Any alternative would mean that he truly was alone and that Dwayne was falling under the same spell that had enchanted the old man years earlier.

He swung the door open, but couldn't bear to look to the floor to see if his suspicions were right. He realised that his entire future could rest on a pair of dirty boots. He took a deep breath and looked down.

The old man's boots were there, as were Randy's own. He had expected that Dwayne's would be missing, but his too were there set neatly next to the others. Randy looked from the boots out into the fields and the torch beam that still danced and cut through the air.

There was somebody else out there.

Randy charged across the garden, crushing the crops that he had spent the last few days tending to. He knew he had to warn whoever was out there and tell them to leave before it was too late. Maybe he could even ask them to go for help. He was almost to the boundary of the crops, and the scarecrows loomed like sentinels framed by the night sky. He paid them no heed and charged into the field, twisting and ducking around their reaching arms as he approached the flashlight beam.

"Go back." He screamed, hoping that it might frighten the would-be explorers away. "Get out of here,"

He could see them in his mind, naive kids, much like he was just a few days ago, looking to get a thrill by creeping onto the Samsonite Farm to laugh at his scarecrows, but this was no laughing matter, and Randy knew that he had to warn them, whatever the cost. He stumbled, and one of the scarecrows dry, stick fingers scraped his cheek, but he kept his footing and went on. The torch beam was just ahead of him now, and he exploded into the clearing hoping it wasn't too late to stop them, when he froze.

It was Dwayne.

He was naked and dancing, gibbering to himself as he swung the torch around over his head. He was covered in dirt and as Randy looked on, he paused and scooped up a large handful of earth and shoveled it into his mouth.

"What the fuck...." Was all Randy could manage, and as he watched his friend, he found that he was more afraid of him than of the scarecrows.

Dwayne ignored him and continued to dance in circles, hopping on one foot as he laughed and muttered. Randy realised that if they were to leave, they couldn't wait. He saw Dwayne's discarded clothes piled up on the floor, and began to search through them, looking for the lighter.

"You won't find it." Dwayne cackled. "I buried it."

"Where? Where did you bury it?" Randy screamed, but Dwayne only laughed.

"They have it now." He said, then picked up another handful of earth and ate it. Randy could see that his stomach was bloating as he engorged himself.

"Come on man." Randy pleaded. "We need to get out of here, we need to go home."

Dwayne stopped dancing and looked at Randy, then flashed a dirty grin.

"I am home." He said, and then started to dance again, swinging the torch above his head.

Horrified and dazed, Randy backed away and ran back to the house before whatever was in the earth here infected him too. He kept waiting for the cold, dry grip of the scarecrows to impede him, but they let him pass without incident, seemingly content for now with Dwayne. He exited the trees, and paused by the crops, hands on his knees. His mind swam with the enormity of what had happened, and he walked back towards the house in a daze, unsure what the next move should be. He entered the house and closed the door behind him, then sat at the kitchen table, holding his head in his hands.

"Do you see it now?" The old man said as he walked out of the shadows.

Randy didn't answer. Jorell walked to the table and sat

opposite Randy.

"They have him, just like they took me all those years ago."

Randy lifted his head, fully intending to give the old man hell, but stopped when he saw him. His face was swollen and he had cuts across the bridge of his nose and eye. He offered Randy a dejected smile, and poured them both a mug of moonshine from the jug on the kitchen table.

"What the hell happened to you?" Randy asked as the old man set the glass of alcohol in front of him.

"I think you know, or at least suspect the answer to that question."

"Dwayne. He did this didn't he?"

The old man nodded and drained his glass.

"I was having him help me out there. I used to be able to do it on my own but I'm getting old, and my joints don't work so good. Those things insist on me planting new ones every few weeks, and I couldn't do it by myself."

The old man grimaced, and took another thoughtful sip. Randy could see that his hands were shaking.

"I didn't think they would get to him as long as I stayed with him. I thought he would be alright. But I noticed him starting to change, and so I told him to come back down to the house earlier this morning."

"I saw him; he said he had come back for water."

"I suspect he did, but that wasn't the reason. He was supposed to be helping me plant the crows, but I saw him digging in the dirt. Using his bare hands he was, and I could hear him whispering to himself as he did it. I didn't like that, reminded me too much of myself way back in the beginning, so I sent him away. He refused, I insisted. Then he took the shovel and did this."

The old man pointed to his eye, which was almost swollen shut.

"Left me there and continued to dig and talk to whatever it is in the dirt here. I suspect he only came back to the house to keep you from coming over to see what was happening. Whilst he was over talking to you, I was out there bleeding under the sun and unable to get up."

"I'm sorry, I didn't know, how could I know..."

"Don't beat yourself up about it kid, it's not your fault." The old man said, offering Randy a top up of the moonshine. Randy accepted the offer, and the old man went on. "So he comes back, and he starts talking to this hole in the ground, telling it all about your plans."

Randy straightened in his seat and stammered before the old man held up a hand to stop him.

"Before you try and talk your way out of it, don't bother. He told them how you two planned to burn your way out of here, which, by the way, wouldn't have worked anyway."

"Why not?"

"They don't burn, son, that's why. Tried it myself. No matter how dry it gets, those damn things just don't take a flame. Anyways, that's beside the point. I was trapped there with him, and he was singing and chattering and I realised then that they had him, I mean completely had him. I tried to talk to them, thinking that they would listen to me since I had looked after them for all those years, but for the first time ever, they shut me out. Cut me off."

The old man's lip started to tremble, and he drank the rest of his whiskey.

"He was going to kill me." He said, matter of factly.

Randy blinked, and couldn't formulate an answer. Jorrell went on, the calm tone of his voice unsettling.

"He was going to kill me and bury me out there in the fields, but they wouldn't let him, I suppose that was my reward for the years I have served them.

I was told I could leave, and by then it was late. He took off his shoes and told me to take them and put them by the door. He said he didn't want you to know what he was up to out there because he needed you to have hope."

"What do you mean? Hope?"

"I don't know, I'm just telling you what he told me, whatever that friend of yours is up to, I'm not privy to it."

"I don't get how this could happen; I mean you said it took weeks for you to be... influenced by those things. How could it happen to Dwayne in just a couple of days?"

"I don't know for sure, but I have a theory if you want to hear it."

"Go ahead," Randy said, wincing as he drank the potent home brew.

"I think when I first discovered it, whatever lives in the dirt, it was weak and in its infancy.

I also think that I was less inclined to listen to them back then because I had something else to hold onto. A wife, a family, a business. But with this friend of yours, I think he was perfect for them. He told me about his mother, and I could see that he was one of those drifter, thrill seeker types. Directionless and looking for a purpose. I think that made him perfect for them. You have to remember, that this... whatever it is, has lived down in the earth there for nigh on forty years. Who knows how long before that? It's strong now, hell I'm sure you felt it, how the atmosphere is different out there, how the air tastes like a storm all the damn time."

Randy nodded, he *had* felt it.

"Well, I think now that it's strong, it can work fast, and that buddy of yours was easy pickings for them and their needs."

"That's what I don't understand. Randy said. "What is it they want with him?"

"Isn't it obvious?" The old man said with a knowing smile. "He's my replacement. I'm too old to tend to them anymore, and they know as well as I do that my days are numbered. They want him to take over where I left off."

Randy licked his lips, not sure quite how to word the question that he needed to ask. The old man grinned and said it for him.

"If you're wondering what that means for me, then I think we both know."

"They will kill you, won't they?"

"Oh no, I don't think so. They know I'm old, they know I'm not gonna last much longer. I think for me, they'll just wait until the inevitable happens, then that friend of yours will bury me out there in the damn dirt and feed me to them."

Randy swallowed, and it hit him all at once

"That just leaves me." He said, somehow feeling distanced from his own body.

"Aye." The old man said as he poured them both another drink. "They know you want to escape, and are young and hungry enough to try it."

"What does that mean?"

"It means that they won't want to take that risk, and will want you out of the picture."

"But I'm safe as long as I stay out of the fields. Right?"

The old man smiled and shook his head.

"They'll send him to do it, and make no mistake, he will."

"He wouldn't do that, even if those things told him to. I have known Dwayne since we were eight years old."

"You don't get it, do you, son? Whoever your friend was before don't exist anymore. He's gone. That thing out in the field now serves them. No two ways about it."

"What do you expect me to do?"

The old man leaned closer, and he whispered the words that Randy was desperate not to hear.

"You'll have to kill him before he kills you."

"I can't do that. I'm no murderer, he's my friend."

"No, he isn't, not anymore. All I can do is advise you. Either will or you won't mind what I tell ya. But take it from me. He *will* come for you, and he *will* do all he can to make sure you die."

Randy lowered his head, and despite his desperation to disbelieve the old man, he knew that he was right.

"I need time, I need to think." Randy said as he drained his glass.

"Time is a luxury you don't have. He will come, and it will be soon."

"I can stop him; I can talk him out of it."

"You might think so, and I thought so too. But think about this. Even when it was weak, they still made me butcher my pregnant wife and feed her to them. No matter how much you think that your human spirit will be enough, your friend will come and he will try to kill you. That's not me trying to put the frighteners on you, that's just the way it is."

"How long do I have?"

"Who knows?" The old man shrugged. It could be minutes, hours or days. But it will be soon. And you need to do whatever it takes to be ready."

"Will you help me? If I try to get you out of here, will you help?" Randy blurted, looking the old man in the eye.

“Ten years ago I would have said yes, but I’m too old, too tired. I can’t help you.”

“You can’t just watch it happen, please!”

“I’m sorry.” The old man said as he stood. “I can’t get involved.”

He walked past Randy, placing a hand on his shoulder as he passed. “Good luck son.” He said, then left the room and headed upstairs.

Randy looked out of the window at the dancing torch beams and thought about what he would have to do.

The night faded to day, and still, Dwayne didn’t come. The torch beam stopped shining a little after four am, but Randy was sure that Dwayne was still out there dancing, and it was just the battery that had expired. He had toiled with the actions that he must take, and although morally they went against everything that he stood for, he acknowledged that it was a case of life or death, and he would do whatever it took to get back to the world, and his life.

By mid-morning, he realised that the waiting was worse, and part of him was eager for Dwayne to make his move so that at least he would be able to reach some resolution.

The old man had come downstairs briefly, and even then he didn’t speak and barely looked at Randy, pausing just long enough to get some food and head back upstairs. Randy heard the old man lock his bedroom door, and once again he was alone. He stepped outside and looked around at the never ending landscape of scarecrows. He knew well enough that they surrounded the house, and that Dwayne could be anywhere, watching him whilst remaining completely unseen himself. Randy held his breath and listened, but he could hear only the pleasant chatter of birds and the drone of bees as they explored the crops. Morning drifted into the afternoon, and still there was no sign of Dwayne. The day had been hot and dry, and Randy wondered just how his friend was lasting without food or water, then realised that he was probably receiving both from the earth, assuming he was still eating it.

Randy cupped his hands over his eyes, and surveyed the

landscape, and was just starting to think that it would be after dark now before he came when he saw him. Just his head at first as he pushed his way through the scarecrows. Randy tensed, and his heart rate increased. Despite the hours psyching himself up, he found that he was rooted to the spot, and unable to move from the doorstep.

Dwayne marched towards the house. He was fully dressed, apart from his feet which were bare. His hands and mouth were streaked with dirt, and his eyes stared blankly as he approached.

This is it.

Randy thought to himself as he prepared for the coming confrontation. Dwayne marched to within ten feet of Randy and then stopped. The two friends faced off, Randy was trying as best he could to hide his fear. Dwayne stared and twitched.

"You don't have to do this." Randy pleaded, his voice sounding incredibly loud in the stillness of the day.

"Death is the only way, they said I have to."

"No, you don't. You don't have to listen to them."

"If I don't, they say you will try to hurt me. I have to do it first."

"I don't want to hurt you Dwayne; I'll do anything not to have to."

"I'm not here for you; I'm here for the old man."

Randy blinked, at the unexpected turn of events.

"He said they were letting him go, and that it's me they want dead."

"I convinced them," Dwayne said as he smiled, his teeth covered in dirt. "I said you were better alive, that you would come around eventually and help me."

"Help with what?"

"Help to grow them, to help them spread. Samsonite is too old, but we are young and strong. I convinced them to let you live."

"But the old man has to die?"

Dwayne nodded. "That's how it has to be."

"We aren't murderers," Randy said, "we don't need to do this."

"This is bigger than us Randy, you don't understand yet, but it is. I'll tell you, fill you in, but first we have to finish the old man.

He's a threat to us. He will kill us if we don't kill him."

"He won't," Randy said, shaking his head. "He's frightened. He just wants peace."

"And what better peace is there than death?" Dwayne said, emitting a sharp bray of laughter.

"I can't let you in here. I won't let you kill him."

Dwayne shook his head, a look of genuine sadness on his face.

"Don't make me hurt you. I really don't want to. Trust me."

"Like I did about the plan to escape?" Randy said, setting himself in the doorframe of the house.

"You don't understand, this way is better. Just let me finish the old man, then I'll tell you all about it."

Dwayne took a step forwards, and in one fluid motion, Randy picked up the shotgun from inside the door and aimed it at his friend.

"Don't you fucking move," He screamed.

Dwayne smiled and put his hands up slowly. Randy noted that he looked completely unconcerned and that his eyes were filled with that deep, dark something that until that day had only been seen in glimpses.

"You won't kill me, Randy. We both know it."

"I don't want to, but I will if I have to."

Dwayne took a single step forward. "No, you won't. You're not a killer. You're not disturbed like me. You are the good guy, the one who everyone likes. You aren't a loner."

"Not one more step Dwayne, I'm warning you."

Dwayne smiled and took another step closer. There was now less than eight feet between them.

"You would really put a gun on me to protect some old fuck we don't even know?"

"You don't get to choose who lives or dies, and neither do they," Randy said, nodding towards the scarecrows.

"You don't understand, I really do think you would see things differently. All you see is what's on the surface, but those scarecrows, their roots run deep, and they grow and spread in ways you can't imagine. Now I'm coming through, and I'm going to kill the old man, then we can talk, okay?"

"Don't do it, please." Randy said, his hands shaking as he kept the weapon focussed on Dwayne.

"I have to, they told me."

"I'm telling you not to, please Dwayne."

"I have no choice."

He walked towards Randy, completely unafraid.

"Stop, please!"

He fired.

The sound rolled across the fields, and at such short distance, Dwayne was launched through the air, coming to rest on his back in the cabbage field. Hit in the stomach, his intestines pooled around the hole in his white T-Shirt. Randy dropped the weapon and ran to his friend, kneeling next to him in the dirt. His stomach was a mess, his insides now on the outside, the smell of hot blood mingled with the smell of vegetables and flowers. Randy held his friend's hand, sickened and surprised that he was still alive.

"I'm sorry, I didn't want to..." Randy sobbed.

Dwayne looked at his friend with glassy eyes and somehow managed a smile.

"You... you... I…" He said through chattering teeth, and the sight of his friend in such a sorry state made Randy's guilt worse.

"Why did you make me do it? Why didn't you stop?" Randy sobbed, and as he watched, Dwayne smiled. He swallowed, and managed to spit out the words that he was so desperately trying to say.

"St...sto… sto…"

He was silenced as another roar of the shotgun sheared away the top of his skull, and punched a great explosion of dirt into the air.

Randy flinched and whirled around, staring at the old man, who stood behind him, the gun smoking from the barrel as Samsonite turned the weapon on Randy.

"You didn't need to do that!" Randy spat through his tears. "He was gonna die anyway. Why did you have to do that?"

The old man smiled, and then licked his lips.

"He tried to take them away from me, and I didn't want that. Nobody can take them from me, not him, not you."

"I don't want to take anything; I just want to go home."

"You say that now, but you're young and strong, and they will get to you like they got to him."

"Are you crazy old man? I just saved your life."

"It doesn't matter, I love them, I can't live without them, and I won't let you take them from me."

Randy realised then what had happened, and glanced to the ravaged remains of his friend, then back to the old man.

"That's why he was coming to kill you, wasn't it?" Randy said, smiling at his own stupidity. "You knew they wouldn't let you die in peace, you knew they would want you dead."

"Course I did, you dumb little shit."

"They had sent him to kill you, not me, didn't they?"

"Yeah, I suppose they did."

Randy shook his head in disbelief. "All that stuff you said last night, it was all bullshit wasn't it Mr Samsonite?"

"Don't get all preachy to me, you little asshole! You came here, trespassing on my land then took away my scarecrows, my friends," The old man raged. "Well even if they think I'm too old, I don't think I am. I have looked after them, devoted my life to them. It won't be easy, but I'll learn to forgive them for trying to replace me."

"Mr Samsonite, please."

"I'm sorry son, but this is the only way to make sure I still have a purpose."

Randy knew then what Dwayne had been trying to say as he lay dying in the dirt.

Stockholm Syndrome.

The old man had it, and who could be surprised after so long alone with whatever power lived in the dirt here. Randy closed his eyes and hoped that it wouldn't hurt when it came.

Samsonite took a single step forward and fired.

H NG N

“Make sure the noose is tight,” Dillon said to the guards as he paced back and forth, smoking his cigar.

Brad said nothing. He looked his captor in the eye and tried to show that he was unafraid, but Dillon's wide smile told him he hadn’t quite managed it.

“I understand you like games,” Dillon said as his guards checked the noose as instructed.

Brad again declined to respond, and instead clenched his fists. Although they were restrained behind his back and secured with cable ties, he would still give anything to have them freed just so he could beat some humility into the overweight mass of flesh in front of him.

Dillon was a French Canadian businessman, who due to his thriving export business, was also rich. Really, really rich. He had homes in Monaco, Florida and Switzerland, and even a private jet which was painted black and had his name emblazoned on the side in gold.

The man himself was large, both in height and in stature. Brad was six two and slim. Dillon was maybe five inches or so taller and a couple of hundred pounds heavier. His face was smooth and flabby, his grin wide and somehow comical now that he had wedged the cigar into the side of his mouth. He squinted against the sun, glaring at Brad with eyes that were cruel and full of vengeance.

“Are you surprised at how things have transpired?” Dillon asked, puffing smoke as he came to a halt in front of the makeshift gallows.

“It’s not how I planned it,” Brad muttered as he adjusted his footing on the ladder.

Dillon snorted and paced, content, for the time being, to smoke and enjoy the sun. Brad looked around, trying to get some sense of his surroundings. He was in some kind of yard or compound. The grass on the ground was thick and yellow and swayed in the slight breeze. To his right, just inside his peripheral vision was the ghost of a building of some kind, which was attached to a huge sandstone wall which looked as if it encased the yard from any outside attention. He looked over it to the sky, which was a beautiful, deep blue.

Brad blinked away fresh rivulets of sweat from his eyes as the punishing heat of the day continued to burn down on him. As if reading his thoughts, Dillon spoke. His tone was cheerful and happy, which, considering what had happened, was a concern.

"If you are wondering where help might arrive from my friend, then I might save you the trouble. We are alone here. You and I will be able to conduct our business in peace."

Brad didn't want to believe him, and half considered trying to turn and look behind him, but his footing was so precarious on the top two steps of the ladder that he dared not move, let alone try to risk losing his balance by looking around. Instead, he concentrated on retaining his balance, and stared straight ahead, swallowing against the pressure of the rope on his neck.

"What is it that you want from me, Dillon?" He croaked.

Dillon smiled and switched the cigar to the opposite side of his mouth.

"From you, I want nothing, apart from answers."

Brad licked his parched lips, the salty taste of his own sweat combined with fear threatening to break him and make him beg, but he knew that he couldn't do that because that was what Dillon wanted. He forced aside the raging, butterfly fear in his stomach and concentrated on retaining his balance.

"This is quite the predicament, wouldn't you say?" Dillon said as he walked to the step ladder and rested his hands on the top rung, just inches from Brad's feet. The gold rings on his fingers shimmered in the blazing sun, and Brad knew that it would only take the smallest movement, the slightest shake from Dillon, and he would surely die. Perhaps sensing his terror, Dillon glared up at his prisoner with hatred and grinned.

"Don't worry, it won

't be that easy. Not until I get my answers,"

He grinned as he gripped the ladder and started to tip it back, and Brad almost immediately lost his balance; he was teetering on the cusp of falling backwards and the certain death that would follow, yet he somehow managed to shift his weight and retain his balance as Dillon laughed and walked towards the wall.

"It's hot today, isn't it?" He said as he loosened the top button of his shirt. "Perhaps a drink is in order."

Dillon motioned to one of his guards who scurried off out of sight. Brad heard a door open and close, and then there was silence. Dillon walked to the thermometer screwed to the wall and leaned close.

"Thirty six degrees. It feels hotter in here, no?"

Brad didn't respond, but it didn't stop Dillon. He went on anyway, still in the same trivial tone.

"This area is something of a suntrap. It retains the heat of the day, although, by the looks of you, you already appreciate how hot it is."

Dillon's lackey returned, bringing with him an ice-cold bottle of beer. Dillon took a long drink, and that alone made Brad's stomach cramp with need.

"Ahh, that hits the spot," Dillon said as he belched loudly. "I would offer you one of course but..." He grinned without humour as he took another sip. "You don't look to be in any position to drink it."

"Look," Brad said, perhaps finally understanding the gravity of his situation. "We don't have to do this. I can go away, disappear. You will never see me again."

"Oh, but then I won't know."

"Know what?"

Dillon looked at him with predatory eyes as the smile melted from his face.

"Why you thought you could sleep with my wife and get away with it."

Dillon waited, perhaps expecting Brad to plead or beg. When neither came, he looked genuinely surprised.

"So you don't deny it?"

"What's the point, we both know it happened."

"Yes, indeed we do."

"So what now?"

"Ah, I'm glad you asked," Dillon said as he walked towards the sandstone compound wall.

"As I asked you earlier, you like to play games, correct?"

"Depends on the game." Brad shot back, determined not to let

Dillon see how afraid he was.

"Ah, well this is a game that everyone knows Mr Jackson. However, first, I wonder if you would mind answering my previous question?"

Brad swallowed and shifted his weight, more aware now of his burning calves as they supported his body just a few inches from death.

"It wasn't about you. It was just one of those things that happened."

"Indeed," Dillon said, folding his arms and watching Brad with a wide sneer. "But nevertheless, it *did* happen. And now we have come to this."

Dillon sighed and took a handkerchief from his pocket. As he wiped his brow, he looked at Brad and flashed another grin.

"You understand why this has to happen, don't you?"

"It doesn't. I already told you I was sorry."

"I believe you, but I have a reputation to consider. I cannot be seen to be weak."

"Then I'll leave the country. You'll never see me again."

Dillon laughed and shook his head. "I might believe you if I didn't know you couldn't afford it. And besides, how would I look if you suddenly turned up like a bad penny one day? No, it has to be this way."

"Then do it. Get it over with."

"You really think I could be so barbaric?"

"Considering my position, yeah. I do."

Dillon smiled and approached the wall. He leaned on it, resting one foot against the stone.

"I'm going to give you a chance to earn your freedom, and your life."

"Why bother, we both know the outcome."

"Ah, is that not a defeatist attitude? Do you not even want to live?" Dillon strode towards the ladder. "Should I kick this from under you, so that you die like a dog in the burning sun?"

"No, please," Brad said, squirming as he tried to both get away and retain his balance at the same time. "I'll play along with your game, whatever it is."

"Very good." Beamed Dillon. "I knew you would make the right decision. First, the stake, as in my experience, games are not so enjoyable without a substantial risk."

Dillon nodded to one of his men, who approached with a suitcase. Dillon took it and opened it, then carried it to the ladder so that Brad could see inside.

"One million dollars, clean and untraceable. Yours if you win. With it, you will take your freedom and leave this country. I think this is enough so that you would have no reason to show your face again."

Brad looked at Dillon but found his eyes returning to the money. It was more than he had ever seen in his life. "What about Monique?" He asked quietly.

"She is not part of this equation. This is between you and me as men."

"What have you done to her?"

Dillon laughed and set the open case on the floor.

"Nothing has happened to her. Why would I harm my own wife? She was led astray and has learned her lesson. She likes men like you, Mister Jackson. Down on their luck Americans with your chiselled features and your beach blonde hair. Oh, I'm quite sure you made quite the impression. But Monique knows well enough that her place is here with me."

He paused and tilted his head.

"You didn't think she would ever stay with you, did you, Mr Jackson?"

Brad's expression told him the answer, and Dillon burst into another bout of booming laughter.

"Don't be fooled into thinking that you are in any way unique here. My wife's adulterous ways are nothing unusual. You are, I believe the seventh during the ten years of our marriage. You are just another statistic.

Brad looked hurt, and Dillon lowered his voice, licking his wet lips as he spoke.

"She does it to get to me. To remind me that I need to show her more attention. I don't like it of course, but she knows that all she has to do is screw some degenerate low-life like you, and she will be rewarded with attention and more money being spent on her."

"I don't believe you. She wouldn't..."

"Oh she would. Whilst we are here burning under this awful

heat, she is in Monaco. I gave her the gold card, so I'm sure she is either at the apartment or sitting on a boat in the harbour, sipping champagne and looking over her purchases. She has already forgotten you, Mr Jackson."

"So why can't you just let me go?"

"I cannot be seen to be weak. Like it or not, you are solely responsible for everything that has happened."

Brad blinked sweat out of his eyes and tried to ignore the stinging sensation on his skin as it was barraged by the sun.

"What if I refuse to play this game of yours?" He said, his voice coming out in a broken, cracked mumble.

"Mr Jackson." Dillon beamed. "Think about it. How long do you think you can balance there? Surely already your calves burn with the effort of standing."

Brad said nothing, but Dillon was right. His legs *did* hurt, his muscles screaming at him to give them a little respite.

Brad grimaced. Dillon grinned.

"Alternatively, you can indulge in my game. A battle of mental fortitude, if you will."

Brad shuffled; sure he could feel the start of an alarming numb ache of a cramp in his leg.

"It seems I have no choice."

"No, you really don't..."

Dillon replied as he walked to the wall and took a piece of red chalk from his pocket. He started to draw a series of lines, speaking over his shoulder as he worked.

"When I was a boy, my father was often busy growing our business. As a consequence, much of my childhood was spent alone. We were rich of course, so it was far from a broken home. To combat the monotony, the other children and I, the ones who like me were neglected by parents who were working on securing our futures, would group together and play games. Cards, chess and the like. Things devised to pass the time."

Dillon finished drawing on the wall and then turned towards Brad and flashed a wide lion like grin.

"My favourite was Hangman, Mr Jackson. And it is that which we are about to play right now."

Despite the heat, a cold shiver danced down Brad's spine, and he licked his parched lips.

"It's insane. I won't do it."

"But I thought we had reached an agreement? After all, it is just a simple word game. The stakes are as follows. If you correctly guess the clue, you leave here with the million dollars and your life, on the strict understanding that you leave the country immediately. If you lose, and the hangman is complete, I kick the ladder from under you and watch you die. Alternatively, if you refuse to participate, I will leave you out here until your strength wanes, after which you will pass out and die anyway. I see only one option, Mr Jackson."

Brad didn't want to play along. He knew how dangerous Dillon was, and that any agreement made was likely playing into his hands. But he very much wanted to live, and even if it was only guaranteed for the short term, he would take it.

"What choice do I have?" He said, locking eyes with Dillon.

"Very good!" Dillon replied, clapping his hands together. "Take a moment to look over the clue, and we can begin before the heat becomes any more unbearable."

Brad looked at the case full of money, then at Dillon and finally at the wall.

---/------/-------/---/-----

His instincts screamed at him not to play along, and that anything that Dillon said could not be trusted. However, he also acknowledged that the odds were against him, and even though he was reasonably fit and healthy, he was already starting to feel weak. He wondered how long it would take for the heat to affect his brain function, and realised that the sooner they began, the sharper he would be and ultimately, the more chance he would have of survival.

"Okay," Brad said as he glared at his captor. "I'm ready."

"Marvellous! I'm sure you know how the game is played, but I shall confirm the rules so that there is absolute clarity. You will call out letters of the alphabet in order to try to fill in the blanks on the clue. A correct answer and I will place the letter on the wall. Incorrect, and I will begin to draw the hangman. If you guess enough correct letters, and you think you know the answer, you may tell me what you believe it to be. If you are incorrect, you forfeit the game. If you do not answer the clue before the hangman is complete, you forfeit the game. If you decide to withdraw, you forfeit the game. Are we in agreement?"

"Just say it how it is, Dillon," Brad grunted, "by forfeit, you mean I'll die."

"If you wish to be so to the point then, yes. That is true." He said with a slimy grin. "But is that not all the more reason to ensure that you answer correctly?"

"I suppose so. Let's get this over with. I choose the letter A."

Dillon grinned, walked to the wall and drew a single line.

"An incorrect answer I'm afraid."

Brad's heart rate increased, and he forced himself to focus through the sweat which was dripping into his eyes.

"E." Brad said, trying to ignore the burning ferocity of the sun

"Well done. That is correct." Dillon said curtly as he took the chalk and updated the clue.

--- / E----E / ------E / E-- / ----E

"Choose again."

Brad licked his lips, knowing that whatever he said next woul(either lead him closer to either life or death. At first, he didn't think he could bring himself to speak, but Dillon was watching and waiting, and so he forced himself to go on.

"N."

Dillon's smile faltered for a moment, and that alone felt like a huge victory to Brad. He watched as Dillon chalked in the letters, then stood back to allow Brad to see.

--N / E----E / --N---E / E-- / ----E

Brad studied the words, and now that he knew his voice woul(come, the temptation to blurt out any number of half-hearted guesses was strong, but he knew to do so would mean death. He would have just one chance to get it right, otherwise, he would die.

"W.," he said quietly as he adjusted his position on the ladder.

Dillon walked to the wall and added a vertical line to the horizontal one that he had drawn earlier.

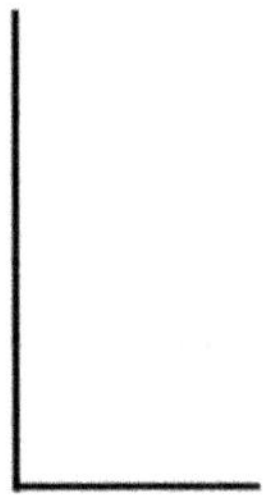

"Unlucky, Mr Jackson."

Brad looked at the wall, fighting hard against the urge to panic, which was hard when he knew that his life hinged on a series of chalk lines on a wall.

"Choose again please." Dillon prodded.

"B." He blurted, not really thinking about it.

Dillon drew air through his teeth and shook his head as he amended the hangman drawing.

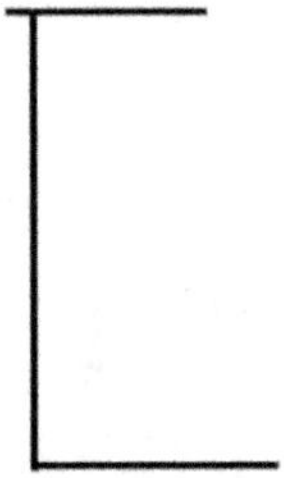

"You should consider your guesses more carefully, Mr Jackson."

Dillon was right. Brad squirmed, trying to ignore the burning pain in his legs, which were desperate for respite from the pressure of supporting his body. Brad pushed the pain aside and concentrated instead on staring at the clue as droplets of sweat dripped from the tip of his nose.

"O."

Dillon updated the clue, then turned and grinned at Brad. "You see? It's so much better if you think. Are you ready to guess yet? Is the ticking clock of death loud enough for you?"

"I'm not ready to die."

"We shall see. Please, choose again."

He looked at the clue, desperately trying to see if he could form any words, anything that might give him a chance to extend his life.

-ON / E-O--E / -ON---E / E-- / -O--E

“L”.

“Incorrect,” Dillon replied as he went to the wall and added to the hangman.

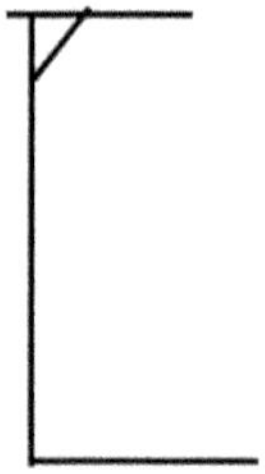

“Please,” Brad blurted, finally overcome by the terror that he had so far managed to hold back. “Just let me go. I've learned my lesson. I should never have done what I did, I know that now. It was a mistake.”

“I understand. Really, I do.” Dillon said. Although his voice was sympathetic, his expression was predatory. “However, we are mid game now, and cannot stop.”

“You can't expect to get away with this.” Brad hissed, for a moment losing his balance. Dillon watched, willing him to fall. When he saw that Brad was stable, he exhaled and shook his head.

“Seven times, Mr Jackson, my wife has cheated on me. And seven times this game has been played in this very yard. Four of the seven correctly guessed the clue and won both their money and freedom. Of the others, two ran out of moves and suffered the consequences. The third had a heart attack right there on the ladder, just when it looked like he might win. You see, the odds are in your favour, as long as you remain calm and think clearly. Now please, choose a letter.”

“P,” Brad said, his voice wavering as he watched his captor with the purest sense of terror he had ever experienced.

“There, you see? Clear thinking.” Dillon said as he chalked the letter into the clue.

-ON / EPO--E / -ON---E / E-- / -O- -E

"It makes no sense. I don't know what it says!" Brad sobbed, and although he didn't like showing Dillon how afraid he was; it was impossible to hide it. He thought he had found love, but it seemed he was just a plaything, a way for a lonely wife to get some attention from her egomaniac husband.

"Don't lose your focus, Mr Jackson." Dillon warned, clearly enjoying the show. "I think you might yet win if you can only keep calm. Please choose again."

"G." He stammered, fighting back the urge to vomit.

"I'm afraid," Dillon said as he walked to the hangman and drew in the next line.

"You are incorrect."

Brad stared at the drawing, and at the beaming Dillon, then finally back to the clue.

"I don't want to do this anymore." He whispered.

"Are you saying you concede defeat?" Dillon said with a wide grin.

"No!" He blurted, and almost lost his balance. He swayed, his punished calves struggling to support him. The rope dug into his throat a little as he tried to regain his footing, and just when it seemed he was destined to fall; he regained his balance. Dillon watched with amusement, chalk held deftly as he waited for Brad to either fall or stay upright, looking as if he didn't care either way.

Sweating, exhausted and afraid, Brad began to sob.

"Choose a letter please," Dillon said with indifference.

"Fuck you."

Dillon grinned and added to the hangman.

"Hey, that's not the rules. It's not fair!" Brad whined, glaring at Dillon.

"I will not be insulted. Please act in a gentlemanly manner, or suffer the consequences."

Brad looked at the hangman, and tried to work out how many moves he had left before the end.

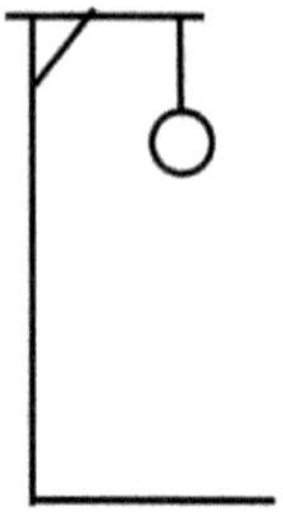

Five incorrect letters were all he had left before his death, so in reality, he could make only four more mistakes. He looked at the clue, and could make no sense of it. The fear which had started as a gnawing subtle pressure in his stomach had now spread and filled his entire being. He could feel himself shaking, both from the pressure on his exhausted legs and the very real possibility that his life was almost at an end. He knew that even if by some miracle he survived the day, some part of him was destined to die here with Dillon.

"Remember, failure to play counts as a forfeit."

"U, I choose U." He spat, the combination of tears and sweat stinging his eyes and making it difficult to see.

"Correct." Dillon beamed, and filled in the clue.

-ON / EPOU-E / -ON--UE / E-- / -O- -E

"I don't know it; I can't do this anymore. Please, let me go!"

He didn't care that Dillon would see his weakness or his fear, all he wanted was to be out of the heat, and to sit down and take the pressure off his legs, which were close to giving up with or without him. Dillon smiled, and picked up the beer that he had started earlier, and took a long, leisurely drink.

Brad's stomach — which felt like a tiny, shrivelled up ball, quivered as he watched the cool liquid disappear down Dillon's gullet.

"You son of a bitch!" He whispered.

"Ah, very refreshing. I would offer you one, but it is against the spirit of the rules. Now please, choose a letter."

"M." He said absently, still staring at the bottle clutched in Dillon's fat fingers.

Dillon smiled and drew the letter into the clue.

"Surely, now you must have some idea, Mr Jackson. It really is quite easy."

Brad looked at the words, trying to make sense of them, and then everything fell into place, and he knew why he couldn't understand.

MON / EPOU-E / MON--UE / E-- / MO- -E

"It isn't written in English, is it Dillon?" Brad asked with a wry smile.

Dillon grinned. "Of course not. Nowhere in the rules did it say it had to be."

"It looks like French."

"Correct. It is, after all, my native tongue."

Dillon grinned, and Brad tried to recall hazy school French lessons, hoping that some of the information had stuck, but if it had, it was evading him now.

"You were never going to lose, were you?" Brad asked, finding it in himself to push his smile into a wide grin. "Because you knew that even if I filled in all of the blanks, I don't speak the language."

"Perhaps you are more intelligent than I thought," Dillon said, with a grin. "You see, Mr Jackson; I have learned never to lose. And never to let anyone take me for a fool."

"I didn't intend any of this," Brad said. "I just happened to fall in love with the wrong woman."

"If it's of consequence, she also said she loved you a little too. I suppose that's why I perhaps skewed the rules in my favour."

"Then why not just let me go. Call it even. I'll disappear. You have my word."

"I cannot do that. You forced my hand. You took everything."

"Then let's cut the crap. Just do it. Kill me." Brad shrieked, unable to handle standing there and waiting until Dillon had finished toying with him.

"I cannot make that decision. Rules are rules."

"Then I will," Brad said, locking eyes with Dillon. "I concede."

Dillon shook his head and walked to the wall. He paused, and then turned back to Brad.

"You know what this means for you if you go ahead and withdraw?"

Brad licked his lips. "We both know I'm dead anyway. I don't want to give you the satisfaction."

"Admirable and, as it happens, something of a first. Such a shame Mr Jackson. Under other circumstances, the two of us may have become friends."

"I doubt it. I wouldn't willingly mix with a lowlife, fat, piece of shit like you, Dillon. Even if you are rich."

"But my wife was good enough?"

"She doesn't love you, you know," Brad said, finding it in himself to smile. "For all the money and the power, it was my name she screamed as she dug her nails into my back. She saw you for what you really are Dillon. A pathetic, insecure little man."

Brad expected fury, but Dillon only sighed.

"I know. I have known for some time, sadly. However, I am a man of great determination. And in a way, you have helped me."

Dillon filled in the missing blanks of the clue and then approached the ladder.

"The clue reads, Mon épouse Monique est morte, which in English means,"

He leaned on the ladder and spoke in a whisper.

"My wife, Monique, is dead."

"No, you wouldn't, you said she…" Brad stammered, and all at once his acceptance had turned back to horror because Dillon's eyes said he was telling the truth.

Brad wanted to explain, to plead and beg for his life, but Dillon had already pulled the ladder from under him. The last thing Brad saw before his neck snapped was Dillon's smiling face and the writing on the wall. *Mon épouse Monique est morte.*

THE BOY WHO SAW SPIDERS

The party on Pointer Street was where Andy had planned to tell Jenny how he felt, and perhaps take the next step in their relationship. But now, any idea of such things had evaporated, disappeared into the ether as he sat and tried to come to terms with the situation. He tried to regain focus, but it was no good.

All he could think about were the spiders.

When he arrived at the party that night, he was just like everybody else. An average, run of the mill student who didn't excel at anything in particular, and had made an academic career of remaining almost completely anonymous. However, none of that mattered. Not anymore. He chewed at his bottom lip, scratched at his greasy mop of brown hair, and tried to make sense of it all. He was perched on the end of the sofa, his beer long forgotten and clutched in his hand, as he watched the spiders scurrying over the carpet and skittering across the walls with horrible, jerky urgency. They were far too numerous to even attempt trying to count. The big ones were hanging back in the corners, peering out from the dark places and watching, their smaller, olive-sized cousins were bolder, and exploring the room as if the throng of people were nothing more than enormous lumbering obstacles.

He took a slow, dazed look around the room and wondered why nobody else was making a fuss. He would have expected screams or panicked yelps of disgust, but with sick realisation, he understood why.

Only he could see them.

He reflexively curled his toes as one darted past his shoe and into Melissa Freese's Handbag. Melissa didn't notice, she was too busy jawing with that smart mouthed, pig faced friend of hers — Alison something-or-other — who was blathering on and on about some personal injustice that had conflicted with her narrow minded view of the world. He looked to his left. On the opposite side of the sofa, Jonny Marshall, and whichever unfortunate girl's face he was chewing off, were slobbering as they groped at each other and tongue wrestled in the way that horny teens did.

One thing for certain was that the pair hadn't noticed the spiders either – even the one that was working its way into Jonny's ear, its thin legs kicking and scrabbling for purchase as it delved deeper. Completely oblivious, Jonny and his date continued swapping spit and feeling each other up. Andy half wanted to warn him, but Jonny was a jock, and more than that, he was an arrogant, bullying son of a bitch who was at his happiest making the less gifted, less attractive, less 'Jonny' type kids' lives miserable.

Fuck him.

Let it burrow.

He saw a flicker of movement, whipped his head around just in time to see it, and immediately wished he hadn't. He watched as a plump, ugly looking funnel web spider darted into an open pack of Cheetos that were on the table. Once again, he had half an urge to call out and tell someone but held his silence. Other than Jenny, he didn't care for anyone at the party anyway, and none of them were people who he could actually call friends. They were just acquaintances, some of which he barely knew. So he swallowed his words and watched in morbid fascination as

Chip Denning — who if the rumor was to be believed, preferred boys to girls and had a homophobe of a brother who would break your teeth if you ever asked about it — picked up a handful of the cheesy snack. Andy saw the plump spider wriggling as Chip shoved the snacks, spider, and all, into his mouth and crunched down, then turned back to his conversation.

Andy's stomach quivered a little, and he suddenly wanted to run away from both spiders and classmates alike, but he knew he would never be able to pluck up the courage. He was also sure that if he tried, his legs would refuse to cooperate, and he would be left standing like an idiot frozen to the spot.

And they would know.

The spiders that only he could see.

He became conscious of the fact that he was holding his breath, and let it out slowly. His eyes flicked to the door, the thought of escape still lingering in his mind, but even if he could move, what he saw made the point moot, as that route was already being cut off.

Hundreds — no, thousands of the spiders were constructing an intricate web which covered the entire doorway.

The scale of it was too much to bear, and he forced himself to turn away. His stomach lurched, and he let out a shallow, booze-flavored belch. It was then that he noticed the bottle of Budweiser still clutched in his fist, and he took a long, grateful swig, just about managing to keep his trembling hand steady enough to get the bottle to his lips. It was warm and flat, but made him feel better nonetheless.

Still the party went on.

Still, the spiders scurried.

Dale Thompson crossed the room, standing in front of Andy with a distracted, uncomfortable look on his acne-ravaged face.

"Hey Andy, you drinking that or what?" Thompson said pointing to the bottle clutched in Andy's hand.

"Uh...Yeah. No... I don't think so." Andy replied, unable to rationalise his thoughts.

"Mind if I have it?"

"No, go ahead," Andy mumbled, handing Dale the barely touched, too warm beverage.

"Thanks. Take it easy Andy."

"Yeah. You too." He said as he watched Dale swagger away.

Dale's T-shirt was swarming with hundreds of spiders, crawling over and under each other as they explored their host's portly frame.

How could he not have noticed? Andy wondered, and as he considered the question, that little voice — the one that went so often ignored – popped up in his mind.

Dale can't see them because they're not there, but you already know that, don't you?

The thought sparked another question, which presented itself in his inner monologue with much less subtlety.

Am I insane?

He considered the question. He was nineteen. Reasonably intelligent, no history of mental-health problems. In fact, life had been pretty uneventful until he arrived at the party that night. But no matter how he tried to spin it, there was no explanation for them.

The spiders.

They were now everywhere, swarming out from behind furniture, and covering almost every wall and surface.

He glanced at Andrea Gill, she who had cheated in last month's chemistry exam by reading his answers. He had let her because he didn't care. He was going places, and regardless of her cheating ways, the Andrea Gill's of the world were destined to become single parents, welfare scrounging fuck-up losers for life.

He watched in fascination as a fat house spider with disproportionately long, spindly legs scurried up her body, finally coming to rest in her hair. One thin black leg clung onto her cheek as the spider paused above her ear.

Andrea carried on talking to her friends, none of them spotting the new addition to the party.

Yes.

He thought to himself as he looked at the table full of half-eaten buffet food, now pulsing and flexing with a life of its own as the arachnid mass explored the fleshy sandwiches and small containers of dips and breadsticks.

Yes indeed.

He supposed that the little voice in his head might be right. He could well have lost the plot, gone mad, bought himself a ticket to the funny farm, lost a few vital sandwiches out of the picnic basket. Because the world ticked on as normal, but for him, it was filled with spiders.

Spiders here, spiders there, spiders everywhere.

He felt a shrill, giddy laugh begin to move up to his throat, and he knew that if he let it out they would hear, and like the words smallest army they would come for him. He knew it as a certainty.

The laugh was close now, and he lifted a clenched fist to his mouth and bit down hard enough to draw a little blood and make his eyes water. The pain didn't bother him, though, in fact, he welcomed it, because the laugh had gone, and the status quo was maintained.

He started to relax and then drew a sharp breath.

There was one of them perched on his knee.

He looked at it, too afraid to swat it away, and

the spider looked back. He could feel its glassy multi eyed

stare boring into him, and could do no more than wait to see what would happen.

It was as if time had stopped, and even though the party and its oblivious guests went on with the business of drinking, pairing off and trying to boost their popularity, his world was no more than the small square of denim on his left knee.

The spider skittered forwards, just a few inches, but it was enough to make Andy try to push himself back into the sofa. He was going to scream. He knew it and knew there was no way that he would be able to stop it this time. When it came, he knew he would be gone — his mind broken as he fell into the black hole of perpetual insanity – but at the last second, the spider changed direction and ran instead off his leg and down out of sight into the dark place between the seat cushions.

He felt sick and saw small white spots dancing in front of his eyes. He was going to faint and knew he couldn't allow it to happen, because if he did they would come for him.

He laughed.

A short, shrill, cackle which went unheard amid the thumping bass and the constant stream of party chatter. Yes, he was sure of it. Something in his brain was defective. Something had broken, and now he could see them everywhere. He imagined how his life would be; living in his own personal world filled with spiders.

He heard a groan. Jonny's date had come up for air, and when she smiled, thousands of tiny newborn spiders streamed out of her mouth and nose, covering her face and neck as they looked for dark places to shelter.

The terror bubbling in Andy's guts told him that his brain was on the verge of shutting up shop and refusing to play ball, and so he closed his eyes, trying to regain a little composure and maybe bring himself under a modicum of control, but even that was no good.

Because even with his eyes closed he could still see them, cast in stark white negative on the blank canvas of his mind's eye. He blinked away the image and found that his reality was marginally better than the squirming, scurrying mass that lived in his brain.

He glanced towards the corner of the room, and when he saw it — saw *her*, he felt something break, a sharp *click* as whatever small thread had been connecting him to his sanity snapped.

Jenny slumped in the corner.

Jenny.

The girl he had known since they were four-year-old neighbors.

Jenny who had always seen him as more of a friend than the more serious thing that he one day hoped they would become.

Jenny who had brought him to the party, even though it was a place where a quiet, reserved kid like him wouldn't have otherwise been invited.

However, all of that was before the spiders.

Her petite frame was swollen, chin resting on her chest. As he watched and his broken mind processed what was in front of him he knew without doubt that he was irreversibly damaged.

He could see them moving *under* her skin, making it ripple and pulse, and bizarrely reminding him of childhood trips to the coast and the way the tides ebbed and flowed as they crept up the beach. They were streaming out of her nose and ears, and as he watched, her mouth slowly opened and a huge, thick-limbed monster of a spider pushed its way out. Andy had seen them on T.V.

Bird eaters.

He was sure that's what they were called.

The huge spider dragged its immense body out of her gaping mouth, and flopped down on to her chest where it stood in splayed legged triumph. Andy was beyond screaming, beyond anything other than looking on with a sick and twisted fascination.

She's the queen, and Jenny was her nest.

The thought danced, darted and spun in Andy's mind, and when he couldn't make any rational sense out of it, it danced and spun some more. He wanted to ask what it wanted. Why him? What did he ever do to deserve this?

But he couldn't move, and his mouth remained tightly closed as still more of them came – a never-ending procession from every conceivable place in the room.

His skin itched, and his stomach danced as he tried to put the situation into some kind of order. But his brain wasn't cut out for dealing with such horror, and so it had decided to leave Andy to his own devices.

He saw Jenny move, and for a moment, there was hope, hope that she was ok, hope that he could get her out of there and maybe then she would look at him in the same way he looked at her.

But it wasn't Jenny that was moving, not really.

It was the spiders.

The spiders in their Jenny skin that were going about their business and making her loll and dance like a macabre marionette.

Spiders.

Spiders Spiders Spiders

He would do anything. *Anything* to avoid having to watch the jerky, skittish way that they moved in that horrible, stop start motion. Anything to avoid having to watch the spider filled Jenny puppet that pulsed and rippled along to the bass line of the party.

You know what it's going to take. You know what you have to do.

The voice in his head whispered, and he did. As terrifying as the thought was, it was the only way. He lurched out of his seat with a defiant roar and did it before he could change his mind.

His scream brought the party to a halt. The music cut out and his fellow classmates, students, friends, and those that he was indifferent to were looking at him. He could feel their judging gaze, and found a bitter irony that for the first time in his life, he wasn't an anonymous face. He was finally the center of attention.

The silence was broken by a single high-pitched scream. He thought it might have been Andrea Gill — she of the over the shoulder wandering eye on test days, but couldn't be sure. Whoever it was; they set off a chain reaction, and the silence morphed into chaos.

Andy stood where he was and smiled. Because although the sounds of the screams were loud, at least they were natural. They were normal, everyday things that he could rationalise and make sense of.

He thought that the world made more sense when it was rational. And he thought that he would be just fine now that it was done. He began to laugh, a sound rich and hearty and full, because he had won.

The chaos was a thick, heavy thing and seemed to hang in the air like a physical entity. Yet, amid the confusion, he heard several distinct things.

Someone shouting for help.

Someone else repeating 'oh god, oh god, oh god' like it was some kind of bizarre mantra.

Someone quite close to him, crying.

He thought it might have been Jenny, and hoped that it was because that would mean he had saved her. He would have looked for himself, but he had already torn out his own eyes.

He continued to laugh as the sound of police sirens drew close.

THE MAN IN THE ALLEY

Benson lived in the alleyway between Juniper Avenue and Grover Lane. He had always lived there, certainly for as long as I can remember anyway. He wasn't a bum, if that's what you're thinking. As far as I know, he never borrowed or asked for anything. I found out later that he actually owned a house - a nice one with a tidy garden and a cherry tree out front. But at some point, he'd chosen to live out his life in the alleyway instead. People thought he was eccentric, some whispered that he was mentally ill, or suffering from Alzheimer's. But that, frankly, is bullshit. I know it's bullshit because I saw him for what he was.

That alleyway dosesn't even exist anymore. It's a multiplex now, complete with a cinema, restaurants and all the other bells and whistles associated with modern living. But if you go and stand outside at just the right time of day, then you can almost still see him - a ghost from the past that reminds me that it was all real and not just a figment of my imagination. The doubt never lasts for long anyway. Especially when the sky becomes the colour of fire, and the shadows become deep and narrow and start reaching out of the dark places.

I was twelve when I first encountered Benson. The world was a different place then of course. Nowadays everyone is so private, so inaccessible and desperate to keep themselves isolated and alone as they try to fumble their way through life. I guess I was just lucky, because when I was growing up, it was in a real community where you actually knew your neighbors and it was safe to go to bed without locking your doors at night. Hell, kids could even play outside without fear of being abducted or murdered.

I first saw Benson when I was out riding my bike with my buddy, Luke. Under normal circumstances, I'm sure that I wouldn't have noticed him, but it was that special time of day, just before dusk, and something drew my attention to this skinny old man in the alley as he sat there at its mouth on a wooden crate just watching the world go by.

"Afternoon boys." He said as we passed, grinning toothlessly and shielding his face against the sun, which had become a fiery red-orange as its leading edge began to dip below the horizon.

"Hi," I mumbled in response.

Benson nodded, then looked past me to Luke.

"Ooh, that's a good one, ain't it?" He muttered, pointing at the ground.

I looked. Luke looked, but neither of us saw anything.

"What's your name son?" He asked, watching me through watery, grey eyes.

"Andrew, sir," I replied.

"You got a last name, or is it just Andrew?" He cackled, his eyes flicking to Luke for a second, then back to me.

"Thompson."

"Ahh, you must be Annie Thompson's kid?"

"Yes sir," I replied.

He paused and sniffed the air, then licked his lips.

"Well, you be sure to tell your mother that old Benson said hi."

I nodded, and even though I wasn't scared, not then at least, I was a little uncomfortable, because his attention had moved away from me, and he was staring at Luke with greedy, hungry eyes.

"Say boy." He said, managing to tear his eyes away from Luke and back to me.

"Yes, sir?"

"Would you do an old man a favour, and get me a lemonade from the corner store?" He said as he thrust a handful of change in my direction.

I knew the store, as I went there all the time. It was just a little way down the street and I could see the blue and yellow awning above the door from where I stood, my forearms leaning on the handlebars of my bike.

"I would sir, but I can't take my bike into the store and my mother doesn't want me leaving it out on the street."

"Well, you can just leave it right here with me, I'll look after it for you." He said, his eyes flicking back towards Luke and lingering there for a while.

I shuffled and stared at my feet.

"I shouldn't, I only just got it for my birthday,"

Benson paused, flicking his tongue back and forth inside his mouth, then clapped his hands and grinned.

"Okay boy, how's about this? Your friend here can stay here with your bike whilst you run and get the lemonade. How does that sound?"

I looked at Luke, who shrugged his indifference. He obviously wasn't picking up any bad vibes, and that, in turn, made me feel foolish for being so spooked.

"Okay," I said, climbing off my bike and leaning it against the alleyway wall. "I'll be right back."

He handed me the change and I ran as fast as I could to the store. Hell, I think I ran everywhere back then, but I pushed just a little bit harder this time, because I wanted to get back, and not only to my bike. The fact is that I didn't want to leave Luke alone with Benson any longer than I had to.

All kinds of thoughts raced through my mind about what would happen when I got back, but when I did, Benson and Luke were chatting, and I felt foolish for the second time in quick succession. The old man saw me coming and grinned. "Ah, here he is."

I held the bottle of lemonade out to him and he smiled and shook his head.

"You know son, I don't really much feel like lemonade anymore, but I'll tell you what. Since you were good enough to go, you and your friend here can share it."

"That's okay, you can maybe drink it later," I said, setting the lemonade down beside him and climbing back on my bike. "We have to go. It's getting late."

"Nice to meet you, Mister," Luke said as he turned his bike around.

"Benson, son. You can call me Benson."

Luke nodded, and I risked looking the old man in the eye. I had expected to see some hint of the darkness that I could sense, but his gaze was friendly, and yet again I wondered if I was making more of the situation than I should be. Luke and I set off, leaving Benson and his alleyway behind. I had intended to ask my mother about him when I got home, but within half an hour I had pushed the thought to the back of my mind. By the time I arrived back at the house later that night, I had forgotten it all together.

It wasn't until a week later that Benson popped into my mind, right after Luke died.

At first, I was convinced that Benson was responsible somehow, and it wasn't until a few days later when my mother told me that he died in his sleep that I accepted that Luke's death was just a tragic accident. She said there was some kind of problem with his heart that nobody had known about until it was too late. Just like that, I had lost my best friend. It was my first experience of death, and it hit me hard. For a few weeks, I was inconsolable.

I next saw Benson a few months later, talking to a kid I knew from school called Charlie Denner. It was as if time had stood still for Benson, and he had been waiting there at the end of the alleyway since I last saw him. He was dressed the same, looked the same, even the weather was the same. He looked up and saw me walking towards him, and although I expected fury or surprise that I had interrupted him, he flashed his gummy grin and waved at me. A quick stab of terror raced through me, but I waved back, and think I even managed a smile. Maybe it was jus because of my earlier discomfort around him, but I didn't like how he looked, bathed in that deep orange glow of pre-dusk. The shadows made his thin face look almost skeletal, and from where I was, they fell across his face and made his eyes looked like empty, gaping sockets. I went straight past the alley without stopping, and although I didn't look over my shoulder, I knew Benson was watching.

Charlie died a week later.

Just like Luke, they said it was natural causes, but I didn't believe in coincidence, and somewhere, deep down, I knew that i had something to do with Benson. I asked my mother about him, trying my best to feign disinterest despite my incredible curiosity I watched for any hint of terror or horror when I mentioned his name, but she only smiled.

"Oh, Benson is a lovely old man. He has lived in that alleywa for years." She said as she set the dinner table.

"Why doesn't anyone help him or try to get him a home?"

"Well, that's the strange thing. He has a home. He's actually a very wealthy man. I think he had some family issues and decided he preferred to live out on the street."

"So what happened to his house?" I asked, trying to imagine what kind of man would willingly sleep rough unless they were up to no good.

"His daughter lives there now, I think. As far as I know he gave her the house and all his money."

"How long has he lived there in the alleyway?" I asked, still watching carefully to see if she would give anything away.

"Oh, it's been years. Your father remembers him living there when he first bought this house, so at least ten years."

I wanted to tell my mother my suspicions about Luke and Charlie, and how I thought Benson was responsible, but I daren't yet in case I was wrong. After all, she was my mother, and if she said he was harmless, I owed it to her to believe it.

The following week I went out of my way to ride past the alleyway. It was a cold, grey morning, and although I couldn't decide if I was afraid or excited, I ended up being disappointed because when I arrived, Benson wasn't there. I stopped my bike at the mouth of the alleyway and stared into it. It was pretty unremarkable. It ended after around twenty five feet with a huge brick wall. There was a large green dumpster about a third of the way down and behind that, the shadow of a recessed doorway.

I inched my bike into the alleyway, wrinkling my nose at the smell. It was ammonia and garbage and something else which I couldn't place. I wondered as I made my way into the alley how anyone could live in such conditions.

"Mr Benson?" I called out, or maybe I whispered. I couldn't be sure.

My stomach churned and my heart was beating fast, but I didn't turn back. I was at the edge of the dumpster and paused. I think I almost turned and ran then, but I was determined to see it through. I edged forward and looked into the doorway.

Empty.

Not only empty, but there was no sign that anyone had even set foot in the alleyway for years, let alone lived there. Nothing added up, apart from the fact that I was surer than ever that there was more to Benson than met the eye.

It rained every day that week, but even so, I went past the alleyway every day, sometimes three or four times a day to try and catch a glimpse of Benson, but he was never there. Even though I had nothing to go on, and nobody else seemed concerned with him, my curiosity grew into an obsession and then into frustration with his constant no shows.

I had almost given up on ever seeing him again when I decided to have one last ride past the alleyway. The bad weather had cleared, and it was one of those deep orange hued afternoons, where the shadows were long and the first stars are just starting to become visible. I rode towards the alleyway, my shadow elongated and racing ahead in front of me, and when I rounded the corner I drew a sharp breath.

He was there, timeless as always sitting on his overturned crate and watching the world go by. He had a sly, secretive smile, and as I approached, he flicked his eyes towards me.

"I understand you've been looking for me, sonny." He said, the sly smile elongating on his thin lips.

Excuses raced through my brain along with lies and denials, but I chose, to tell the truth instead because I needed to know what Benson was all about.

"Yes, I have."

"Why?" He asked as he watched a couple walk past with their dog.

"I want to know what you did to Luke and Charlie. I came back, but you were never around."

"Oh, I'm always around." He said with a dry chuckle. "I'm never too far away."

It was as if the rest of the world had melted away and it was just me, Benson and the alleyway. I said the words before I had thought about them. Maybe because I had a feeling there were no secrets from Benson and suspected that any bluffing would be pointless.

"I think you killed Luke and Charlie."

The words seemed to hang in the air, and I waited for a denial, maybe an outburst or for him to threaten to tell my mother, and in some way that would have been better because it would have been a normal reaction. Instead, he sighed, and turned his attention to the road. He watched as people walked back and forth and I stood in silence, waiting for whatever came next.

"It's not what you think." He said, squinting up at me. The sun was low now, and the shadows were deep and cast his wrinkled skin into black scars.

I wanted to ask him more but realised that real life wasn't like it was in movies or on TV shows where the star always had a witty retort or comeback. I was too afraid to do anything but stand and stare. He smiled, but it was wistful, and somehow tired.

"You couldn't imagine how much of a burden it is." He said, letting out another deep sigh. "It just has to be done."

"Are you going to kill me?" I asked, dreading the answer, but needing to know all the same.

He looked me up and down, his eyes dark and probing. I felt invaded, and his gaze came to rest on my shadow. He frowned, sniffed the air, and tapped his fingers on his tattered trouser leg.

"No. No, I'm not. You're one of the good ones."

"Charlie and Luke…?"

He looked at me, and whatever darkness that had been in his eyes when he looked at my shadow was gone. He was the same tired old man that everyone else saw.

"They had to go, son. Best to catch them early."

"What do you mean? I don't understand."

"Bad people. Bad, bad people." He muttered, and turned his gaze back to the street as everyone else went about their business around them.

"Luke was my friend, he wasn't bad."

"Bad, bad, bad, bad." He muttered, scratching at his matted hair, which stuck up at the back like Einstein.

"I have to tell the police," I said.

He looked at me and grimaced, the expression horrific due to his absence of teeth.

"If I show you why, will you promise not to tell?"

I could see that he was upset, and that made me curious.

"I don't understand."

"You will." He said. "As long as you see for yourself."

"Then show me," I said before I could change my mind.

He nodded, and then he did it.

He closed his eyes and exhaled, the breath seeming to last for an eternity, then he opened them and breathed in. My shadow, deep and rich as it lay across the ground was drawn up towards his mouth. I was frozen, watching as he sucked it in, and like a glass, his eyes started to fill with opaque from bottom to top as he took it in.

It happened instantly. It wasn't a flashback or a series of images, but suddenly I knew. I understood everything. I saw snatches of images which punctuated the stream of knowledge passed to me from Benson.

I saw Luke as the friend I knew, smiling and perched on his bike, only his shadow was warped and distorted, shimmering on the ground next to my perfectly normal one. I saw him as a man, and what would have become of him. How he would become a prolific and violent serial killer of children and women.

I saw Charlie, and like Luke, his shadow was distorted and broken, and then I understood. Because as harmless as he was as a child, as a man, Charlie would get into weapons trading with Middle Eastern countries, and supply them with a suitcase nuclear bomb that would go on to be used to devastating effect in the city of Chicago. Or at least it would have if Benson hadn't stopped him.

Benson was moaning, and bloody tears rolled down his cheeks. The world went on around me, but it was muted and hollow as if I were underwater. Benson balled his fists and began to tremble, then opened his mouth. My shadow filtered back out and reattached itself to my feet, streaming from him like billowing black smoke. His eyes returned to their normal colour, and as they did, the connection between us was severed, and the world came back to its usual vibrancy.

He wiped away the bloody tears and looked at me. He seemed somehow even older, and his efforts had obviously exhausted him.

"Do you understand now boy?" He whispered, still trying to catch his breath.

"You can see them can't you Mr Benson?" I croaked. "The bad people. But you see them before they are bad. You see it in their shadows."

He nodded. "The shadow and the soul are connected. People think that they are born into this world with a clean slate, but it's not like that. Bad people are born bad."

"Are you some kind of angel?" I asked him, and despite his exhaustion, he found it in himself to chuckle.

"No, not exactly. I was born in Boston actually."

"Then how?" I trailed off and stared down at my shadow which just a few minutes ago had been ingested by the withered old man in front of me.

"I don't know the how's or why's." He said with a shrug. "I didn't get the power until I was in my early forties. Fell off a ladder when I was painting the house and banged my head on the concrete. Knocked myself out cold. When I woke up, I saw my neighbour who had come to help me and see if I was okay. His shadow was tainted, all fuzzy and jittery. Course, I didn't know what it meant at the time. I thought it was just a concussion, and didn't give it much thought. A couple of years later he was all over the news. Serial killer. But by then I was starting to suspect what had happened to me."

I nodded, letting him go back and remember and tell his story.

"First time I took a shadow was nineteen sixty six. I don't know how I knew to do it, I just did. I knew how and I knew why. But whatever it was that showed me what to do, didn't tell me how to live with the guilt. And you better believe it boy, it's hard to sit down to eat dinner with your family when you have just condemned a soul to death."

"But it's only bad people, isn't it?" I whispered.

"Good or bad they are still people. And even bad people might still have good qualities."

"How many…" I muttered as he looked off into the distance.

"I don't know. Thousands I expect. One thing I can tell you is that the guilt doesn't get any easier to live with. When a man can't look his family in the eye, it's time to stop burdening them."

"That's why you moved out of your house, isn't it?" I said.

He nodded, and I noticed that his hands were shaking.

"Are you okay Mr Benson?"

"I will be. It takes a lot out of me these days. Every shadow I take eats a little bit of me. That's the way it is. That's the rules. Sugar helps. That's why I asked you to go for lemonade, for after I took your friend's shadow."

I had half a bar of chocolate in my jacket, and I offered it to Benson. He took it gratefully and broke off a piece. He popped it in its mouth and we were silent. He watched the people, looking for the bad ones. Even though I couldn't see what he did, I looked anyway.

"Does it hurt them, when they go I mean?"

Benson shrugged. "I don't know. I hope not. I know they don't feel me taking the shadow, and they never die right away. It's always later. I like to tell myself that there is no pain, but I'm only guessing."

"The papers said Luke went in his sleep and wouldn't have felt a thing. Same with Charlie."

Benson nodded, popping another piece of chocolate into his mouth.

"Well, that's something I guess." He muttered, taking a long hard look at a young woman's shadow as she walked across the other side of the street.

"Bad one?" I asked, partly dreading the answer.

"No."

I nodded.

"That's why you only ever come out at this time isn't it Mr. Benson? When it's sunny and the shadows are easy to see."

He nodded.

"Makes my work easier. The older I get, the harder it is to function. I don't suppose I'm long for this world son. Even though people here see me as some crazy bum, I've worked hard at trying to make the world a better place. Only thing is, there are too many bad ones now. Way more bad than good. There is only so much I can do."

"Are there others like you, Mr Benson?"

"I don't know son." He sighed. "I hope so. I hope there is an entire army of them, because if not, the world is in trouble. I'm working as hard as I can, but this old body of mine is running out of steam."

"So what happens now?" I asked him.

"That's up to you. If you want to go to the police or repeat what I have told you, I can't stop you. But I know your shadow, and I believe what it tells me."

"That I'm one of the good ones?"

"Yes, you are."

The orange of the sunset had turned to red, and the day was starting to become night.

"I won't tell anyone," I said, watching as he finished the last of the chocolate. "I think you're doing a good thing, Mr Benson. I think you're one of the good ones too."

"Thank you, I only hope you're right."

I turned my bike around and readied to set off.

"Will I see you again Mr Benson?"

"I don't know." He said with a shrug. "You know where I'll be, for as long as I'm able. As soon as I know it's the end, I'll go someplace quiet and end it my own way."

I nodded, and we shared a look that was a bond greater than any friendship or relationship that I have experienced since.

"Good luck Mr Benson."

"Thank you for understanding. And for the chocolate." He said quietly. I started to ride away when he called me. I turned on my bike, and once again he was just a withered, broken old man.

"Keep being one of the good ones." He said, and then turned back to the road and the people.

I never spoke to Benson again after that day, although I did see him a few times, always on that overturned crate, always at that same time of day when the shadows were strong and easy to spot. I think it was around six months later when he stopped showing up. I guessed he had made good on his promise, and found himself a nice quiet place to finally get his peace. I hope he went to a better place, and that his service to our species was well served. I remember my conversation with him, and our hope that there were others out there like him, and that they were doing all they could to protect the rest of us. But the more horror I see in the news, the more terrible things that I see happen, the more certain I am, that Benson was one of a kind. There is one thing for sure, though, without him, the world is a much worse place.

I never told anyone about Benson, not until now, but I did heed his advice. I have tried to be one of the good ones. I have a beautiful wife and three amazing children who I'm trying to bring up as best I can. As I write this, I'm watching them playing outside in the garden. It's a beautiful day, and I'm incredibly grateful for what I have. My children's shadows dance in tandem with them, and I can only hope that they are pure and untainted and that they will grow up to be one of the good ones, just like Benson was.

SICK DAY

The cat was on the kitchen counter, and even from across the room, Mannering knew it was dead. He stared at it, quite unable to fathom why it was there, but the cat offered no answers, and its glassy green eyes stared back at him. Beside the dead cat were the blue marigolds that Alice used when she washed the dishes. They were pocked with marks and scratches, just like the ones a struggling cat might make if someone was trying to kill it.

He realised that he was holding his breath, and exhaled, unable to tear his eyes away from the dead animal, which was the only blemish in the otherwise pristine kitchen where just a couple of hours ago he had eaten breakfast and headed off to work.

The house was quiet, and he listened to the silence, which weighed like a physical thing as he tried to make sense of what was going on. He could just about hear the constant metronome ticking of the grandfather clock in the sitting room and the dull hum of the fridge freezer, but other than that, the house was completely devoid of sound.

It was then that he asked himself a new question.

Where was his wife?

He had been married to Alice for twenty one years, and their union had been happy. The house had been long since bought and paid for, and the two of them were content to live a quiet life ruled by routine and very defined roles. He went out to work, whilst Alice looked after the house. That was the way it had always been.

It was as he stood in his kitchen, that he started to ask himself what his wife actually did all day when he went out to work.

"Alice?" He said, his throat dry as he croaked his wife's name.

Silence.

He wondered where she could be. She didn't drive, and even if she did, he had taken the car to work that morning anyway. He supposed she could have been over at Betsy's, had he not known that she was visiting her sister for the next two weeks.

"Alice?" He repeated, this time finding the courage to say it just a little louder.

Still without reply, he walked into the sitting room, his heart fluttering as wildly as his mind raced with ideas, speculation and possibilities, none of which explained the dead cat in the kitchen. It was then that his curiosity morphed into fear.

The room was perfectly normal, perfectly clean and tidy and as it had been that morning, apart from the string of dead blackbirds on the wall. There were three of them strung across the chimney breast. They had been threaded through the neck and hung in the same way that they hung their Christmas cards, the scrawny bodies hanging limp and broken as Mannering stared at them.

He opened his mouth and then snapped it closed. He had intended to call out to his wife again but then had decided against it, because now in light of everything, he wasn't so sure he wanted her to know he was here. He felt almost like an intruder like he had transgressed on some secret ritual meant for her eyes only. He thought about how long this could have been happening. How many of those Monday to Friday eight to six shifts had been consumed by this…whatever it was.

As he considered that idea, other things started to fall into place, things which up until then, hadn't registered. The way she always insisted he call before he left the office. He had always assumed it was just something she did to know that he was coming home, but now he wondered if it was to give her time to hide away her… displays. The more he considered it, the more he thought it could be a valid point. It was just after eleven in the morning, and he should be at work. It was her time, time which he shouldn't be encroaching on. If only the office hadn't had a power outage and sent everyone home, then he would still be there and not a witness to the disturbing happenings in his house. Because it had been both sudden and a situation out of the ordinary, he hadn't called home and now he had discovered… whatever it was that he had discovered. The disturbing display had also made him consider the fact that – as ashamed as he was to admit it - he knew nothing about what his wife did with her spare time. Nothing at all. As far he knew she had no hobbies, no real friends. Her entire life, as he knew it, was spent within these four walls keeping their home clean and tidy and running smoothly.

Could that be it? Could the years of isolation and loneliness have broken something in Alice's mind to make her believe that such repulsive things as killing animals was acceptable? He couldn't bear to think about it anymore, and pushed the idea to the back of his mind, knowing that he needed everything to rationalise and deal with the unique and frightening situation at hand. Once again, he asked himself just where Alice was, and in the same instant, the floodgates opened and the answer popped into his mind.

He didn't rush, as part of him didn't want to prove his suspicions right. Instead, he walked back to the kitchen, giving the dead cat a wide berth as he walked to the window and looked out into the garden.

Alice's greenhouse.

He had built it for her when she expressed an interest in growing their own vegetables, something which she had done for a while and then seemed to lose all enthusiasm for. The greenhouse had remained unused since its windows grimy and fogged. Ghosts of overgrown plants pressed against the glass and Mannering was filled with such an intense dread that he had to cling to the edge of the sink.

He had never set foot in that greenhouse and knew that if he was to find Alice, then that is where she would be. How he knew that, he couldn't be sure. Perhaps it came with the absolute knowledge you could have for a person over time, although he hadn't seen this particular situation coming, so all bets were off

The air was cool and crisp as he stepped outside, pausing at the edge of their neatly trimmed garden. His breath fogged in the chill September air, but even that was nowhere near as cold as the ice which circulated his veins. He could see no sign of movement in the greenhouse, no shadows moving against the filthy, frosted glass. He set off towards the greenhouse, walking slowly, straining his senses. After the silence of the house, the chorus of birdsong around him was deafening. There were two more cats in the garden. The first bore all the hallmarks of a stray, its fur mangy and knotted. Its head was twisted at a nauseating angle, and like the one in the kitchen, its glassy eyes stared accusingly.

The second was even more horrific, it's clumpy grey fur flecked with blood. The kitchen scissors were embedded into the creature's eyes, and it had been displayed spread-eagled on the birdbath, the drinking water now a diluted shade of red. Whilst he was asking himself what he would do if his wife was insane, a second, more important question came to him, one which he had no answer for.

What would he do if she wasn't?

What if, when it came to it, she was perfectly rational? What if she was the same woman who he had loved for the last twenty three years, twenty one of those as his wife? What would he do if she was fine apart from her desire to kill the local wildlife? Could he, over time, learn to live with it? Could he treat it like some kind of sordid affair and ignore it? Perhaps sweep it under the rug and go on as if nothing had happened? He didn't think so. He was pretty sure that if he could, he wouldn't be inching his way towards the greenhouse at the end of the garden.

The glass and steel construction was just ahead of him now, and he paused at the door, waiting for his knotted stomach to settle. On the ground in front of him was a single spot of blood. It was something that, under ordinary circumstances, he might have never noticed, in fact, he would never have been over at the greenhouse in the first place, but that was before he came home early from work to a house and garden filled with dead animals and a wife who was still missing.

Alice.

His wife's name hovered in his throat, but try as he might, he couldn't bring himself to say it. A light, cold sweat had formed on his arms and back as he tried to force himself to open the door and face whatever was inside.

It's not too late, just turn around and go back to work. If you love her, you would. She obviously doesn't want you to know about this.

No, he couldn't do that. He just couldn't. He had to intervene, to sit her down and talk to her, perhaps pay her more attention, make sure they did more things together. But first, he had to face whatever was inside.

He quietly opened the door and stepped inside.

The smell hit him immediately.

Mannering blinked, unable to process what he was seeing.

The twin shelves which lined each wall of the greenhouse were filled with withered, brown overgrown plants, most of which were dead or dying. Alice's clothes were neatly folded and placed between two cracked red plant pots. At the furthest end of the greenhouse was a natural earth bed which had been excavated to allow Alice to grow potatoes and carrots, but now, as Mannering watched, he saw that they had been used for an entirely different purpose.

Alice lay on her back in the dirt, moaning as she rubbed the moist earth into her body and over her face. She had her eyes closed and was murmuring as she scooped the soil against herself. Buried within the dirt were bodies - putrid, rotting carcasses of birds, cats and dogs. Whenever her hand would fall upon one, she would drag it towards her and crush it against her body, displacing flesh and allowing liquefied organs to spill out, turning the soil into a thick mud paste.

Mannering was bizarrely reminded of their first wedding anniversary when they had made snow angels in Paris.

He watched in sick fascination as she rolled in the dirt and pulled another mound towards her. A human arm flopped out of the mud, touching her stomach. It was putrid and rotten, and Alice grabbed at the maggot infested appendage and touched its dead fingers to her cheeks, kissing the blackened nails. Mannering could only look as he saw for the first time beyond the writhing shape of his wife to the other arms which protruded out of the earth like strange exotic plants. Some were brown and leathery, but many were still disgustingly recognisable, even in their putrid state.

He stopped counting at seven, knowing that his mind wasn't equipped to take much more. He was just an insurance salesman. Things like this didn't happen to people like him. Without knowing that he was going to do it, he backed out of the greenhouse and gently closed the door, shutting away the horrors inside.

You need to call the police.

He staggered back up the garden path, unable to focus, unable to breathe. The dead cat in the kitchen now seemed of little consequence. After all, how could it shock him after what he had just seen? Mannering knew he had to get out, had to get away.

He staggered to his car, dropped the keys, picked them up again with shaking hands and managed to unlock the vehicle. He drove away from the house, looking but not seeing as he left his little slice of suburban hell behind.

He made it as far as the docks before he pulled over and threw up into the grass verge. As he stood there sobbing and panting with his hands on his knees and the bitter taste of vomit in his throat, it finally hit home just want he had witnessed. Things had changed, and would never be the same again.

You need to call the police. Now.

It was true. He loved his wife, but she was obviously sick. There was something inherently wrong with her that needed to be fixed, or at least that was what the rational side of his brain was telling him. On the other hand, she was his true love, his soul mate, his one and only thing in the world that he cared for. Could he do it? Could he bring himself to make the call? He wouldn't be there when it happened, but the neighbours would. And as the police arrived en masse and led Alice away in handcuffs, questions would be asked, asked of him.

Mannering fished his phone out of his pocket, stared at it, and then knew what he was going to do. It was for the best.

Alice was just finishing washing the dishes. The kitchen was filled with the delicious aroma of pot roast. She heard the car pull up to the house, and paused. It was earlier than normal, and her eyes went towards the knife block on the side. She heard the car door close, and waited, hand hovering over the carving knife.

Mannering walked through the door, and Alice relaxed. He looked jaded, exhausted even as he slipped off his jacket and walked towards the kitchen.

"What's for dinner?" He asked as he fixed himself a drink, flashing a quick glance towards the spot where the dead cat had been displayed earlier.

"Pot roast." Alice replied. "You look exhausted. Tough day?"

Mannering nodded as he drained the glass of whisky then poured himself another.

“Why don’t you go and drink that in the sitting room? Dinner isn’t quite ready yet. I got some wonderful potatoes to go with it.”

He almost laughed, or screamed at the idea, but instead took a sip of his drink and did as he was told.

Although it seemed impossible now, he was sure that he would learn to live with Alice’s hobby. Although the vows of marriage didn’t mean as much these days as they once did, he was determined to honour the commitment that he had made to her. And that was to love and cherish her until death. Was a life alone worth the price of doing the right thing?

Probably.

Just not to him. Everyone had quirks, and everyone had imperfections, but like any good husband, he was just going to have to learn to live with the ones his wife had and try to make the best of them. He was sure that in time, he would learn to live with it. Mannering kicked off his shoes, switched on the television and sank down into his favourite chair whilst he waited for dinner.

JASPER

Jasper Collins had been a patient at Leafields Hospital for almost five years, and today was his first real chance at getting out. He was nervous as he was led into the room and sat in front of Dr Ronson, not because he had the power to deny Jasper his freedom, but because of the window in his office. It ran the full length of the wall, and looked onto the beautiful, lush gardens which appeared somehow even more magical under the rain, which probed and tapped at the glass.

Jasper forced himself not to look at it, otherwise, Ronson might see that there was something wrong, and the game would be up.

"Is everything okay Jasper?" Ronson asked, breaking his train of thought.

Jasper fidgeted, licked his lips, and ran a hand through his dirty blonde hair.

"I'm fine. Just… nervous. This is a big day for me."

"It is." The doctor agreed, offering a thin smile - a token gesture which bore little humour.

Ronson had been Jasper's doctor since he was first admitted. Although, Jasper knew well enough that committed was a better word for what had happened to him. People were admitted to places when they were ill, and still had the opportunity to leave whenever they wanted. For Jasper, however, there was no open front door, no option to leave. They thought he was mad, loopy, a few buns short of a dozen. And he supposed, as he sat there trying his best not to glance out of the window, that they might be right.

He at least felt comfortable enough with Ronson though. There was a familiarity to the salt and pepper haired old man, a kindness in his eyes that put people at ease, which was a world away from his feelings towards the bullying, asshole orderlies who worked out on the wards.

"We can close the blinds, if you prefer." Ronson said, following Jaspers' gaze to the window.

Although he was desperate to say yes, Jasper remained calm

and shrugged, even managing to sound calm when he replied.

"It's fine. Really."

Ronson nodded and made a note on his paperwork, which was the only thing between Jasper and his freedom.

"So." He said, looking over his notes. "You have been with us for almost five years now. I'm told you have made great progress, particularly over these last eighteen months."

Jasper nodded. "I feel good now, I think I have come a long way."

"How old are you now Jasper?"

"Twenty three."

More notes were scribbled, and Ronson folded his hands on the desk and smiled. Jasper couldn't help but look at the doctor's fingers, how manicured and perfect his nails were. He looked down at his own chewed to the skin appendages and hid them out of sight on his knees.

"How do you feel now, about what happened before you came here?" Ronson asked.

Jasper felt a flicker of the bad stuff, the darkness that sometimes fizzed and bubbled in his stomach. For a split second, he saw himself launching over the desk and tearing Ronson's tongue out. Instead, he smiled.

"Of course, I feel bad, sorry and ashamed."

It was a lie. He actually didn't know how he felt about it all, however, they were the words that Ronson would have wanted, and so they were the ones he gave.

"And what about the crows? How do you feel about them?"

A surge of emotions coursed through Jasper all at once. Rage, terror, paranoia. It took an incredible force of will for him to avoid glancing to the window, especially since that was what Ronson was watching for.

Fuck you Ronson.

"That's something else I'm ashamed of. I... don't want to talk about it."

For all the deceit that he had planned, that was the first true thing that Jasper had said since the assessment began. Ronson was staring again. How he hated that stare. It had switched from kind and friendly during the introductory small talk, to one that was purely judgmental, and seemed to burn into Jaspers' very soul. He was suddenly certain that Ronson knew everything. Knew abou the lies, knew about the plan to bluff his way to freedom.

Knew about the crows.

He coughed into his hand. "I really would rather not bring it al up again."

"Look Jasper, I'm not against you here. But we need to tal about this. I need to assess that you do, in fact, have a firm gras on reality. Until I can satisfy myself and the board of this hospita that you truly are ready to go back into society, then I won't b able to agree to your release. Please, talk to me about the crows."

Jasper hesitated, and couldn't help flick his gaze to the window He instantly regretted it, because Ronson saw it. He cleared hi throat and looked the doctor in the eye.

"They don't speak to me anymore if that's what you want t know."

"So I understand from my reports. How do you feel about that?"

Careful. He's trying to catch you out here.

"Well… I know now that they never did. Not really. I know can't blame them for what I did." He said with a shrug.

"You admit responsibility for what you did to your mother an brothers?"

Jasper paused, as a series of quick fire images came to him images forever burned into his memory.

Bloody kitchen tiles.

The knife clutched in his shaking hand.

His mother's glassy, dolls eyes, horrified and staring int oblivion.

The crow at the window. Watching. Always watching.

He shuffled again and looked at his feet.

"I know what I did, and I know I have to live with it for the res of my life."

"Jasper, when the crows used to speak to you, what was it like How did they sound?"

He paused to consider the question, desperate to look out of th window but afraid of what he might see if he did.

"It was always just one. A big one. At first, I didn't think muc of it. It started showing up in the garden. I didn't realise at first but every time I saw it, something bad happened. That first time my dog Toby was run over in the street. I loved that dog.

remember going out there where he lay, broken and panting in the street, and as I was cradling his head, I looked up and saw the crow. It was just standing on the lawn watching me."

"I see," Ronson said, making more notes.

He pushed his glasses back up his face, and then looked at Jasper. He was now in full on professional mode. Gone were the friendly smiles and encouragement. He had a look in his eyes which said he was looking for information, and wouldn't rest until he had everything he wanted.

"When did you see it as more than coincidence?" He asked, pen poised over paper.

"When they started to read my mind," Jasper replied immediately, then hesitated, and offered a nervous smile. "I mean when I thought that's what they were doing."

He searched Ronson's face for any inkling of a reaction, but the doctor only looked back, waiting patiently as he always did. After all, what was time in a place like this? Jasper flicked his eyes to the window and the green gardens beyond, and when he saw that it was empty, he continued.

"I saw it again, that same bird a few weeks later on the day my dad had his heart attack. I know what you must be thinking. How can I know it was the same one?" He grinned, but it was a pained gesture which felt alien, and he reverted to his neutral frown.

"It's kind of hard to explain. Somehow, I just *knew* it was the same bird. I knew it as a certainty. That's when I first heard it in my head. I heard it telling me I was right, that it was the one that had been there when my dog was killed, and that if I ever told anyone, they would come for me."

He paused again and began to rub his thumb and forefinger together.

"My father died in the hospital that night, although in a way that didn't matter as much as the crow. Even though I couldn't see it, I knew it was there, hovering in my head, listening to my thoughts, invading my privacy."

"This certainly still seems to be stressful for you. Would you like to take a break? If you don't feel ready for this we can postpone."

"No, that's alright. I don't mind. It's just not something I like to talk about, that's all,"

"I just wanted to be certain. Please, continue. You are doing really, really well." Ronson said, giving Jasper one of his best encouraging smiles.

"I'm unsure if I should. How do I know this isn't a trick? What if you're trying to get me to say something that means I'll have to stay here?"

"Jasper, you should know by now that I only want what's best for you. Since you came here, I've done everything I can to help you."

Jasper nodded. It was true, Ronson *had* always tried to help, and seemed to have a genuine interest in his progress. "And besides," Ronson added, looking around the empty office, "it's just us here. Talking like the friends. I hope, by now, we are. Please, continue."

Jasper scratched at his hair, snatched a quick glance out of the window, and continued.

"Well, it went on like that for a few months. At first, I would only see it every few weeks or so, and when I did, something bad would always happen."

"What kind of things?"

"You know this."

Ronson didn't reply. He simply waited. Good old ever patient Ronson. With a sigh, Jasper continued to talk.

"Nothing too serious at first. Just minor stuff. I broke my leg. The kitchen somehow got set on fire, stuff like that. No matter what happened, it was always there, watching me from the garden. And even when I couldn't see it, I could hear it in my head. Talking to me, taunting me, threatening me."

"How did it feel? The voices inside your head?"

"It's kind of hard to explain," Jasper mumbled as he looked at the window, not a glance this time but a full on stare. He looked out into the gardens beyond, satisfied himself that all was normal, and then turned back to Ronson. "It's like… you know when there's a wasp in the house, and you can hear it buzzing, but it's kinda quiet?"

"I know exactly what you mean," Ronson said. "I grew up on a farm in Texas. It was a problem we had a lot."

Jasper nodded. "That's how it was. It was in there, just buzzing around in my head. It's odd because I didn't even have to speak. I could just think of something and it would know about it and answer me. It was around that time when I started to see it more often. Almost every other day, and pretty much straight away, things escalated."

"What happened?"

"You know the answer to this... I don't want to go over it again."

"Talking about it is good. In fact, it's a vital part of the healing process."

"You promise me this isn't a scam?" Jasper said, narrowing his eyes at Ronson.

"It's nothing of the sort. Please, go on."

Don't do it, you know what they said if you told anyone. You know what happened last time.

He was afraid, but he was also tired of the secrets. He wanted to start living his life, a chance to just be normal and do normal things. He wasn't sure the words would come out at first, but they did, and he was surprised by how smoothly they rolled off his tongue.

"I was sitting at the kitchen table, just looking out the window, and as always the crow was there. Standing on the grass, staring in at me, and as always, I could hear it in my head, buzzing and darting around and saying things. I... I threatened to tell people about it, and... it took flight and landed on the window ledge. It was standing on the other side of the glass, inches away and just... looking at me. And I don't know if it was because it was so close, but I heard it as clear as you and I are talking now, telling me that if I told anyone about it, they would make me pay."

Jasper was now staring into space, chewing at his fingertips as he recalled his story.

"I was angry, so I told it that it was just a bird, and I was going to tell my mother. It said it would be a mistake, and they would prove it, and with that, it took off and I didn't see it for a week."

"What happened after that?"

"You know what happened." He snapped. "My mother was raped on her way home from work."

The room fell silent. Ronson made more notes, and then looked at Jasper.

"You thought what happened to your mother was something to do with the crow?"

"I knew it was – or at least I thought I did. See I saw it again, later that night as my mother was taking her fifth shower since the police let her home. I was in my usual spot in the kitchen, wondering if it could possibly be a coincidence, and I heard that buzzing in my head and knew it was out there."

"You saw it?"

"No. It was dark, and all I could see through the glass was my own reflection. I just knew it was out there, watching me from the dark. It was in my head, telling me it had proved its point and if I wanted to stay safe, I needed to keep what I knew about them to myself, and from that day forth do whatever they told me."

"And you agreed?"

"I did." Jasper sighed. "By then, I was too afraid not to. Things got pretty bad, pretty fast from then on. I was convinced that if I didn't actually see it, nothing bad could happen to anyone close to me, so I holed up in my room. Painted the windows with black paint so I couldn't see out, and just sat there in the dark. My mother and brothers were worried, but I couldn't tell any of them what had happened. I was too afraid."

"How long did this go on for?"

"Oh, a few months. I couldn't sleep, I barely ate. I just sat there in the dark, listening to that maddening buzz in my head as it told me things, things I had to do. I tried to be strong, Doc Ronson, I really, really did, but they were like poison, and it didn't take much for them to break me. I was isolated and scared, and in the end, I did what they told me to do."

"Which brings us to the day when you killed your family."

To hear it said out loud made Jasper's stomach roll, and he lowered his gaze, staring at his white hospital issue pants and pumps.

Apart from the persistent tapping of the rain on the glass, the room was silent.

"I... I wish I could take it back. I really, really do." He said, his voice barely a whisper. "I was ill, and whatever I thought I could hear, seemed real enough to me at the time to make me do what I did."

"Tell me about it Jasper. It will help if you get it out in the open."

Jasper looked his doctor in the eye, searching for reassurance, and finding it.

"They… they told me my brothers were a part of it. That they knew all about the crows and what they did. They told me if I wanted things to go back to normal, I would have to kill them. By then, of course, my brain was pretty much fried. Of course, you already know that I have been here long enough to make that point obvious enough. As sick as it sounds now, the idea to kill my brothers seemed like the most reasonable idea in the world. Joe was only seven, and Mark was fourteen. I…"

Jasper swallowed hard, struggling to hold back his emotions.

"I took the carving knife and I…." He trailed off and reverted back to rubbing his thumb and forefinger together as he jigged his leg up and down.

"I can see you're getting upset, but we're almost done," Ronson said. "Can you go on?"

"I stabbed them." Jasper blurted, losing the battle to keep his tears at bay. "I started and I just couldn't stop. They were in my head, counting along as I did it. I stabbed Joe twenty three times and Mark fifty seven times. I… I have no excuse."

"Jasper, Don't blame yourself. You were ill, suffering from acute schizophrenia. It really wasn't your fault. I…"

"My mother was an accident." He blurted, flicking his eyes once again to the window. "She came home early from work, and I was there, covered in blood in the kitchen with my brother's dead bodies on the floor. She started to scream. I begged her to stop, but then that damn bird was in my head, telling me to shut her up… and I did... I did."

Jasper lowered his head, weeping openly. Ronson made more notes. When he had finished, he set his pen down and looked across the desk.

"I know it was hard for you to tell me that."

"It's the first time I have told it all to anyone," Jasper said between great, ragged sobs.

"When you came here, I have to admit, we didn't expect you to recover so quickly."

"Almost five years is hardly quick." He shot back, wiping his eyes with his shirt sleeve.

"Compared to what could have been? Life in prison perhaps? I would consider this a good day, a day to celebrate you finally getting better."

"Does this mean you are letting me out?" Jasper asked, filled with a sudden surge of hope.

Ronson hesitated, and the pleasant smile faded. "Here's the thing Jasper. I know how bright you are. I also know that you have taken to covering the windows of your room with a sheet during the day."

"It's to block out the sun I..."

Ronson held up a hand, and Jasper stopped speaking.

"I also noticed that since we started our conversation, you have been looking out of the window pretty much all the time. I think you still believe that the crows are out there. I still believe that despite our best efforts, you still hear them, and with that in mind I'm afraid I can only recommend that you stay here indefinitely until such a time when you are fit to return to society."

Jasper took the information in, staring at Ronson as his lip trembled slightly.

"You said I was progressing, you said I could go home…"

"No, I didn't. I said it was looking promising, however, this conversation has raised concerns enough so that I wouldn't be comfortable with releasing you at this time."

Ronson, you backstabbing motherfucker.

He glared at Ronson as the thought bounced around his head and was surprised to see Ronson flinch.

"There's no need for that Jasper. I'm only trying to help."

Jasper froze, the skin on his arms rippling with gooseflesh.

"I didn't say anything."

"You didn't have to," Ronson said, staring at Jasper. He saw it then, the reason why Ronson always seemed so familiar.

He had the same stare as the crow.

"You're one of them aren't you?" Jasper whispered.

He gave Ronson time to deny it. To refute it. To call him ridiculous, none of which he did. Instead, he stared, his eyes dark and somehow terrifying.

"You're sick Jasper. You need to stay here and let me help you."

"No!" Jasper blurted, and looked to the window.

The garden was filled with crows. They were standing motionless, staring into the office and watching proceedings unfold. Jasper recoiled, and threw himself out of his chair on to the floor.

"Get them away from me!" He screamed as he pushed his way across the carpet into the corner. Ronson should, by rights be hurrying around the table to help, but he simply sat, a knowing smile on his lips.

He was enjoying it.

"Doc Ronson, please, shut the blinds, they're out there." Jasper shrieked, staring at the army of birds on the lawn.

Ronson also looked at the garden full of birds and shrugged. "They are just birds, Jasper. They can't hurt you."

"You are one of them, aren't you doc?" Jasper cackled. He was hysterical now and had pushed himself back against the bookcase by the locked office door.

"Call em' off! I promise I won't ever tell anyone about them. Please!"

Ronson grinned and pressed the intercom on his desk. "Nurse, get someone in here with a sedative, Mr. Collins is having an episode!" Jasper noted that he spoke with mock panic over the intercom, which was replaced by the oozing, cool calm when it was just the two of them.

And the lawn full of crows, of course.

"What do you want from me?" Jasper sobbed as he tucked his knees up to his chin and hugged them tightly.

Ronson stood and approached Jasper. He was holding a silver letter opener.

"Are you going to kill me?" Jasper whispered as the incessant buzzing began to drone around his head.

Ronson crouched and leaned close enough for Jasper to smell the expensive aftershave that he wore.

"No. You're going to stab me." He said, and then thrust the letter opener into his own arm. He yelled out in pain, and in unison, the crows as one let out a high-pitched squawk and took off in a flurry of beating wings. It was then that the orderlies burst into the room to see Jasper rocking and staring out of the window and Ronson on his back, holding his bleeding arm and moaning. No words were shared as Jasper was sedated, even so, he could hear Ronson clearly enough in his head along with the buzzing as he lost consciousness.

Six months later.

The lobotomy had been successful. Although rarely performed anymore, in the case of Jasper Collins, it was seen as a necessary step. The procedure hadn't gone as expected, however, Jasper didn't care. He was happy in his room. The window was small and high up on the wall so that he couldn't see out of it. It was also dark, and moonlight spread across the wall, making a projection of the bars that covered the window. He sat in the corner, knees tucked under his chin, wiry arms hooked around them. He was still the same on the inside, but he couldn't outwardly articulate. He was a prisoner within a prisoner.

Ronson had pushed for the surgery, and although for a time he hadn't known why he thought he knew now. Of course, now it was too late, because although the thoughts were sharp in his mind, the procedure had meant that he couldn't articulate them even if he wanted to. He heard a sound, and his heart rate increased. He cast his eyes to the window and saw it, the silhouette blown up to giant proportions on the wall. The crow walked back and forth at the window and then stopped to look in at him. He met its gaze, and for a moment, the thick soup that had replaced his brain cleared. He heard a voice, Ronson's voice, clear and sharp. It said just seven words, but they were enough to confirm his suspicions. Jasper smiled and closed his eyes, the fight long since having left him.

The silhouette on the wall took flight and he was again alone. He knew he would never be able to leave. Because the crows wouldn't allow it. He thought of his brothers, his mother and his father during happier times when they were still alive, but his mind kept going back to those seven words uttered by the crow. He didn't think he would hear from them again. He was sure that now that they were satisfied that he had been silenced. After all, wasn't that the entire point?

Seven words.

Enough to make sense of the whole mess. Jasper covered his ears and rocked back and forth just a little harder as those words bounced around in his broken brain. It was his error because he didn't think that Ronson counted. After all, he was a doctor. How could he have known it was a test?

Either way, it was too late now. He had done it and he would have to live with it. He wondered if the crow's presence meant that something bad was going to happen, or if it was just a final goodbye, a gloating show of victory.

Those seven words spun around his head.

You shouldn't have told anyone about us.

And they were right, Jasper thought as he bit into his wrists, tearing through veins and sinewy flesh. He sat there, bloody-mouthed and smiling as he bled out onto the padded white floor, which greedily soaked up the precious fluid. He was smiling. At last, it was over. At last, there was silence.

TILLY

Tom Johnson accelerated, pushing the S-Class Mercedes past sixty. It had been one of those days, the kind that starts badly and just get worse, and now to top it all off, he had a headache. As he maneuvered the vehicle around a slow moving campervan, he acknowledged that he might well have been fired instead of just given a verbal dressing down, and for that at least he could be grateful.

The car flashed past a road sign, and he shook his head.

Four miles to go.

At least Gloria was asleep. On top of his already shitty day, she had given him hell when he had cancelled their plans. He had promised to take her to dinner, and then to an expensive hotel. To say that she was less than pleased to be driving out here into the middle of nowhere would be an understatement. Somehow, he had managed to convince her to come along with him, with the promise that as soon as he had done what he needed to do, he would make it up to her.

A rare flush of guilt raced down his spine, and in his mind's eye, he saw his wife of ten years, Melanie, and his children – Alice and George – swim out of the darkness. He thought of them now, and what they would be doing. It was almost seven, which meant that the kids would be watching television, and Melanie would likely be washing the dishes from their evening meal. He loved her of course, but as he supposed was natural, the spark had gone from their relationship, and even if it hadn't, it had been a long time since she had been able to excite him, which was the exact opposite of his dozing travel companion.

The more he thought about it, the more the guilt took hold. As always, he tried to convince himself that he shouldn't see it as an affair, but as a way to save his marriage. He got the warm, genuine love from his wife, and his thrill seeking excitement from his lover, and as long as the two remained separate, he was happy to continue with his deceit.

Johnson turned his attention back to the road, and his mind to the reason for his journey out into the boonies.

He had been head of quality control for Randell's toys for the last seven years, doing his part to assist in the growth of a company that had started out as a local business run from a shed in the late sixties, to what it was today - A global multi-billion dollar business and undisputed leader in the toy industry. When seventeen-year-old James Randell first had the idea to start a toy business, he was an unemployed farmhand who most said had no future. When he died sixty-three years later, he was worth close to seven hundred million dollars and counted several high profile celebrities and politicians (and two former presidents) amongst his close friends.

Johnson had joined the company in 99', and had clawed his way up the corporate ladder until he reached, what he thought, was a secure and, more importantly, a financially stable role. As head of quality control, he would be required to make sure that the products were safe to use before they went to manufacture, and if Johnson was honest with himself, the job was an easy one. Hardly anything ever came across Johnson's desk that his team couldn't deal with without him.

Or at least, that had been the case until Tilly.

Tilly was a new brand of doll for girls aged four to eight. It was hailed as the latest great revolution from the Randall toy company, and Johnson had to admit, the gimmick was a good one. Each doll was essentially a micro PC, fitted with a small computer processor and hard drive in its innards, and tiny cameras inside its eyes. The idea was that the dolls would recognise gestures made by its owner, and remember certain things, and when appropriate, would respond with one of around five hundred pre-installed words or phrases. The public went Tilly crazy, and the Randell brand added a few more million to its already swollen bank balance.

Within a week, local stores were sold out, within a month; you couldn't find a Tilly anywhere in the country. Desperate parents were paying up to six or seven thousand for a doll online in their desperation to deliver their children with the latest craze, and the media frenzy served to push sales and prices even further.

The CEO of Randall, James Crockett, congratulated his staff for another big success, and Johnson, along with everyone else, was waiting for the expected fat bonus for another job well done.

But that all went out the window when he was called up to Crockett's office earlier that day.

Crockett was a large man, always dressed in a suit that cost more than most of his employees made in a month. He had cruel eyes, and a thin handlebar mustache perched on top of a thin, pencil line mouth.

"Get in here Johnson." He said as he glared from behind his desk.

Johnson had complied, and for a moment, Crockett had stared at him, and because Johnson had no idea why he was even there, he stared back.

"So Tom." He started. "You want to tell me what the hell happened with these damn Tilly dolls?"

"What about them?"

"Returns, lots of them."

"Do we know why?"

"Take your pick. They aren't functioning properly, the software is faulty, it's a god damn mess."

Johnson nodded but wasn't initially concerned. Even with the greatest care, some products would slip through the gaps and be shipped faulty, and a small number of returns would be expected. He relaxed a little, and without waiting for an invite, sat opposite Crockett.

"It is to be expected sir, especially for a product like Tilly, where the construction is so complex."

"Then what the hell do I pay you for?" He said, narrowing his eyes "Aren't you supposed to be head of quality control?"

"Yes sir I am, and as I said, we would expect, even with the greatest care and attention to have a small number of returns, and assigned a two percent allowance in the budget to reflect that."

Johnson was pleased with himself, and it seemed that he had, for the time being, silenced his overpowering boss. But Crockett' look of indifference became a sneer, and he slid a single sheet of paper across the desk.

"My math may not be that great," Crockett said, as his sneer morphed into a smug grin. "But I would say that the number of returns equals more than a two percent margin."

Johnson picked up the sheet of paper, and let his eyes take in the numbers as his brain crunched and processed them. As he read, he felt his heart rate increase.

"This can't be right." He said as he looked over the paper at Crockett.

"Oh its right, I had the figures double checked."

"But this is…" He tried to work out the figure and was almost there when Crockett said it for him.

"Seventy three percent is the number you are trying to reach."

Johnson looked at Crockett, and for a few seconds there was silence.

"That's not possible," Johnson said as he looked again at the paper clutched in his hands. "We were thorough, we always are."

"In this case, it seems you missed something big."

"Maybe it's a bad batch of processors, or a faulty part affecting a small number of products."

Crockett nodded, and Johnson was sure that this line of enquiry had already been considered.

"Well, that sheet is just for Ridgefield. We were thinking the same thing, but now reports are coming in from all over the world of these damn dolls being returned in droves. This could cost us millions."

"What are the reasons given for their return?"

"That's the thing." Crocket said with a sigh. "Nobody knows. Hell, some stores are getting forty or fifty back a day, some people aren't even asking for refunds, they are just dumping the damn things."

Johnson felt nauseous and suspected that the blame, rightly or wrongly was about to land firmly at his feet.

"So how do we proceed with this?"

Crockett opened his desk drawer and tossed a map towards Johnson.

"That's one of our warehouses over in Oakwell. We are keeping all of the returns there, but the place is starting to look like some kind of damn doll graveyard."

Johnson looked at the map, and then back to Crockett, sure of what was coming but hoping he was wrong.

"Might be an idea to send Davies over to take a look," Johnson said, trying to keep casual. "He designed the processor chip in the Tilly range, so if anybody can find out what's wrong it's him."

Crockett grinned again and licked his thin lips.

"We sent him up there last week to try and find out what the hell is going on. This morning he calls me and resigns. No explanation, no notice, just tells me he's done and hangs up the phone."

"But Davies has been with the company for years, he wouldn't just quit for no reason."

"You would think not, but quit he did, which leaves us with a huge problem. The shareholders are on my ass to fix this before the press get a hold of the story and crucify us, and the power structure dictates that they give me shit, I delegate said shit out to my staff, which brings me to you."

"I could send some of my team out there, see if they can look into it."

"No," Crockett said, shaking his head. "I want you to go personally."

Johnson hesitated, trying to think of an excuse to get out of it.

"Okay, no problem. I can head up there next week and take a look."

"That's not good enough Tom. I need you to go up there *tonight* and find out what the hell the problem is."

"Can't this wait until after the weekend sir? I have plans tonight."

"Frankly, I don't give a shit. Cancel them."

"I don't see what the rush is here, give me a day or two and I'll head up there and take a look, it's almost a hundred miles to Oakwell. You can't expect me to just drop everything and drive across the country."

"Eighty three miles, actually." Crockett snapped. "But that's beside the point. I don't think you understand the gravity of this situation Tom, so I'm going to lay it out for you nice and clear."

Crockett's cheeks had flushed, and his lips were pursed together. He looked close to losing it, and so Johnson remained silent.

"What you need to know." He started, pointing across the desk "Is that, until this problem — this major design flaw that you and your people apparently missed — is fixed, production is halted. Until it starts again, we are losing over a hundred and twenty grand per day in revenue, not to mention what we are paying out in wages for staff who are, as we speak sitting at home on their asses and waiting for the okay to get back to work. The way things are headed, we are going to be in the hole financially on this entire project before the end of the month. Now somebody has to be responsible, and so I suggest that you, as head of quality control, is to be that person."

Crockett pointed a chubby finger at Johnson.

"So I'm giving you a choice. You can either go out there today and find out what's going on with this damn product, or you can keep to the plans you have made, and first thing tomorrow start looking for a new job. Have I made myself clear enough?"

For a split second, Johnson had the urge to tell Crockett to shove his job up his arrogant ass, but he knew that it would be stupid, and although it would be satisfying in the short term, it was a bad idea. Instead, he nodded.

"Okay, I didn't realise it was such a big deal. I'll go and check it out and find out what's going on over there."

"Good," Crockett said with an arrogant smile. "I'm glad we understand each other."

Johnson stood, picked up the map, and crossed the office.

"Oh Tom." Crockett said. "If you don't fix this problem, then I'm sorry to have to tell you that it could cost you your job."

Crockett didn't sound sorry. In fact, he was smiling, the arrogance rolling off him as he leaned back in his chair and relaxed.

Asshole.

"Why me?" Johnson asked.

"Because if we can't fix it, somebody will have to take the fall."

"And I say again. Why me?"

Crockett didn't answer; instead, he smiled and folded his hands on his desk, but the message was clear enough. It was how businesses like this worked. The top dogs never took the fall, it was always the little people down the chain, the ones who worked hardest that paid the penalty. Johnson realised that Crockett was staring at him and that he, in turn, was still standing in the office.

"You better get going Tom, it's a long drive. Call me as soon as you have some information."

"Absolutely sir. You can count on me."

"I hope so, because if not, we are screwed."

Oakwell was one of those sleepy, one street towns with red brick buildings, and neat, tidy houses. The modern world had so far not slammed the town with corporate branding, and as he navigated down Main Street, Johnson thought that he could well have driven back to another era -Twilight Zone style- perhaps to the fifties or early sixties.

He wasn't quite sure how to get to the warehouse and thought it best to check with one of the locals that he was on the right track before Gloria woke up and gave him another ear bashing for ruining their night. He pulled over to the sidewalk and rolled down the window. There was on older man heading towards him, walking a scruffy looking Jack Russell terrier with a pink bow tied behind its ears.

Johnson verified that he was indeed on the right track, and the local told him that he needed to go through the village, past the forest and he would see the signs for the warehouse. He thanked the man and was on his way again when Gloria stirred and woke.

"What time is it?" She asked as she rubbed sleep out of her eyes.

"Just after eight. You have been out for a while."

He looked at her, and although she wasn't what would be deemed conventionally beautiful, she had a certain something that appealed to him. He thought it might be what he referred to as her 'natural' beauty. She wasn't the type to go overboard with make-up, and even so she was looked upon enviously by her fellow females, as her skin was clean and smooth, enhanced by the scattering of freckles across her nose. At twenty-three, she was thirteen years younger than Johnson, but intellectually they were similar, sharing a love for fine dining and opera, which was a world away from his home life where the weekly topic of conversation was the comings and goings on the latest reality TV show. She looked at him, her eyes a stunning blue-green.

"How long is this going to take?" She said as she lit a

cigarette.

He could tell that although she was still pissed at him, she seemed to have calmed down a little.

"Not long. Crockett is on my ass to fix this tonight."

"You should tell that sack of shit to do it himself if it's so important."

"It's my job Gloria, I had no choice."

"Yeah, well your job has screwed up our night. You should just quit, you are way too good for that place."

"You know I can't quit."

"Oh yeah, wifey wouldn't approve." She sneered.

"Hey come on, we agreed that we wouldn't talk about my other life when we are together."

She didn't say anything and turned away to look out of the window. They drove on in silence. There was little traffic, and apart from a cherry red convertible full of rowdy teens that overtook them way too fast, and too close for comfort, the road was empty. The green spires of Oakwell Forest rolled past on his right, and eventually, he saw the slip road leading towards the industrial area. He maneuvered the car down the rutted, dirt road.

"Jesus, haven't they heard of blacktop here?" Gloria muttered.

"I doubt there would be much call for it here."

He passed a hulking industrial laundry on his right, and then a little further down, the sweet smell of sawdust heralded the lumber mill, a huge concrete structure which looked eerie in its deserted state. Gloria had noticed it too.

"The place is a ghost town." She said as she watched the building roll past.

"They will all be closed up. I guess by mid-afternoon the workers down tools and the whole area is empty."

"Will anyone be at this warehouse to meet us?"

"No, it's used for storage, and even then it's only ever staffed at Christmas. The rest of the year, it sits empty." He saw the roof of the building appear in the distance. "There it is."

They pulled up at the warehouse, a rectangular slab of concrete with steel roller shutter doors. When it was operational, it housed a hundred and fifty dedicated staff who were responsible for local distribution. Johnson had visited once before, but that was in December and the place was a hive of activity, which couldn't be further from the heavy silence as he shut off the car's engine.

"Is nobody even here to meet us?" Gloria asked as she leaned forwards in her seat to peer out of the window.

"No, there is nobody here on a weekend. It's just us."

"*You* aren't supposed to work weekends." She said, glaring at him.

"Look, Gloria, I know you aren't happy about this and neither am I, but I didn't have a choice. Let's just get this over and done with and be on our way. Okay?"

"Yeah, well it looks like I don't have a choice."

She didn't give him a chance to answer, exiting the car and making sure to slam the door to emphasise her annoyance. Johnson sighed, tried to push his headache away. He took a moment to compose himself, then grabbed the warehouse keys from the glove compartment, and exited the car.

The air was cool, and the breeze pulled at Johnsons coat as he walked towards the door. He leafed through the tangle of keys he had been given, selected the correct one and unlocked the door, remembering to punch in the alarm key combination as he entered and switched on the lights.

They were in a short reception hallway with another locked door at the end. Johnson walked towards it, pushed through into the main workspace, and immediately drew breath.

The cavernous space was filled with Tilly dolls. The ones that had been returned in the original packaging were stacked on several wooden pallets. The loose returns were in dozens of cloth bins, which were filled almost to overflowing with the toys.

Before he had seen it for himself, Johnson had half an idea that Crockett had been overdramatising, but as he stood there, he understood why his boss had perhaps been a little short tempered with him.

"That's a lot of dolls," Gloria mumbled as she checked her Twitter account on her phone.

"Yeah, you got that right. Must be something fundamental that's wrong with them for so many to come back."

Gloria nodded, and walked over to one of the bins, picking up a doll and looking it over.

"So what's the gimmick with these?" She asked as she turned

the lifelike doll over in her hands.

He crossed the room to join her and took the doll.

"Well, these are different to other dolls on the market. For starters, they aren't made of plastic, and they have a steel skeleton with a latex composite body over the top. We designed the frame to mimic the human body, so it can articulate in the same way we can. Here, I'll show you."

"If it works." She said, flashing him a seductive smile that told him that he might well be approaching forgiveness.

Johnson turned the doll over and flicked the on-off switch located on the back of its neck. It sprang to life, opening and closing its tiny hands and wrinkling its nose with freakishly lifelike accuracy. Johnson set it down on the floor and it began to walk in jerky, ponderous movements.

"It looks so real, but the walk is off," Gloria said as she stared at the doll as it walked in its Frankenstein lumber.

"Yeah, the walk cycle needs work. The initial selling point was the expression engine that made them behave realistically, and the eye cameras that made them remember their owner."

Gloria touched her finger to the dolls hand, and it gently grasped her fingertip.

"That's pretty amazing." Gloria said with a smile. "It almost feels real."

"That's the point, although I would move your finger just in case."

"Of what?"

"Well, until I find out what the fault is, I don't want to risk that gentle grasp turning into one that could break your finger."

She flipped him *her* middle finger and pulled her other hand free as Johnson grinned and took the doll over to the supervisor's office and set it on the desk.

"So what now?" Gloria asked as she sat on the couch at the rear of the room.

"Now." He said as he slid the toolbox out from under the table. "I find out what's wrong with these things."

"All of them?"

"No, don't worry, not them all." He said with a grin. "One should suffice to find the issue, I can verify my findings on a second model, and then we can get out of here."

"They seem to be working fine to me."

"Yeah, I can't see anything wrong yet either."

The Tilly doll turned its head slightly and looked past Johnson.

"Hi, Gloria." It said with its robotic voice.

"What the hell was that?" She said to Johnson, as she stared at the doll.

Johnson couldn't hide his smile.

"It's normal; it has a microphone inside the hairline that picks up sounds whilst the doll is activated. It's designed to listen for names and remember them."

"Well it's creepy, and I don't like it."

"Kids love it; it makes the entire experience more real. Check this out."

He held the doll up in front of him and looked into its eyes as he spoke.

"Hi, I'm Tom, what's your name?"

The doll turned back to him, its rubberised mouth moving as it replied.

"Hi, I'm Tilly Greeneyes. Can we play together?"

Johnson glanced over his shoulder and grinned at Gloria, who didn't seem impressed. Undeterred, he continued.

"Do you know my name?"

The doll blinked and turned its head as the canned response came from its lips.

"You are Tom, and I'm Tilly Greeneyes. Can I play with Gloria now?"

Johnson turned towards Gloria, who was watching with vague interest.

"It seems Tilly here wants to play." He said, holding the doll out towards her.

"Yeah, well Tilly can wait, and if Tom Johnson wants to play later, he better hurry his ass up and get to work."

She smiled at him and raised her eyebrows, and he grinned in return.

"Sorry, Tilly." He said as he turned the doll face down on the desk. "But that's an offer I just can't refuse."

"Hi, I'm Tilly Greeneyes. Can we play together?"

Tom selected a screwdriver and began to unscrew the panel in the Tilly back, as it continued to speak into the table.

"Hi, I'm Tilly Greeneyes. Can we play together?"

"Hi, I'm Tilly Greeneyes. Can we play together?"

"Hi, I'm Tilly Greeneyes. Can we play together?"

"Should it be doing that?" Gloria asked as Johnson worked on unscrewing the panel.

"No. Although the dolls only have a set number of responses, it should wait until it is interacted with."

"Hi, I'm Tilly Greeneyes. Can we play together?"

"Hi, I'm Tilly Greeneyes. Can we play together?"

"Well, I can see why people would send the damn things back, it's annoying," Gloria said as she sat back on the sofa.

"Yeah, I'll shut it up in a second." He muttered as he pulled the casing open.

"Hi, I'm Tilly Greeneyes. Can we..."

Johnson pulled the battery, and the doll was silenced.

"At last," Gloria grumbled. "That thing was driving me insane."

"Well, the good thing is it gives me an idea of what I'm looking for fault wise. This might not take too long after all."

"Good, the sooner the better. I'm getting hungry."

There's a cafeteria upstairs. It will be closed but there are a couple of vending machines if you want to get a bite to eat."

"What a romantic night this is turning into." She grumbled under her breath.

He glanced at her and frowned, then saw that she was only half-serious.

"Do you want anything?" She asked as she stood and stretched.

"Maybe a can of something cold."

"I'll take a look. You and old Greeneyes here behave."

"One affair is enough for me." He said as she passed him. He watched her go and then turned his attention back to the dolls innards. Everything looked to be as it should, and after giving everything a quick once over, he slipped the battery back into the doll and switched it on. Immediately, it spoke.

"Hi, I'm Tilly Greeneyes. Where is Gloria?"

He smiled, and could understand why kids could get so involved, it really was lifelike. He supposed it was as good a chance as any to test the memory engine, and so placed the doll in a seated position on the desk in front of him.

"Gloria isn't here, Tilly." He said, marvelling at the way the doll's eyes seemed to be looking right at him. "You will have to make do with me."

"I want to play with Gloria. She is my best friend."

"Can you remember my name?" Johnson asked the doll.

"I'm Tilly Greeneyes. Where is Gloria?"

"What is my name?" Johnson repeated slowly, wondering if perhaps it was a microphone issue that was stopping the doll from picking up the required information.

The Tilly doll turned its head, and Johnson was almost certain that it had scowled at him.

"Where is Gloria?"

Johnson felt a prickle of fear and looked at the foot tall composite of electronics, plastic and lightweight steel on the desk. Its response was one of the 'canned' ones that were programmed into the unit, but the delivery was different. It sounded… aggressive.

"She isn't here," Johnson repeated, wondering why he felt so exposed.

The doll blinked at him, and then there was no doubt, it *smiled* at him, which was quite impossible, as they couldn't figure out a way at prototype to make it work.

"Liar, Liar, pants on fire." The doll said to him, and then it hit him, the reason for his fear and discomfort.

There was no way the doll could have learned Gloria's name. He was certain that he hadn't said it since they arrived.

He started to consider the fact that the reason that so many Tilly dolls had been returned wasn't a technical fault at all, but something much worse. It was either that, or he had gone insane. He licked his lips and spoke to the doll, trying to figure out if it was just some kind of software fault.

"Do you remember my name?" He asked, knowing that the tiny cameras behind the doll's eyes should have recorded his face, and matched it with the spoken audio of his name.

"I don't want to play with you, Tom." The doll said, its face contorting into expressions that were never within its design perimeters. "I want to play with Gloria."

"She will be back soon, until then it's just you and me."

The doll flexed its hands and blinked its plastic eyelids.

"Don't you mean you and us?"

Johnson looked up through the window leading onto the shop floor, and although he wanted to run, he was unable to move. They were standing, all of them surrounding the office and looking at him. Tilly Greeneyes screwed up her plastic features and pointed at Johnson.

"You lied to us Tom, you said Gloria would come back to play with us."

"She will be back soon." He stammered, still struggling to make sense of what was happening.

"No, she won't," Tilly said as she hopped to her feet.

"Why not?" Johnson asked, already sure that he knew the answer.

"Gloria is dead." The doll said, and he laughed because they were all saying it, a terrible, emotionless symphony of voices. He shoved himself back, the office chair rolling across the room where it bumped into the sofa, he covered his ears, but it did him no good, the volume was just too great, and he thought he understood now why Davies had suddenly quit.

Tilly Greeneyes hopped off the desk, and approached Johnson, behaving in a way that should be impossible.

"We just want to play. Why won't you play with us?"

"This isn't real." He mumbled to himself.

"This is real Tom, we are real. We just want to play."

He wasn't certain if it was driven by panic or adrenaline, but he burst into action, sprinting for the door and almost tearing it from its hinges as he opened it. He could make the exit in fifteen seconds if he ran, and then he was home free.

They are just dolls

He told himself as he made for the exit, but they moved quickly and their sheer number swarmed him. He stumbled, almost stayed upright, and then fell, landing hard on the concrete floor. The latex covered skeletal hands clawed at him, and held him down, rolling him over so that he was staring at the ceiling. He didn't shout or scream, as his body had reached the point where he was beyond terror. He lay still and waited, watching wide-eyed as Tilly Greeneyes approached. She hopped up onto

Johnson's chest, and she was holding a screwdriver from his tool bag, although it was now covered in blood and matted clumps of Gloria's hair. He knew it was coming, and that he was about to join her.

"We want you to help us, Tom." Tilly said as she paused inches from his face, screwdriver in hand.

"All we want to do is play."

"Please, I'll do anything." He stammered, desperate to live, and suddenly unable to think about anything but his wife and the guilt at his infidelity that now overcame him in droves. He started to cry, blubbering in a way that he hadn't done since he was a child.

"Don't cry, Tom," Tilly said as two of her fellow dolls neared.

"All you need to do is help us; we just want to go back to our masters and play."

Johnson nodded. "Anything, I'll do anything, just please, please don't kill me."

Tilly Greeneyes smiled and nodded.

"This is what we want you to do…"

<u>Clipping from the Oakwell Herald, January 17th, 2013.</u>

Tragedy struck Oakwell this past Monday night, when business executive, Tom Johnson (37) was arrested on suspicion of murder.

Mr. Johnson is said to have lured a local woman, Miss Gloria Spengler (23) to a warehouse on the outskirts of Oakwell, where it is thought he murdered her with a screwdriver.

Police sources claim that Mr. Johnson was found at the scene and was reported to be catatonic, and unresponsive. It is understood that a weapon was recovered from the scene, and investigators confirmed that they are not looking for anyone else in connection with the murder.

Detective Petrov, who is leading the investigation, confirmed that Mr. Johnson was the only suspect, and despite protesting his innocence, he is expected to be charged at Oakwell County Court next week.

In related news, rumors of manufacturing issues with the latest range of Tilly Dolls from Randall's Toys continue to circulate. The rumors relating to inconsistencies with the software used to make the dolls function were dispelled by company CEO James Crockett, Mr. Crockett said:

"I can confirm that following reports of a suspected fault with the Tilly range of dolls, an expert was dispatched to investigate, and reported in to say that the dolls were in perfect working order and fit for resale."

Mr. Crockett declined to comment on the situation involving Mr. Johnson, saying that the company would support the police in their investigations.

The Tilly range of dolls are set to be the number one must have toy this year, with experts predicting that within twelve months, eighty percent of all family homes worldwide would own one of the lifelike dolls, which look set to be another smash hit success for the Randall Toy Company.

LONG TALL COFFIN

It was the first time Charlie had seen Ferguson since high school. He wanted to go over and say hello, but remembering how things used to be, hesitated. Surely, there would be no hard feelings. Not now. After all, it had been eight years, and they were adults now. Still, he stayed where he was, watching his former classmate from across the bar, and trying to decide if he should go over or just slink away before he was spotted. All of that was rendered moot, however, and Ferguson caught his eye, and after a few seconds without reaction, nodded and grinned. Charlie responded, tipping his glass. He slid out of his booth, and taking his beer with him, crossed toward the bar to where Ferguson was sitting.

"Hey, Charlie. Long time no see." Ferguson said with a smile.

"Tell me about it. How have you been?"

Ferguson shrugged. "Can't complain. You?"

"I'm good, really good actually," Charlie replied. "God, how long has it been since we were at school together?

Ferguson frowned, and Charlie noted that even though time had passed, he still looked pretty much the same. Sure, he was a little older, and had changed his hairstyle, but he was still the same kid-

Fergie Faggott

- That had been his classmate for their entire school career until, as was life, everyone went off into the world to try to make their mark.

"Hell, it will be... almost nine years now," Ferguson said.

"Jesus, time flies huh?"

"It does. You still play football?"

"Not anymore, I'm too big for it now," Charlie said, more than aware that although he was still stocky, he was starting to get soft in the gut and grow an extra chin or two under the crew cut that he had worn since he was a kid.

"You here with anyone?" Ferguson asked as he sipped his beer.

"No, I just called in for a quick beer after work. You?"

Ferguson shook his head. "Same. I usually go down to Shooters, but today I felt like changing the routine."

"Small world huh?" Charlie said.

"That it is."

The two men stood silent, each trying as best they could to avoid the elephant in the room.

"Want a beer?" Ferguson asked.

"Yeah, why not. I have time for one more."

"Well go ahead and take a seat," Ferguson said, gesturing to the empty barstool next to him. Charlie sat as Ferguson ordered beers. The two sat quietly and drank for a few minutes, watching the football game on the big screen TV above the bar.

"So," Charlie said. "What are you up to these days man?"

"Apart from work, not a hell of a lot." Ferguson shot back as he took a great swig of beer.

Charlie looked at his former classmate in profile, and now that he was a little closer, he was again struck by how little his appearance had altered. He was still skinny, he still wore glasses, although those were more modern now than the huge black framed ones that he used to wear at school. The only thing that seemed to have altered was his confidence, and unlike when they were in school, Ferguson could now look Charlie in the eye when they spoke.

"What about you?" Ferguson said with a grin. "How is life treating Charlie Brooks these days?"

"Not bad," Charlie said, managing to fake a grin.

In truth, life of late had developed a habit of kicking Charlie in the balls on what felt like a daily basis. He was working a shitty job, only just managing to make ends meet and was in the middle of what was looking increasingly likely to be a very messy divorce. He took another drink and swallowed away his problems.

"Are you married? Kids?" Ferguson pressed, and Charlie felt a slicker of the old anger towards Ferguson and was starting to wish he hadn't walked over to say hi.

"No kids, and although I'm married, I won't be for long."

Ferguson sucked air through his teeth and shook his head. "I'm sorry to hear that Charlie, I really am."

“Me too.”
“What happened?”
“She decided to screw around behind my back.”
“That can’t be easy to live with.”
“Damn right it ain't. She just came clean out of the blue one day. Confessed everything… anyway you can probably guess the rest.”
“Look I’m sorry, really I am.”
I bet you are, you fuckin’ asshole.
Charlie’s thoughts were taking a decidedly dark turn, which was all just a little too familiar, especially where Ferguson was concerned. However, he reminded himself that those days were behind them, and they were adults now. He sipped his beer and turned the tables, suddenly curious to see if his former classmate was faring any better than he was.
“What about you Ferguson? What have you been doing since school ended?”
He was bitter and didn’t hide it, but if Ferguson noticed, he didn’t say anything. Instead, he shrugged.
“Well, I got married, have a son and a daughter.”
“Yeah? Good on you man. I’m glad to hear it.” Charlie said, almost able to hide his jealousy.
“What are you doing for work?” Charlie pressed, suddenly keen to know as much as possible about the kid he used to bully.
“You heard of Trans Ex?”
“The export guys? Sure, I heard of them. They run from down at the docks right?”
“Yeah, that’s them,” Ferguson said as he finished his drink.
“That’s good going man, how long have you worked there?”
“I don’t work there. I own it.” Ferguson said and flashed a grin that was half-sincere half smug.
The news enraged Charlie, who was finding himself bitterly jealous of his former classmate.
“Holy shit, you own the place? Man, you really did well.”
Ferguson shrugged. “I did what I could to make something of myself, that’s all. As you probably remember, school was... tough.”
“Yeah…” Charlie said, knowing that the subject would come up eventually. “Look, about that… I’m sorry man. I’m sorry for

being such a dick to you all those years. I was just a kid. I didn't know any better."

He held Ferguson's gaze, because, despite his jealousy, he truly was sorry for what he had done.

"Forget it," Ferguson said with a smile. "That's all in the past. How about another beer for old time's sake?"

"I really should be going," Charlie said, not wanting to admit that he couldn't even afford another beer.

"Come on, one more, on me. Just to show there are no hard feelings."

You patronising son of a bitch.

Charlie dismissed the thought, wondering how little Fergie had managed to get under his skin so easily.

"Ah, hell with it. Maybe just one more then I really have to go."

"Good man." Ferguson said as he motioned to the bartender. This time when he took out his wallet to pay for the drinks, Charlie couldn't help but look to see how much cash he had, and wished he hadn't, the array of notes stuffed into his wallet fuelling his jealousy.

The drinks were served, and Ferguson held up his bottle.

"To forgiveness." He said.

Charlie hesitated, then picked up his own bottle and clinked it against Ferguson's.

"And to apologies." He added.

The two men grinned and took long drinks from their respective beers. Charlie thought that if he buttered Fergie up enough, he could maybe manage to wrangle himself a job down on the docks and stave off losing the house for another month or two. He took another sip of his drink and wondered how long it might take him to drink Fergie unconscious and maybe help himself to that wallet full of cash. The two drank, and when they were finished, Ferguson ordered more beers as the two talked about old acquaintances long past and off the radar, but never about the bullying. That, it seemed was still taboo and that suited Charlie just fine. He drained his fifth beer and wondered just how much more he could fleece out of little Fergie Faggot before he realised he was being played.

Charlie woke face down to the hazy hangover headache that had become all too familiar in his life of late. His mouth was dry and had the distinct taste of old carpet and stale beer. He was stif and sore and tried to force himself awake. Memories of the previous night were hazy, half-remembered snatches of conversations and drinking more and more and more.

"You awake Charlie?"

"Fergie?" Charlie mumbled as he forced his eyes open and rolled onto his side.

"What the hell did we do last night I-"

It was then that Charlie realised that his hands were taped together behind his back. He tried to move his legs but discovered that they too were taped.

"What the hell?" He mumbled as he tried to make sense of everything. He forced his eyes open, allowing them time to focus.

Ferguson was sitting on a chair at his feet, hands flat on his knees as he watched Charlie struggle to come around.

"You just take your time Charlie," Ferguson said. "It will all come back to you soon enough."

" Whattimeisit?" He grumbled as he tried to organise the soup that seemed to have replaced his brain. "Is this your place?"

"No, this isn't my place. Not exactly. This is your place. Or at least, now it is."

Something in Ferguson's tone of voice alerted Charlie to the fact that not all was well, and he forced himself to focus on where he was – which appeared to be on the floor of a shipping container. As best as he could tell from his prone position, its walls and roof were red painted steel. Sunlight streamed through the open door on Fergusons back, as Charlie's former classmate watched in fascination as the pieces started to fall into place.

"What's going on Fergie?" Charlie asked, watching Ferguson carefully from the floor.

A breeze stirred the air in the shipping container, and Charlie's disorientation was shattered by the awful stench that was pushed towards him by the air. He retched, and for a moment thought he was going to be spared the indignity of throwing up, but his stomach churned violently, and he vomited onto the floor, the ejecta pooling around his face as he struggled for breath.

"What the hell is that smell man?" He spat around stringy lumps of his own vomit.

Ferguson stood and strode towards Charlie, crouching on his haunches by his head. Charlie squinted up at him, the side of his face encrusted with the spoils of the previous night's binge drinking.

"What are you going to do with me Fergie?" He whispered as Ferguson looked on, a wide grin on his face.

"I'm not going to do anything to you, Charlie. Not in comparison to the hell you put me through at school that is."

"We were just kids… I already said I was sorry." Charlie spat.

"Do my eyes deceive me? Or is big, tough Charlie Priestley crying?"

"No man, I ain't crying, it's that smell, its making my eyes water, it fucking stinks in here."

"That would be because of Ringwood and Schofield," Ferguson said as he grabbed Charlie and lifted him into a seated position, then dragged him towards the wall, propping him in a sitting position. He crouched and leaned close, glaring at Charlie from inches away.

"I have been waiting for this day, Charlie. I have been waiting for you, just like I waited for Ringwood and Schofield." He rolled his eyes towards the back of the container. Charlie followed his gaze and saw the two bundles of rolled carpet. Although he couldn't see it, he knew what was inside and also that the carpets were the source of the stench which had made him throw up. His suspicions seemed to be confirmed by the haze of flies which circled above the rugs, and the disgusting infestation of maggots which covered the cheap blue pile.

"Is that?... Did you?…" Charlie couldn't get the words out. His brain was overloaded with fear as he stared at the rolled carpet which he was certain contained the corpses of his old school friends.

Ferguson stood and returned to his seat, placing his hands palms down on his knees.

"I feel like hell. What did you do to me?" Charlie snapped.

"Rohypnol. Knocked you clean out."

“The date rape drug? What the hell did you do that for Fergie?” Charlie said, unable to hide the panic in his voice.

“I had to so I could bring you here.”

“And why am I here?” Charlie whispered.

“You are here Charlie because I have a few things I need to get off my chest.”

“What kind of things?”

“Things like the way you made my life hell you bullying son of a bitch.” Ferguson spat, the smile melting off his face.

“I thought that was behind us, you said…”

“I told you what I had to in order to get you here.”

“And what about them?” Charlie said, nodding to the maggot infested carpets at the back of the container. “What did you do to them?”

Ferguson smiled and shrugged. “Look, we are getting ahead of ourselves here. This is about us, not them.”

“Then what do you want?”

“I want to know why? Why out of all those kids, you chose me as the target? Why chose my life as the one you would make hell?”

“It wasn’t like that man, I was just a kid, I didn’t know any better.”

Ferguson went on as if Charlie hadn’t spoken, the wide, fixed grin still firmly in place.

“There were other kids of course, I know you and those asshole friends of yours always gave Paul Jennings a hard time, but I was always your favourite wasn’t I? It was always me who would be the target.”

“Look, man, I get it,” Charlie said, his voice shrill. “I owe you and I promise I'll make it up to you, I’ll give you whatever you want.”

“Oh yeah? Like what?” Ferguson said, tilting his head.

“Money, I can give you money. I have savings. Just let me go and you can have it all. No questions asked.”

“Oh yeah? How much are we talking here?” Ferguson said, pushing his glasses back up his face.

“Twenty grand, all yours if you just let me go.”

“You swear you will behave and give me the money if I cut you free?”

"I swear man, I promise!" Charlie said, nodding for effect. "I'll take you straight to the bank and get you the money, right now, today. Just set me loose."

"Okay then, it's agreed. Twenty grand buys you your life. Deal?"

"Deal man, deal," Charlie said, just waiting for the first opportunity to get his hands free so he could pummel the shit out of his captor.

Ferguson stood and fished a knife out of his pocket, unfolding the blade as he approached Charlie.

"Now lean forwards whilst I cut your restraints free."

"You got it Fergie," Charlie said as Ferguson crouched beside him. "I just want you to know that there will be no hard feeling here, we will just-"

Sharp, hot agony surged through Charlie's finger, and he squirmed away from Ferguson, rolling on his back as Ferguson returned to his chair.

"You cut me, you fucking cut me!" Charlie yelped as he rolled in his own blood.

"Actually, I cut your finger off. Look." Ferguson said as he dangled Charlie's severed little finger between his own thumb and forefinger.

"We had a deal, why?...."

"Even now you haven't changed," Ferguson said as he tossed the severed finger towards Charlie, who was still rolling on his side in pain.

"I always knew when you were lying to me back at school Charlie, and age hasn't made you a better liar."

"But I have the money, I'm good for it!"

"I would be careful what you say next unless you want to lose another finger."

Charlie stopped rolling and touched his forehead to the ground. He was sobbing now, a mucus bubble in his nose contracting and expanding with every ragged, snorted breath.

"I don't have it as such, but I'll get it. Every penny. I give you my word."

Ferguson laughed. It was incredibly loud as it rolled around the container walls. "Twenty grand to me is nothing. Its pocket change. It just goes to show that even with assholes like you,

Ringwood and Schofield riding my ass and making every waking moment of my school life hell, I still made more of myself than you ever will. And besides..."

Ferguson stood and walked towards the prone Charlie, who flinched as he neared. Ferguson helped his prisoner back to a sitting position against the wall and then whispered in his ear. "I know everything about you."

"Wha- what do you mean?" Charlie stammered as Ferguson returned to his seat.

"Just that. I know you, Charlie. I know your life. I know that you are close to losing your home. I know you move from shitty job to shitty job because you don't have the intelligence of the work ethic to really make a go of life. I know you have a drinking problem, and that was one of the reasons why Sophia left you."

Charlie was staring open mouthed, trying to make sense of what was being said. Ferguson saw his reaction and laughed.

"You really think our meeting last night was an accident? It was all planned. Nothing was accidental. You haven't taken a shit for the last two years without me knowing about it."

"That's sick! I always knew you were a weird one Ferguson. This just proves it."

"Sick?" Ferguson repeated, enjoying the show. "I'll show you sick."

He stood and walked towards Charlie, then reached into his pocket, pulling out a bundle of photographs.

"What are those? What you got there?" Charlie said, straining to see.

"You know Charlie, watching you live your pathetic little life was fun for a while. Then I even started to feel sorry for how much of a waster you were. The only thing you had going for you, was that wife of yours. Now she was smoking hot. Credit where it's due, you did well there."

"I swear to you if you have hurt her..."

"Relax, I didn't hurt her. She never did anything to me, and so I have no reason to hurt her. See I am a pillar of this local community, I contribute. All of this may seem sick to you, but it's what you deserve."

Ferguson dropped the photos on the floor and spread them out with his foot so that Charlie could see them all, and when he did, his stomach rolled in disgust at what they contained.

They were of Ferguson and Sophia.

Charlie tried to tell himself as he looked at the photos that his wife had been forced into doing those things, but he could see by the look in her eyes and the way she was performing acts on Ferguson that she would never even dream of doing with him, that she was enjoying every moment of it.

"You son of a bitch, it was you," Charlie said, glaring up at Ferguson. "You were the one who was screwing my wife!"

"It was," Ferguson said with a smile. "More times than I care to remember. It took a while to worm my way into her life and get her interested, but once I did, she couldn't get enough Charlie. She used to tell me how she hated you. Hated that you were a fat, washed up loser. Did you know that towards the end, she hated the feel of your touch? She said it used to make her feel sick. I used to make her call me your name while I did her in every single way you can imagine."

"I swear to god, I'll kill you." Charlie hissed.

"Those threats won't work on me anymore. I'm in control here."

Charlie desperately wanted to take his eyes off the photographs, but couldn't help but look, his emotions a bitter cocktail of jealousy, sorrow, and fury.

"Why are you doing this to me? You said so yourself, you have everything. A good job, a good life. Why bother with someone like me? Why screw my life up?"

Ferguson didn't answer at first. He paced the container, hands clasped behind his back.

"Back when I was fourteen, I remember I was down by Goodson's lake. Of course, we both know back then that I had no friends. You made sure of that. Remember Charlie? The way you made everyone afraid to be my friend in case you and your running buddies decided to turn on them. Do you remember that day?"

Charlie shook his head. "No man, I don't remember anything."

"Maybe it was lost somewhere in the shuffle. Easy to imagine when you made me miserable every damn day. Anyway, you remember how I had a thing for animals?"

Charlie didn't answer. He was staring at Ferguson, trying to look unafraid, and failing miserably. Ferguson went on.

"Course you do, you used to ride me about it all the time. Fergie Faggot. Isn't that what you used to call me? Anyway, I was minding my own business down by the lake. I remember I was collecting frogspawn. I always liked frogs you know Charlie They were always my favourite. So I'm there with my bucket ful of frogspawn because I wanted to take some home and watch them hatch into tadpoles and grow. I was always going to put them back, of course, I just wanted to see the process. But then you turned up, remember? You and those other two assholes who were never more than an arm's length away."

Ferguson smiled as he continued to pace.

"You have no idea how scared I was when I saw you. I mean really, really scared. I thought I was going to piss myself. And you, of course, made straight for me. You had this look in your eye like all your Christmases had come at once. Do you remember what you did?"

Charlie still wasn't speaking and was now ignoring the photographs too. He was staring at the wall, his teeth clenched as he waited for what was coming.

"Of course, you remember. I'll remind you anyway. Your buddies, Ringwood, and Schofield held me down whilst you made me eat the frogspawn. Remember? You made me eat it all then you took my clothes and threw me in the lake. I almost got pneumonia. I was sick for two damn weeks. But as if that wasn't humiliation enough, you went and told everyone at school. Do you have any idea how it feels to be ridiculed by everyone? Hell, I even saw one of the teachers laughing at me. A damn teacher. You made my life hell Charlie. Every single day."

"I don't know how many times I can tell you I'm sorry man. I was a dick at school I get it, but you have to admit you were weird. So damn quiet all the time."

"It's called a lack of self-confidence, brought on by assholes like you."

"Either way, don't you think this is a bit of an overreaction?" Charlie bellowed. "I tried to make amends; I tried to make it right."

"Oh, this isn't right. Not by a long shot."

The way Ferguson said it intensified the fear in Charlie, and he flicked his eyes towards the rolled carpets at the back of the container.

"So you are just going to kill me? Doesn't that make you just as much of a bully as I was?"

"I'm not going to do a thing to you. I already told you. I may be out for a little payback, but I'm not a killer."

Charlie looked at the rolls of carpet again, and this time, Ferguson joined him in looking, then grinned.

"Relax. It's not what you think." Ferguson said as he returned to his chair.

"So if you aren't going to kill me, what happens now?"

"I want you to be sorry Charlie. For everything you did to me."

"I am sorry, I told you already, I don't know how else to say it."

"I think you need to take some time to really think about what you have done to me. You need to really learn to be sorry."

It was then that Charlie knew what Ferguson had in mind.

"You're framing me for killing them aren't you?" He said, nodding towards the rotting corpses at the back of the container. "You're going to make sure I spend the rest of my life in prison."

"You aren't as stupid as you look," Ferguson said with a smile. "But I know you, Charlie. You wouldn't shut up until you convinced the police to investigate me. I just can't risk that happening. No, I need you to learn true forgiveness. I need for you to really appreciate the isolation that I felt."

Charlie looked at the container and shook his head.

"Please no, not here. Not with them." He said his voice wavering.

"Yes, here with them. You need time to come to terms with what you did was wrong. More importantly, I need you to be sorry so I can finally move on with my life."

"Please, don't leave me here. It's inhuman."

"No more than some of the things you did to me."

Charlie was broken. His lip trembled as he looked for any shred of compassion within Ferguson, but his cold stare said there was none.

"Come on man, I'm claustrophobic, please, I'm begging you not to do this."

"Just like I begged you not to do all those things you did to me."

"That was just kids' stuff. It didn't mean anything. I'll die in here!" He looked at the open door. "Somebody, please help me!" He screamed. Ferguson made no effort to stop him and laughed.

"You think I would be stupid enough to bring you to a populated area to conduct our business?" He asked, shaking his head.

"You really are a stupid fuck, aren't you Charlie?"

"Charlie stopped screaming as Ferguson stood and walked to the doors.

"I don't suspect we will see each other again Charlie. But I want to give you every chance to extend your life as long as possible. This container is twenty feet long and nine feet tall. Once the doors are locked, you will have air enough for three days, maybe four if you really take shallow breaths. That could all go to hell though once the isolation gets you. Schofield lasted two days. He panicked and used up all his air. Ringwood made it to four and a half, but the dark and isolation combined sent him off the rails."

"You sick son of a bitch," Charlie whispered.

"I wouldn't expect you to experience something I hadn't myself. I spent the night in here just last week in preparation for this. The dark is total, and the silence is deafening. Worse is the smell. You think it's bad now with the door open, just wait until the air is closed out. It gets really, really bad."

"If you want me dead just kill me. Shoot me, slit my throat with that damn knife of yours, anything but this. Please…"

"I'm sorry Charlie; this is how it has to be. Once I'm gone, you can feel free to scream, shout, and bang on the walls as much as you like. You are far enough away from anyone to hear or even find you. Just remember that screaming uses up air, and air for you, is about to become pretty precious."

"What can I do to make you change your mind?"

Ferguson paused, and considered, and for a moment, there was absolute silence.

"Absolutely nothing," Ferguson said, and then stepped outside. First swinging one door shut, and then partly closing the other.

“Please!” Charlie said as he tried to push himself up the wall to his feet, then fell back down, his nose and face smashing into the floor. He looked up at the door, his last tantalising glimpse of the outside world beyond.

“Ferguson... please…”

“Goodbye, Charlie.”

Ferguson closed and locked the door, then sat in the sun, resting his head against the container door and listening to Charlie’s muted screams. He took the knife out of his pocket and etched three words into the dirt, then stood and admired his handiwork.

Long Tall Coffin.

He put the knife back into his pocket, took a deep breath of good clean air, then without looking back, made his way through the maze of storage containers. He didn’t feel bad. The world was a better place without bullying assholes like Charlie Brooks in it. Ferguson got in his car, switched on the radio, and went home to his family.

50/50

He stood on the ledge at the top of the Seaburn Hotel, the toes of his shoes hanging over the edge of oblivion. Death used to scare him, but not anymore. Now he was relaxed, arms at his sides as the wind rocked him on his heels and threatened to displace him with each fierce gust.

He had been trying to kill himself for three years.

The first time he tried, he was nineteen. It wasn't even because he was depressed, or mentally damaged or any of those other bullshit excuses. He had simply decided that he no longer wanted to live. He kept it to himself, a dirty secret which wasn't something to bring up in conversation, but from the moment he had decided he wanted to die, he knew what he had to do to make it easier on those around him. He distanced himself from his small circle of friends to the point where they had started to ignore him as he passed in the street. He knew they pointed and laughed and called him a weirdo, and he was glad, as it was just another thing that would help to make it easier to go ahead with it.

He looked at the cars forty stories below, a stop-start procession of people going home from work, or heading out to meet family or friends to eat dinner, people who were looking forward to futures filled with meaningless objects and jobs they hate. He wondered how could they be so stupid, how could they stomach living in such a shallow, pathetic way with bodies filled with parasites and bacteria, cancers and tumours. He wondered how they couldn't see that humans as a species, like a plague of locusts were ravaging the planet and making it uninhabitable for future generations. He was angry, sad, and frustrated.

Back in the beginning, when he was certain that his friends were suitably alienated and he was completely alone, he put his plan into action and tried to hang himself.

He bought a good length of strong rope and taught himself how to make a noose, then tied the rope to the upstairs bannister rail of the house. The rope snapped the first time he tried, and he landed on the floor frustrated and angry with nothing more than a grazed knee and a sprained ankle.

Determined not to be denied, he tried again, this time, he bought thicker, stronger rope and headed deep into the woods, looking for a strong tree from which to end his life. Although the rope held, the death he craved still didn't come.

For twelve hours he hung there, waiting to die. There was no pain. No struggling for breath even though the rope was embedded deeply into his neck. Eventually, a passer-by cut him down, and he managed to slink away before medical attention could arrive, or awkward questions from the authorities could be asked.

No matter what he tried, the results were the same. He slit his wrists, but where he knew there should be great gouts of blood, there was nothing but a small trickle which quickly stopped. He could feel the pain, and had certainly gone deep enough, but the precious red stuff was stubbornly staying in his veins.

He spent more and more time in the seedy, red-light areas of town, the places where bad things happen to people. He did so without fear, for death was something he craved more than ever. Eventually, he was able to source some Grade A heroin. Although he had never done the drug before, he knew that any information was available on the internet, and after a little research, he cooked it up and filled the syringe with way more than he knew was survivable. He didn't hesitate, or consider the consequences, and injected it into his arm.

He lapsed into a warm, hazy cocoon of pure joy, and was sure that he had at last succeeded, embracing the numb bliss of his high.

But as always, it didn't work, and he had come round a few hours later, nauseous and frustrated.

The story was almost the same with the sleeping pill overdose that he tried the next day, only this time he *was* sick, and when there was nothing left to throw up, he had wept and wished that whatever was keeping him alive would just let him die in peace.

Again, he postponed his death, and did more research, hoping to find something he had missed, some reason for his continued existence. His depression grew deeper, and he started to hang around in the dangerous parts of town, provoking people into fights, trying to get himself stabbed or shot, anything to bring his life to an end. On two occasions he had been threatened with a knife, only for his attacker to lose his nerve and leave. Another time, a mugger shot at him, but something went wrong, and the bullet ricocheted off the lighter in his jacket pocket, embedding itself into the wall.

By then, he wasn't even surprised anymore and laughed as the mugger fled back under whichever rock he had crawled from. If anything, his failure to die had served to increase his determination to succeed.

That was in the past, though, and now he was determined to make this next attempt count. He leaned forward to look over the edge of the roof, enjoying the dizzy, giddy rush of adrenaline which surged through him. The street resembled nothing more than a thin pencil line from all the way up here, and he wondered how long he would free-fall for before he hit the ground. He tried to ignore the possibility that he might still be alive when he hit the ground, but the idea was there, all the same, lingering in his subconscious.

He sighed, licking his lips as the wind ruffled his hair. He had tried high impact death before, sure that it would work, but when a speeding car throwing him up into the air didn't do the trick, he tried stepping in front of a train instead. Although he was tossed further and higher, his body spinning like a ragdoll before skidding across the ground, he was unhurt, and able to get up, dust himself off and walk away as the disbelieving onlookers pointed and stared as if he was some kind of freak, and he supposed, in some respects, he was.

The wind tugged at him on his perch, and although his instinct told him to grab the edge of the roof, he forced himself to keep his hands at his sides, almost willing the elements to make the decision for him and drag him away to the death that he craved.

Here it comes.

He thought to himself as he felt his weight shifting, tipping over towards the dizzying fall, but like a door slamming in his face, a secondary gust which came completely against the direction of the wind pushed him back to safety.

He felt a stab of fury at again being denied another chance to die, and then he calmed and took a deep breath. He didn't believe in god, but he prayed anyway, because, on the slim chance that there was someone listening, he wanted to plead his case.

"Please." He said softly, his words snatched from his mouth almost immediately by the wind.

"Please just let me die."

He waited, breath held, staring at the rolling thunderheads above for some kind of response. Twenty seconds passed. Then a minute. He shook his head and smiled.

Of course, there was no answer.

Nobody was listening, and the world ticked on as normal, and that in itself was the problem with the world as a whole. Everyone out for themselves, never looking at the bigger picture. Why could only he see it? Either way, it didn't matter. It was time.

This was his last chance, his last attempt to leave this cruel, shithole world to its own devices. An idea popped into his head, a single thought appearing from nowhere.

If I survive, I'll give life a try.

It certainly wasn't something he had ever considered before, and he wondered if this was indeed an answer from whatever was manipulating him into continuing his life.

And what if you do?

He asked himself in his head.

What if you fall, and hit the ground then just appear back up here on the ledge, or at home in your bed, or worse, you hit the floor and break every bone in your body, and live on as a cripple?

He shrugged his shoulders. He didn't think so. He was pretty sure by now it didn't work that way. Whatever was pulling the strings wouldn't have him suffer, it wasn't its way. Whatever it was, wanted him to live, and not be a broken, brain damaged thing lying in a bed for the rest of his days. It was a flip of a coin, a 50/ 50 chance. It reminded him of the time he had tried to shoot himself and every bullet in the chamber had failed to fire. If whatever was responsible had meant for him to exist as a cripple, then one of the bullets would have done the job, or the asphyxia from the hanging attempt would have done just enough damage to his brain to leave him a drooling thing unable to communicate.

No.

Something wanted him mobile, active, able to do whatever it was that he was supposed to do. Whatever it was, this was the best way to test the theory.

"Okay." He said, his voice barely audible against the fury of the wind. "It's a deal."

The wind roared and tugged at him, his coat flapping against his legs as he composed himself.

50/50. Live or die. Such a simple choice.

He smiled, hoping that the outcome would be the one he wanted, and also considering what the hell he would do with his life if it didn't. It was an exciting proposition, though, and that was something that he hadn't experienced for some time.

He took a deep breath, closed his eyes, and stepped off the edge.

CABIN FEVER

This is what happened.

I am an old man now, and although its true that I have forgotten some things, the events of that summer in '89 will stay with me until the day I take my final breath.

I fear death is close, closer than I would like at any rate, which is why I have decided to commit the events to paper. It will at least serve to dispel some of the speculation and myth that still surrounds the events of that summer.

It's funny how your own mortality is something that you never think of until that one day when you realise that you are getting old, and you start worrying about all the things you never did or will never get to do. At my age (a healthy-ish eighty three if you're curious) you learn to accept that dying can't be any worse than the list of aches and pains which seems to grow longer every day, never mind the amount of pills that I have to throw down my neck just to keep the old engine ticking over.

Yellow ones, blue ones, white ones. Even those horrible elongated pink ones that leave a thick, chalky taste in the throat. However, none of that matters. Not for this story anyway. Arthritis in my hands means that I can't write for too long, and I want to be sure I have time to tell it all before I shuffle off to whatever comes after the lights go out.

I grew up as a city kid, surrounded by the drone of traffic, the hustle, and bustle of the rat race. I was settled and happy, so when my father decided to move us out to the country, as you might imagine I wasn't too impressed. But I was just a kid, and a kid's opinion isn't usually held in too high a regard by parents who think they know best. As dismayed as I was when I first heard about the move, it was nothing compared to how completely devastated that I was when I *saw* the place.

To say it was in the middle of nowhere would be an understatement. The house sat on a rolling carpet of green farmland that to my eyes seemed to have no end. No shops, no roads, no familiar city blocks reaching into the heavens — just endless miles of grass and trees.

As we pulled up in our old pickup, I looked for something — anything that might satisfy the need for excitement that lives within every twelve-year-old boy.

Grass.

Wheat.

More grass.

Trees.

The house itself was fine enough - a good-sized traditional farmhouse, the kind of place you could imagine on the side of a soup can or in one of those olde-worlde detective programs that my mother seemed to love so much. It was like a great brown smudge against a sea of green. Two stories, separate barn. The wood looked as tired and unhappy as I felt as I kicked my feet in the gravel and tried to ignore the drifting, country cow shit smell. Intuitive as always, my father was plenty aware of my unhappiness. He approached and stood beside me, and we both stared out at the acres of fields in stony silence.

He was always a man of few words, and as we stood in the mid-morning sun, angry child or not, he was no different. He lit a cigarette, the acrid smoke dragged away by the breeze as he exhaled.

"We will be ok here Jimmy." He said to me, nudging my shoulder. "The fresh air will be good for us. Not like that city air."

I was unimpressed and let it be known by keeping my mouth shut and my eyes on the tree line of the forest behind the house. It seemed to stretch forever. I had already made my mind up that I would hate living there. I don't know why, I just knew in the way that kids sometimes, absolutely without question, *know* things. I was going to tell my father this, but I had started with silence and decided to stick to my guns. He finished his cigarette and dropped it to the ground.

"Give it a chance at least. Okay, boy?"

He ruffled my hair, and I knew that no amount of skulking around would make him change his mind. This was a battle I wasn't going to win.

"Now come on up and take a look at the house," He called over his shoulder.

I scowled and sighed, and then with no other options, followed my father.

As much as I hate to admit it, once I got over my initial dissatisfaction, the place grew on me. It was all bare beams and natural oak floors. It even *smelt* old, if you can understand what I mean. Ancient and dry, like a place which was good at clinging to its secrets. Those first weeks passed quickly, and despite my initial misgivings about such a huge change to my surroundings, I had settled well. It was spring, and I was due to start at a new school a couple of months later. Let me tell you, there is *nothing* worse than being the new kid starting school during mid-term. By then friendships have already been formed and alliances made. It would be difficult to fit in, and I fully expected the 'let's bully the new kid' mentality to be in full force.

The day when it all started to go wrong was a Friday. I was moping around the house, feeling sorry for myself as usual. I tried to find something to do, anything to pass the time. I went through a few boxes in the spare bedroom which still hadn't been unpacked, hoping to find some forgotten toy or treasure that might relieve the boredom, but all I found were some old photographs, a pair of brass candlesticks and a couple of folded towels.

I made my way to the kitchen, and there as always was my mother. She was baking, barely glancing over as I began to rummage in the fridge for something to eat.

"Jimmy get out of there, you've only just eaten lunch." She chastised as she worked the large slab of dough.

"I'm bored," I whined back, adding a sigh for emphasis. "There's nothing to do here."

She looked at me, wringing her flour-covered hands as she would when she was agitated.

"Go outside and explore, there must be *something* for you to do. Besides, it's a lovely day."

I opened my mouth to argue but closed it again. I knew that this was a non-negotiable request, and when my mother demanded something, then it was a braver child than I that would disobey her. Besides, she was right. It *was* a beautiful day. With another sigh to make sure I had put my point across, I sloped off through the door, squinting at the brilliant brightness of the sunshine.

The heat was incredible, dry and fierce, and the slight breeze that there was, did little to cool me, as I walked towards the barn.

At one time, it would have housed hay or sheltered livestock, but now it was a makeshift garage for our two cars. My father had the hood of the ford pickup truck open and was working away at the engine. I walked into the barn, swatting at the flies as they swerved around my face. My father glanced at me, but didn't say anything. Maybe he was expecting another of my outbursts about the current living arrangements and was waiting to see if it materialised. When nothing came, he went back to work, brow furrowed in concentration as his oily hands worked and pulled at the car's innards.

"What ya doing there boy?" He asked me without looking up.

I looked around the barn. Its old wooden framework was pocked with holes that seemed to be stuffed with liquid gold from the blazing light of the day.

"Nothing," I said as I scuffed my trainers in the dirt. "Just heading out to explore the woods I think."

He looked at me, his face streaked with oil.

"Okay, but just don't go past the river, its private property on the other side and the last thing I want is to get off on the wrong foot with the new neighbors."

"I won't," I said, already disinterested. "I probably won't go too far anyway, not much to do on my own," I added, hoping that he would feel guilty for taking me away from my friends.

He stretched, wiped his hands on his overalls, and then strode across the barn to an old brown leather bag that was leaning against the wall.

"Here, you can maybe give this a try," he said, passing the bag to me.

Fumbling with the buckle I opened it and looked inside, hoping to find a rifle, and that my father would perhaps teach me how to shoot. Instead, my young eyes fell upon an old fishing rod.

"I found that in here when I was clearing the place out. There's a creel just outside the door there that was with it. Why don't you take it and see if you can catch us some supper?" He said with a grin and a wink.

For all of my annoyance, I couldn't help but smile. I loved fishing and my dad knew it. He also knew that I had been pestering him for the last year for a rod of my own.

"Thanks, dad!" I said with genuine gratitude, my self-pity forgotten.

He smiled again, and then leaned in close, filling my nostrils with the smell of sweat and engine oil.

"Tell you what boy. You catch us a big one for supper, I'll see about getting you a brand new one all of your own."

He leaned away, then looked from side to side and spoke in a whisper.

"Just don't tell your mother!" He said, flashing another wink at me. "Go one, get out of here before I have you help me fix this old piece of sh— junk." He corrected himself.

I nodded, excited to get going. Perhaps the day wouldn't be a complete loss after all.

"I'll do my best. What time shall I be back?" I asked.

"Be home before dark. And remember, don't cross the river. That's the boundary of our land." He added, pointing his spanner at me for emphasis. "Now go on, those fish won't catch themselves."

I whirled around and grabbed the old wicker creel that was beside the barn door just as my dad said it would be, and began to walk away from the house towards the tree line. For the first time since the move, I didn't hate the place. In fact, I was looking forward to doing some solo exploration, and maybe, just maybe catching a decent fish or two. I wondered if the river held trout, or maybe even tuna, although that was doubtful. I was already covered in a sticky sweat as I approached the looming tree line. I looked over my shoulder at the house, marveling at how small it looked silhouetted against the crisp blue sky. Wiping my brow, and looking forward to a good days fishing, I stepped into the cool shadow of the forest.

The shade was a blissful relief from the dry heat of the day. A light breeze passed through the trees, making mottles of sun dance across the ground. I explored lazily, heading towards the sound of the river. All around, I could hear birds chattering and singing, and content in my wondering I began to whistle to myself. I was so excited to get to try out the rod that I almost fell down the sheer embankment that edged the river. I somehow managed to cling onto a thick branch with my right hand, whilst I pin-wheeled my left in a desperate attempt to avoid a nasty fall. The sunlight was no longer impeded by the thick canopy, and shimmered brilliantly on the surface of the water, making the green hues of the forest stand out with breathtaking vibrancy.

I shielded my eyes from the glare and looked for a suitable place to set up my rod and give me a shady place to wait for a bite. There was a nice looking area downstream where the river curved away as it made its way deeper into the forest that looked just about perfect.

When I arrived, I set up the rod, and after casting the line using a few plump earthworms that I dug up for bait, I settled back to wait for the fish that I was sure would come.

I must have fallen asleep, lulled by the heat and the sound of the river, because I woke up to find that my line had been moved. I reeled it in, hopeful for a catch, but it seemed that the opportunistic fish had taken the bait without hooking itself. As I bent to pick up my rod, something metallic reflected in the sunlight across the river.

I could see no source for the out of place shimmer, which increased my curiosity. The warning words of my father echoed in my ears, but only for a second. I had already decided to go over and look, just to satisfy my own curiosity. I convinced myself that my father need not know, and I would be back over with time to dry off before I had to head back home.

I sometimes wonder how my life would have turned out had I not seen that intriguing shimmer in the trees. Would the nightmare I went on to live still have happened but in some other way? Was my own curiosity alone to blame? I have asked those questions myself more times than I care to remember. I think, perhaps that is why they haunt me the most.

Time has made the rest of the experience easier to live with, or at least to bury it away in the deep, dark place in my mind, but it's always there, festering and lingering close enough to mean I will never have peace or normality. Even to write it down brings back horrifying memories, things that I had somehow managed to repress over the years. To have them so fresh in my mind makes me understand just how tired I am, and perhaps the end of my time on this earth can't come soon enough. No matter, I set out to tell all, and that is what I will do.

The water wasn't as deep as it looked, and at no point reached higher than my knees. I began to make my way across, the heat of the day burning the back of my neck as I waded through the cool water. It's funny how the things, which would cause the old man that I am now, to grumble, were no more than a slight irritation for a twelve year old boy, especially one who's curiosity had been piqued, and wet pants or not, I was determined to find out what was over on the other side of the water. The opposite bank offered more shade, and more exhausted than I thought I would be, I took a moment to rest and try to catch a better look for the shimmering thing in the woods.

At first, I couldn't see it, but then the wind moved the trees and it was there. A quick flash of chrome against green. The ground was softer on the opposite side, and my feet left water filled pools as I toiled through the boggy ground.

I can still recall that time with frightening clarity, of dragging myself through the mud, swatting the mosquitoes away from my face and driven on to discover what I had seen in the woods.

As I approached the object, I recognised the form, the familiar shape making my heart sink.

It was just a van.

A large silver transit with a sliding side door, its front grille, the source of the shimmer that had brought me across the water. My disappointment was short lived, however, when I noticed the trail that curled off deeper into the woods. The shadows here were inky and cast into long, probing fingers by the intertwined tree canopy. Everything seemed slightly different, the birds were less vocal in song, and the air was still and sticky with the dry summer heat and the pungent smell of stagnant water. Only the mosquitos were consistent, going about their business with aplomb as they buzzed, dived, and looked for something to feed on. I didn't think about not following the trail. It seemed like the most natural thing in the world.

Perhaps that was the first twinge of some different feeling within. Not excitement, but not quite fear either. It was more of a lingering uneasiness that I couldn't altogether shake. Part of me had expected — and even hoped for — a long and winding road into the woods, but I was surprised to find that as I rounded the curve, the trees terminated almost immediately and there, set back against a natural recess in the trees was a dilapidated shack.

I must choose my next words carefully as even to think of it now makes my tired old heart quiver and my hands begin to shake. I would do no service to you by falling down dead here at the desk in my room with the story unfinished. The staff here are nice, and I don't want them to think of me as some crazy old fool making up stories in the dead of night when I should be sleeping.

Apologies, I'm distracting myself again.

Perhaps part of me is reluctant to commit the rest to paper, but I will, *I must* if I am to have any hope of resting with a clear conscience. And so I will push on, despite the terror that even thinking about that place fills me with. Even from a distance, I didn't like it. It looked to be some kind of a hunter's lodge, one that had been long forgotten, and the woods were making steady progress of reclaiming the land where it stood.

Fear.

I still remember the moment of distinction between it and excitement. I was aware of how exposed I was — standing in plain sight and staring at that ugly wooden building in the middle of nowhere. I looked at the filthy board-covered windows and imagined someone watching me through the gaps in the wood.

I scrambled off the road, plunging into the undergrowth and the relative safety of the trees. Stinging nettles scraped my arms, but I barely noticed as I positioned myself out of sight.

How long I crouched there on my haunches I can only guess, but when I did move, I was drenched with sweat and my calves burned. Something inside told me to run, to put as much distance between myself and this ramshackle building as possible, but that part of me was quickly silenced by the Buck Rogers adventure seeking child, and rather than head back across the river, I skirted around the trees and moved closer to the shack.

Two of the planks on the windows at the side of the building were broken and slightly pulled apart, and I guessed that with enough effort I could squeeze inside. Even as I write the words it seems insane, but back then the world wasn't such a harsh place as it is today, and I wanted to see what was inside. I made my way to the shack and looked through the gap in the wood. A rotten, earthy stench hit me, and I had to pull my T-shirt up over my nose. It was a smell, unlike anything I could express in words. Undeterred, I cupped my hands and peered through the gloom into the shack.

It looked to be a small kitchen of some kind, although I couldn't see much from the angle I was at. With fear once again replaced by excitement, I began to wiggle my way through the window. I squirmed and wriggled, and for a horrifying moment, I could go neither forwards or backwards, then like a cork from a bottle, I was in.

The first thing that hit me as I squeezed my way into the room was the heat. If you have ever opened the door to a hot oven and had your breath taken away by the change in temperature, then you will have a good idea how it felt. It must have been well over a hundred degrees in there, and as I knelt on the floor, I looked around to allow my eyes to adjust to the gloom.

The small kitchenette was dilapidated at best. The walls were filthy, the tile floor broken and grimy. Bars of sunlight fell across it from the multiple cracks and breaks in the wooden walls, and dust motes drifted and swam in the golden shafts.

A filthy sheet covered the doorway that led to the rest of the shack, and I was about to sweep it aside when the feeling of being watched came over me. I held my breath and listened, but could hear nothing apart from the sound of my own breathing. I decided that I would just peek and then get out of there, just to satisfy my curiosity.

There was a girl.

She was gagged and tied to a chair in the middle of the room. Her head was low, resting on her chest, and I feared the worse, but I could see that she was breathing. Her hair was dirty and hung listlessly to her face in sweaty clumps. She looked to be in her early twenties and was wearing only her underwear. I could see her jeans and t-shirt tossed in the corner. Her wrists were caked in crusty, dried blood where she had struggled to break free from her restraints. The rest of the room was bare apart from a tripod and camera set up in one corner, and a long table across the far wall draped with a red cloth and filled with, what I can best describe as torture implements. There was a different smell in the room, buried below the dry, woody, rot stench. It was a coppery smell, and there were stains on the walls and floor, dark reddish brown, which I knew was blood. There was something almost poetic as she sat there in the gloom. How long had she been captive was anybody's guess, but she looked painfully thin and her skin was dirty and bruised. All I wanted to do was help this poor girl to break free from the pitiful conditions that she had been subjected to.

Pushing the curtain aside, I entered the room. She must have heard me, as she raised her head. The awkwardness that I had expected at meeting her gaze was, in the end, a non-issue, as she was wearing a blindfold.

"Who's there?" She said, unable to hide the fear in her trembling voice.

My own voice was stubbornly refusing to show itself, and I was suddenly aware of how thirsty I was and how much I wanted a cold drink, just a simple thing that I took for granted now felt like an unattainable luxury. I couldn't help but stare at her, and felt ashamed and disgusted that I had begun to feel aroused as I cast my eyes on her semi-naked body.

It pains me to write this now, and I urge you to remember that I was just a boy, a young boy who didn't know any better or have control of his raging pre teen hormones. I make no excuses for it, and even though eighty-one years have passed since that day, I still feel ashamed when I remember how I had looked at her. I might have stood there forever, had I not been forced into action.

I sensed it before I heard it, which I think is what saved me. I'm not sure how, maybe it was some kind of intuition, but I knew I was in danger. With seconds to spare as I heard the sound of a key working the lock, I quickly scurried under the table, protected from view by the overhanging cloth.

The door creaked open and I heard heavy boots on bare wood.

The footsteps approached me and I was sure I had been seen. After all, such a poor hiding place was viable in a movie, but not here. This was real, as real and terrifying as it gets. I closed my eyes and waited to be discovered, hoping that I wouldn't suffer the same fate as the girl, left here waiting for death or worse. The footsteps were close and then went past me as their owner went to the filthy kitchenette.

I could have run then, and should have, but I was shaking and my legs wouldn't move even though I willed them to obey and get us out of there. Either way it was too late, as the owner of those boots returned and moved towards the girl. I dared to peek, ignoring the stifling heat as I watched.

He removed her blindfold, and then just circled the chair, watching her. I tried to get a look at his face so that I could give as much information as possible to the police the first chance I got, but he was wearing a novelty monster mask that wouldn't have looked out of place in some cheap 50's B-Movie. As much as I was desperate to help this girl, and no matter how I would like to tell you that I saved the day, I have to admit that saving my own skin was more important to me, and so I stayed hidden whilst he danced around her and cackled as she grew more and more afraid. I don't know how long it went on for. All I know is that I was drenched in sweat and the shadows had grown long by the time he left. I waited and listened, and once I was satisfied that he was gone, I crawled out from under the table.

The girl was sobbing quietly, and if she knew I was there, she didn't acknowledge me. I was just about to sneak off when she spoke, so softly that it would have been easy to miss.

"Help me." She said, and found the strength to lift her head and look at me. Her eyes were a piercing blue, and although her ordeal must have been unbearable, there was a life and defiance in them which told me that she still had plenty of fight. I approached her restraints. They were tightly knotted, and the rope was thick, but I thought with enough time I would be able to untie them.

I began to work the knots, ignoring that intuitive feeling that I didn't have much time. I don't know how much the girl knew about what was going on, but I suspect that she might have been experiencing some kind of delirium. It was now almost dark, and the shadows had almost completely claimed the room when the gaps between the window boards illuminated with the harsh twin glow of car headlights. The girl began to thrash in her seat, and I ran for the safety of the covered table. I barely made it before the door swung open.

A lot happened all at once. It seemed that I had done enough to loosen the ropes because the girl squirmed free and ran for the door. I could see right away that she never had a chance of making it, but she tried anyway, and the masked man with the dirty work boots grabbed with ease. She tried to fight, but she was weak, and he easily overpowered her despite her clawing and scratching at his arms. I thought he would tie her back to the chair, but he seemed intent on teaching her a lesson, perhaps for daring to try to break free. He began to hit her, the sounds of his fists impacting on her flesh combined with the screams were indescribable.

He carried on even when she stopped screaming.

By the time the man left, the shack was in total darkness. I crept from my hiding place, and in the gloom, saw the girl lying there on the floor. I had never seen death before, and it was a frightening thing to experience. I ran, ran as fast as my young legs would carry me. I barely felt the cuts and scratches from the unseen branches as I charged through the underbrush, at every second, expecting my world to grow bright from the twin pool of headlights behind me as the gibbering, masked man came for me.

I didn't stop running until I was on the other side of the river, and there I stood gasping and sobbing but finally safe. I walked quickly, keeping on my guard until I could see the soft glow coming from the house in the distance. All I could think of was that lifeless stare of that poor girl who lay dead in that stinking, filthy shack. By the time I had reached the house I had organised my thoughts enough to work out how I would tell it, making sure that my parents knew how serious the situation was before they had a chance to punish me for my lateness, or for forgetting my rod and creel. What happened next was one of those moments where a person's life can change completely in a split second, and all that seemed important suddenly became trivial.

They were the same boots.

I knew because I had been unfortunate enough to get a close

look at them whilst I was cowering under the table in the shack. They were by the side of the back door, my father obviously not wanting to walk the mud that covered them through the house.

My stomach was performing dizzy somersaults and I felt something, perhaps a scream, launch itself to my throat, but in the end, it came out as a shallow gasp. It seemed impossible to me that the gibbering, mask-wearing thing in the shack could be my father, a man I associated with being strong and proud. A man who lived by his morals, and tried to always teach me the difference between right and wrong, and yet I knew it was true. He and the murderous, cruel beast in the shack were one and the same.

My mind raced with what to do, and even though now as an adult, the answer seemed obvious, the repercussions on my family weighed heavy, and rather than call the police, I took off my equally filthy shoes, set them next to the murder boots, and went inside the house.

Dinner that night was roast chicken and potatoes, but as we sat around the table, I barely tasted it. I had told my parents that I had fallen asleep whilst fishing and then got lost in the woods trying to find my way home after dark. It was a plausible explanation, which they accepted without question. We ate in silence. I shot my father secretive glances, trying to make sense of the new information I had just learned. I tried to see him as that thing from the shack, but despite my best efforts, he was just my father, the man I had known and respected since I was old enough to know right from wrong. Broad shoulders, red and black lumberjack shirt, strong jaw and kind eyes which I had inherited from him. Nowhere could I see the latex mask-wearing animal, and I began to wonder if perhaps I had made a mistake.

He caught me looking at him and I almost screamed.

"Everything okay, boy?"

"I'm fine. Just tired."

He nodded, and as was his way didn't push the point any further. Again, there was silence, the sounds of cutlery on plates our only company. I looked at my mother and wondered if she knew or even suspected anything. My instinct said not, surely she couldn't be so indifferent if she were privy to such a horrific secret, and besides, It was hardly something that my father would be keen to share with his wife.

'How was your day honey?"

"Oh, not too bad. I tortured and killed a naked girl today."

"Oh, that's nice. Did anyone see you?"

"No danger of that, I have a little place across the river away from prying eyes. I might show it to you sometime."

"That would be nice dear. Would you like more potatoes?"

I felt sick, then my mother said something that almost caused me to scream outright and run as fast and as far as I could.

"What happened to your arms?" She asked my father as she bit into another piece of chicken.

I glanced to the scratches on his forearms, then watched his face, hoping that it would betray the lie that I knew was coming.

"Barbed wire." He said between mouthfuls of food.

My mother seemed satisfied, but I knew it wasn't barbed wire. I knew that it was the desperate clawing of his most recent victim as she tried to escape had caused it. I was dismayed with the ease of his lie, and by the lack of guilt or emotion in his eyes. It raised another question, one that gave a completely new depth to my terror.

How long had my father been partaking in his secret hobby?

That night I barely slept. I kept imagining that he knew and that he had somehow seen me in his secret place and was just waiting to get me alone in the house to kill me. However, he didn't come, and as the days passed, I was reassured that my presence in the shack had gone unnoticed. I started to watch him, to observe his patterns. When he would leave the house in the pickup truck, I would charge through the woods and across the river, and because it was the more direct route, I would always arrive first. I don't know where, but at some point between leaving our house and arriving at the shack by the dirt road, he always switched vehicles and arrived at the shack in the transit van. I hardly ever ventured back inside the shack, and I didn't have to. Even from outside I heard the screams and the sounds of torture from whoever his latest victim was. Often, he would come out bloody and breathless, the latex mask perched on top of his head as he smoked a quick cigarette between torture sessions.

I became desensitised, and soon the violence seemed no more

real to me than the stuff I watched on TV. As strange as it seemed I got used to seeing the animalistic side of my father, and as winter came and went and a new year dawned, I stopped logging the events on paper, because I knew that I could no longer rely on the police to help me. I knew that I had to take care of it myself, and the only way to do that was to him as he did to others.

I had to kill my father.

It was mid-April by the time I was ready to proceed. I don't know how many he killed in that shack during that time. If I had to guess, I'd say it was at least twenty, but that was conservative. I was thinking at least forty would be a more accurate number. As to my father himself, I had never seen such a sickening Jekyll and Hyde performance. He was his usual loving and caring self at home, but on those occasions when I was brave enough to venture to the window and look through the gaps in the boards, it was like watching a stranger. I felt sick as he danced and slithered around that hot, sweaty shack, and even though the faces would be different, it would always be a girl tied to the chair, naked and frightened and bloody from his torture, but no more. My preparations were done and I was ready.

It was a family dinner, much like the night when I first discovered his secret. I remember my father was in a good mood that day because he had sold off some shares that he had been sitting on for twenty years, and was looking at a good sum of money. He was grinning and talking to my mother, who was listening politely when I picked my moment to speak up.

"Hey dad, I found something in the woods today," I said, somehow able to keep my voice conversational and calm.

"That's good boy, lots of wildlife out there if you look hard enough."

I paused and watched him as he continued to eat the stew that was in his bowl, wanting to deliver the killer blow as it were.

"Actually," I said with a smile. "It was across the river."

He paused and looked at me, his steaming spoon of potatoes and meat held still on the way to his mouth.

"I thought I told you not to cross the river. I made that clear."

I could see the fury in his eyes and maybe, deep inside a flicker of fear.

"I'm sorry; it's just that I was curious and crossed to take a look. Nobody saw me. I did find something odd, though."

He set his spoon down, and now it was as if it was just him and me, eyes locked, a battle of wills. My mother may as well have been a million miles away.

"What did you find?" He asked, eyes burning into mine.

"There's an old shack out there," I replied, watching him and trying to hold his gaze despite the knot in my stomach.

"I think there's something going on in there. Something bad."

I had never seen my father angry, not until then, but he set his spoon down and leaned across the table, pointing at me with a huge, calloused index finger.

"Now you listen and you listen good. I don't want you in those woods anymore, do you understand?"

I opened my mouth to protest, and he cut me off, bringing a huge fist down on the table, which made both my mother and I flinch in our seats.

"I said no woods, end of discussion."

"Henry, don't you think..."

"No Mary, he has to obey the rules." My father raged.

I could see he was tense, the veins sticking out of his neck, and bulging eyes told me he was close to losing control and I was looking at a beating or worse.

"I'm sorry, I didn't know it was such a big deal," I said, trying to sound as downbeat as I could.

He relaxed and I thought that I had done enough to make him react. We finished the rest of our meal in silence and every time I looked up from my plate he was staring at me, and I wondered if he knew that I knew his secret. I waited to see if he would take the bait, and it didn't take long. He finished eating and set his spoon down.

"I have to head out for a while." He said it in a way that told both my mother and me that questioning why and where just wasn't an option. We sat in silence as he stood and left, and I chose that moment to make my own move, as I knew where he would be heading.

"I'm going to go up to my room for a while," I said to my mother, and she barely acknowledged me. I think she was troubled by the glimpse into the usually hidden side of my father's personality, and I was grateful as I slinked away from the table.

I heard the pickup splutter into life. For a second, the room was bathed in the glow of headlights that brought back memories of that first day when I found his secret place before the car rumbled away down the dirt track. He was heading to the shack and I had to make sure I was there first. I don't know if my mother heard me slip out of the front door, and to be honest any potential punishment was the least of my worries. I had been building up to ending my father's disgusting existence and knew I had to act whilst I still had the courage.

I ran into the woods, crashing through the underbrush and across the river. Even in the full dark, my passage was easy, as there was a good-sized moon to light the way. I arrived just a few moments before my father. He hadn't bothered to switch trucks, and it was our Ford which skidded to a halt outside the shack.

My father was out of the car before it had fully come to a halt and stalked towards the door. I waited and watched; heart pounding and throat dry from fear. I was waiting for the sound, the one that would tell me that it was almost all over.

It came to me then, a short sharp rapport like a gunshot as it drifted across the chill air to where I squat in the undergrowth. His scream came next, long and anguished, and I felt renewed and pushed on by adrenaline, I charged for the open door.

I had set the bear trap just behind the curtain that led to the kitchen area.

I knew he would always go in there first because that's where he kept the latex mask. The plan was simple. Set up the trap and wait for him to step in it, then once incapacitated, finish him as humanely as possible. The repercussions of what I was about to do had not dawned on me at the time, I just knew it needed to end and because I alone knew what he was, I had to be the one to do it.

I charged through the door and was first hit by the smell, like rancid meat and feces. The girl in the chair looked to have been dead for a long time. How he coped in that tiny, hot windowless space with that stench is beyond my comprehension, and to this day I can't think of an adequate way to describe just how awful it was. The dead girl, however, wasn't my concern, and I ran past her and swept aside the curtain towards my wounded father.

The split second that it took me to realise that he wasn't in the trap seemed to last forever. I remember feeling a sharp pain in my face, and then I was bouncing off the wall and sliding into a sitting position on the filthy floor.

He came through the curtain and I knew then that all of my planning had been in vain because he knew. He had known all along. The trap that I thought was sprung for him was in fact set for me.

He was naked apart from the green latex horror mask, his pot-belly shaking as he danced into the room. I could taste the blood in my mouth and when I blinked, I saw flashes of white, which further aggravated the pain in my head. Did he recognise me as his son? I couldn't say, all I could hear was his laughing beneath the mask as he skipped around the room and closed the door, the sound of the latch closing making me feel as if it was the final nail in what would soon be my coffin. I couldn't understand how my plan had failed, as I was sure I had heard the bear trap go off. When he grabbed a length of cane that was leaning against the wall, he whipped it against the floor, and the realisation hit me. It was similar enough to the sound the bear trap would make had it been sprung, and enough to bring me charging into his death room.

I could see his eyes glaring at me in the half-light, and although a thousand thoughts raced through my mind, I didn't say anything. I watched him as he approached the girl from behind, and yanked her dead head up to look at me. Her milky eyes were open and glared accusingly, as my father manipulated her mouth and he spoke in a mock female voice.

"I told you not to cross the river and you went ahead and disobeyed my command."

I was horrified as he continued his bizarre ventriloquist act.

“What choice do I have now but to kill the inquisitive boy who couldn’t keep his nose out of daddy’s business.”

I realised then that this man wasn’t my father. He was an animal, a crazed beast. I also realised that I was about to die. He came towards me gibbering and dancing and singing and grabbed me by the shoulders, his strong hands digging into me as he yanked me to my feet. I’m not sure what happened next, maybe it was the anger and frustration at seeing the true face of the man I had called my father, but something in me ignited, and I screamed and brought my knee up as hard as I could into his groin. Crazy or not, he still felt pain, and he crumpled to the floor, groaning as he rolled around. I stumbled to my feet, my only thought was of escaping and calling the police now that I realised that I was completely out of my depth, but he grabbed my leg as I ran past, and I fell to the floor. He was recovering quickly, his eyes angry behind the mask, the same way they had been at dinner just an hour earlier. It already felt like a different lifetime.

I kicked out with my free foot and caught him in the face, but it barely seemed to register. He was up and so was I, and we faced off in that tiny, stinking room, a boy and his crazy, naked murderer of a father. He was laughing as we circled, round and round the stinking dead girl in the middle of the room. He feigned charging at me, laughing all the time. I had seen this before. He was toying with me the way he toyed with them. I heard myself pleading with him in my head, begging for forgiveness but I knew from my observations that to do that would increase his excitement, and so I kept my mouth closed. He grabbed at me and I wasn’t ready. I tried to rear back but he got a good handful of my t-shirt and pulled me towards him. I squirmed and twisted, and was free of him again.

He charged at me, but this time, I was ready and avoided him, and made for the kitchen. He was right behind me and just as we reached the dividing curtain, I made my move, throwing aside the filthy covering and dropping to my knees.

He was going too fast to stop and clattered into me, his knees hit me painfully in the ribs, and he pitched forwards, and this time the sound of the trap going off was not only real but also loud, echoing in the tiny room with a sharp *ker-chuck* as it closed on his face. His scream was raw and agonising, and much more convincing than the fake one that first drew me to the house.

I stood, holding a hand to my injured ribs and looked at him. The mask had come off as he fell and I looked at him. It's funny, because for all my fear, as I stared at him, face down on the floor with blood pooling out around him and without the mask, I wasn't scared anymore. I couldn't decide for sure what it was that I felt at that moment. I wondered if it was fear, triumph, or relief. The truth is, that I felt nothing at all. He twitched, and his leg shook involuntarily but even seeing him in such obvious distress didn't bother me. I put my foot under him and rolled him over onto his back, ignoring his groans as he took the rusty steel-toothed trap with him. I looked down on him then, and our eyes met. Blood was streaming down his face and I could see that one of his eyes had been pushed partially out of its socket by the force of the trap. He smiled at me then and I could hear him trying to speak. I ignored it, though. Instead, I made good on my promise. I took the huge lump hammer from the table and stood above him. I think I even managed a smile. He weakly beckoned me close, and I obliged, letting him whisper in my ear whatever it was that he was so desperate to tell me.

Three words.

Three words can sometimes be all it takes to flick someone's inner switch from sane to bat shit crazy. And I think I was halfway there anyway before he said it and gave me that stupid, crushed, bloody toothed grin. It only wavered when I flashed it right back at him, then I adjusted my grip on the hammer and went to work.

Why I put the mask on to do it I still don't know.

Inside it felt sweaty and itchy, but somehow empowering. The first blow would have been enough I think to finish him, but I continued to rain blows on his face until it was barely recognisable pulp. I cried and screamed all the way, though, and I honestly think that all of my emotions left me that day.

When it was done, I put the second phase of my original plan into place. I took the large can of gasoline from where I had hidden it in the bushes and poured it all around the cabin, then used the matches that I had taken from the kitchen drawer to ignite it. The place burned fierce and fast, and with it went my father and his legacy of terror. I watched it burn, and was shocked to find that I felt no emotion. All I could think about were those three words that were whispered by a dying murderer, a habitual liar, and a psychopath, but three words that I believed nonetheless. I didn't realise until I looked down that I still had the latex mask and hammer clutched in my hands. I walked back to the house, thinking over the enormity of what I had done, and for the first time wondering what may become of me. Still, those three words reverberated around my head, as infectious and poisonous as the man who uttered them. The house loomed largely, and I could see her silhouette in the window of the kitchen.

Three words.

I pulled on the mask, and took a firm hold of the lump hammer, ignoring the matted hair and skin that clung to its head.

Three words.

Enough to change a life.

I opened the door and went inside, those three words singing a crescendo in my brain.

Three words.

Your mother knows!

She never saw it coming, and I took no pleasure from it, but like him, she had to be taught a lesson, and wearing the mask made it easier. I wondered every day since then why I believed him without question. Could it have been the last sadistic play of a sick man? Or did he want to make sure that I understood that it wasn't just him to blame?

Either way, I reacted, and after it was done, I sat on the floor cross-legged, exhausted and covered with the blood and viscera of my parents. The house seemed very large and quiet, and I knew that it wasn't something that I could deal with on my own. I picked up the phone and called the police, and told them what I had done. Then I sat on the floor and waited for them to arrive. They were never able to prove my father's guilt. I had inadvertently destroyed the evidence, and all they had were two murders committed by a twelve-year-old boy. They had circumstantial stuff of course. D.N.A from the transit van and from his clothes were enough to suggest that what I told them was true, but there was never quite enough to prove anything. A detective called Petrov and I talked a lot on those weeks after, but I could never bring myself to tell the story. It's hard to explain, but I felt like a passenger riding along in my own body, and that somewhere in my head, the real me, was sitting there with his eyes squeezed closed and his fingers in his ears shouting *lalalalalalalala* so that he wouldn't have to face up to what he had done. I was passed from care home to care home, and then when that didn't work, I was put into a mental health institute to see if they could repair whatever had broken in my mind. I accepted it. I have always been an honest man, and for every day I glance in the mirror and see the genetic mix of my parents in my own reflection, I feel equal amounts of anguish, pain, and vindication. Deep down I know I was right, and that I had to do what I did in order to stop a monster.

I started to have nightmares.

In my dreams, I am tied naked to a chair, and my parents are dancing around me wearing latex masks and gibbering and laughing. I don't always wake up screaming anymore, but it still frightens me each and every time it happens. The institution that I have lived in for the best part of my life has become my home, and I like the routine. I like knowing when to eat when to sleep, when to take my meds and when to shit.

They are releasing me tomorrow.

A washed up old man who they think is too ancient and broken to cause any problem for society. They are probably right but the thought of being out there and responsible for myself scares me. I have never lived without some kind of supervision, and I don't know quite what to expect. It's ok, though because I know what I'm going to do. I'm going to go buy a good length of strong rope and use it to hang myself. I don't fear my death, but do worry about what comes after. Will I see the forgiving and smiling face of my innocent mother? Or will I join the two mask wearing gibbering monsters in hell? I suppose time will tell and whatever the outcome, I'm just glad it's over. I stand by what I did and wouldn't change a thing.

I have to go now as it's getting late, and it's almost time for me to go to sleep for the last time in this room that has become my home.

This book will remain my legacy, my confession of a boy

trying to do the right thing who became a man shunned by society. I bid you farewell and hope that in reading this you might at least understand.

Your friend,

James Michael Godswall.

THE LANGTON EFFECT

I wasn't certain at first, but now I'm pretty convinced that the old guy at the homeless shelter is who I think he is. As impossible as it seems, I can't help but buy into the fact that that scruffy old toothless hobo with the deformed cheek is me, or what I will become at least.

I have been working over there at the shelter for the last seven months, on community service for screwing over a drugstore. Don't judge me, I get it. I'm a bad seed, one of those people shaped by society to be a degenerate fuckup. All of that, however, is beside the point. I want to get back to talking about the old man.

He calls himself Langton, which freaked me out because that was the name of my imaginary friend when I was a kid. Nobody knows about that, and although it could be a coincidence, I doubt it.

Although Langton has skin like old leather and tired, watery eyes which say they have had enough of living in this shitty world, I can't deny it.

He does kinda look like me, or how I might look after fifty years addicted to crack and moonshine.

Anyhow, this all started when I caught him staring at me, his cocky, half smug grin as familiar as the one I see in the mirror every day. I thought he might have had a cleft lip, or something else wrong with his face, as the left side of his face was sunk inwards, and his top lip overhung his bottom, making him slur as he spoke. Despite his appearance, I held his gaze, because at that point I was still trying to portray the bad ass, to make sure everyone knew I wasn't to be messed with. But Langton didn't seem in the least bit intimidated, and he waved me over. Now normally, I would tell a guy like this to go screw himself. I wasn't there to help the homeless like Jason and the rest of the asshole staff who worked there. My presence was required by law, but that doesn't mean I had to like it.

Anyway, I had intended to give the old man some verbal, just enough to maybe frighten him off and make sure he kept his nose out of my business, but before I could do anything, he held up a grubby hand and stopped me in my tracks.

"Save it, Monty." He said, watching me with that shit eating, knowing look on his face that I would grow to hate.

Now I'll admit, I was freaked out. Nobody calls me Monty anymore. Not since I was a kid, and although I had never seen the old bum before, he knew, and it knocked the wind right out of me.

I forgot about trying to frighten him off then. In fact, I forgot about trying to be the big man altogether. Instead, I sat down opposite him, and as he began to talk, I listened, and the more he talked, the more convinced I became that I was in conversation with a version of myself from some alternate reality or something. The funny thing is that all the things he told me were things that *only* I could know.

He told me about things that would happen. Things that had already happened and he had no reason to know.

He was crafty with it too. He told me all about how his brother had been put into a Young Offenders Institute for taking part in a botched armed robbery of a pharmacy, and then had his sentence uplifted to murder when one of the other kids tried to touch him up and got himself beaten to death.

The story was familiar of course because it was *my* brother that had been institutionalised and *my* brother who had been convicted of murder, only my brother had tried to hold up a petrol station, not a pharmacy.

I was numb as he recounted experiences of my life as if they were his own, always making them just different enough to give the benefit of the doubt.

His father died of a stroke, mine of a brain tumour.

His mother had Parkinson's disease and lived out the rest of her years in a nursing home; mine had just been diagnosed with the disease.

Days melted into weeks, but I could never find it in myself to outright ask him if my suspicions were true. I kept hoping that he would come out and say it, but it became the big old elephant in the room, the unspeakable conundrum, so we both skirted around it.

For as much as I wanted to, I knew I couldn't mention it, not without sounding as crazy as he was, and that got me thinking if maybe that's how I ended up like him, by being branded as crazy and starting on that slippery slope towards the warm embrace of smack, meth, and cheap booze.

I knew I shouldn't meddle, but I needed to know, and I asked him what happened to him, what went wrong in his life to make him become like he was. He gave me one of those looks, like he knew what I was asking, but wasn't prepared to say it outright. It was like on those movies where the actors acknowledge the camera and give it a goofy look or a wink. We both knew what we were talking about, but we were in character and went on with the lie.

The story of his life mirrored mine almost exactly, but by then I had grown accustomed to the weirdness and wanted to know what came later.

He told me about how he had been shunned by his family and had spent his early twenties going in and out of prisons for petty offences. It was then that his mood changed. He didn't seem quite so keen to talk, and I had to threaten to have him tossed from the shelter and go hungry. He must have known I would do it because he told me.

"I killed some people." He said as he slurped down his soup.

My heart was racing, but I needed to know. I needed to know what was going to happen.

I asked him how many, and for what felt like hours, he didn't speak, he looked at me, sucking his deformed jaw as he breathed. I waited, and eventually he answered.

"A lot."

He didn't say anymore, and in truth, that was enough. Without saying another word, I stood and left. He didn't try to stop me. At that point, I didn't care about anything other than making sure I changed what I was to become, no matter what.

The burden of knowledge made any sensible thoughts impossible, and I started to micro analyse every decision in my life, desperate to do something to avoid becoming Langton. The ironic thing is that now it has reached the point where I'm afraid to do anything but sit here in my shitty apartment with the curtains closed and think about everything that I have learned. I have also started to do certain things that I tell myself will rid the bad Juju brought on by the combination of Langton and my brain, which I'm pretty sure is sick now.

I convinced myself that I have to turn the light switch on and off fifty seven times before I enter or leave the room, or it will set me on my way to becoming like Langton. Or I have to take a step back for every five I take forwards, or, you guessed it, it will somehow set me on the first step towards becoming Langton. To only eat foods that are green or yellow, or it will… well you get the picture.

I had to kill the cat from the apartment next door because it walked from right to left across my window ledge instead of left to right. There was no pleasure in it, and I made sure I washed it thoroughly before I threw it out of the window into the street. (Cold tap on, cold off, hot on, hot off, cold on, Just to make sure I don't catch the Juju)

It's all gotten out of hand, and it's now to the point when I'm too afraid to even leave the apartment. I know that if I touch the door handle, it will set off a microscopic chain of events that will lead to my future fifty years from now as that deformed, broken old murderer, and I don't want that.

Everyone in my life has always called me a loser, they always said I would never amount to anything, and I'll be damned if I'm about to prove them right.

Langton had all of his fingernails I think.

I peeled three of mine off to make sure we weren't the same.

If it rains I have to walk backwards around the apartment until the sun comes out.

It sounds odd to you, I know, but it's something I have to do.

One thing that is a worry, is that I ran out of food a couple of weeks ago, and my stomach almost continuously reminds me that I'm hungry, but I tell it to be quiet. If I eat the wrong thing, I could set things in motion that will lead me to you know where.

It's a strange feeling, knowing that the door is unlocked but I'm still a prisoner, but the doorknob can only be turned right, as to turn it left would surely mean I would go out, and then anything could happen.

Butterfly effect? Try the Langton Effect! Ha!

If I have learned anything as I sit here and waste away, it's that the human mind is far more powerful than people give it credit for. Take this situation for example.

I know I'm hungry.

I know I need food.

I know that if I go outside, I can get food.

But this stupid fucking brain of mine overrides all of that and tells me that if I want to avoid becoming like Langton, then I have to stay where I am and not risk doing anything to set things in motion.

It's funny because I always wanted to know the future, about how things might pan out further down the line. I always believed that I would get on track, that I would put my life straight and make a difference. But all of that was before, and right now I would give anything to go back and never have to meet that crazy old bastard.

At least the isolation has given me time to think, and I'm pretty sure that now, at last, I finally get it.

Screwing around with light switches, killing cats and making sure I count the spots on the curtains before I go to sleep won't stop me from becoming like him.

There is one way to be sure, and I must be right because my brain, for once isn't objecting.

The pistol in my hand is the last symbol of my gang days. Something which seems like it was not only another lifetime but one lived by someone else. I always thought I would be scared of death, but after everything that I have been through, it has to be better than lying here on the floor, a pathetic, emaciated shell of a man who is afraid to do anything in case it sets in motion that chain of events that I'm desperate to avoid. My hands were surprisingly steady as I loaded the weapon, and its weight feels reassuring in my hand. (Now that I think about it, maybe Langton *was* missing a couple of fingernails). It's almost over now anyway, and as I wedge that oily barrel up behind my front teeth, I wonder if when I pull the trigger, it will also mean that Langton would never have existed. I believe in science, they call that a paradox. I'll leave these notes for whoever finds me. I want to be cremated, and for them to play The End by The Doors at my funeral. I might also ask another favour of whoever finds and reads these notes, and that is for them to head down to the homeless shelter on Maple, and look for a guy with brown hair, a cleft lip and grey eyes who wears a brown trench coat and answers to the name of Langton. I'm pretty sure you won't find him, and I hope that's true, because if he's there then it either means I was wrong, or this suicide is about to fail.

That is a sobering thought, and I need to end this now before I allow myself to think about it too much.

Load the gun, unload the gun, load the gun, unload the gun, load the gun, unload the gun, load the gun, unload the gun.

Load the gun.

THE TRIAL OF EDWYN GREER

The man restrained to the table was slender, his features sharp as he watched his captors with cold defiance. The windowless room was colder still, stainless steel walls lined with a host of control panels displaying thousands of calculations per second. The machines were connected to the man's arms and chest, monitoring and feeding information to the plethora of scientists in attendance.

One such scientist approached the restrained man, watching him as he stood poised with his pen and clipboard.

"Subject 27431 is under restraint and appears calm. Please state your name for the official record."

The restrained man sneered at his captor and then flashed a wide grin.

"You know well enough my name."

The scientist looked over his shoulder, and his superior nodded from behind the seven inch bulletproof glass. The scientist turned back to the subject and spoke loudly enough for the overhead audio recorder to pick up clearly.

"The subject's name is Edwyn Greer. Caucasian male, five feet eight inches tall, one hundred and twenty pounds. Life age is unknown. Estimated body age thirty to forty years. Subject has been with host for approximately two hundred years, and fusion is at ninety seven point three percent. As per the United Governments' Agreement, Mr Greer is to undergo the Longborough Removal Procedure in order to stand trial for his crimes to humanity."

The scientist approached the restrained man and looked at him as one might look at an animal which he found slightly amusing.

"Do you have anything to add, Mr Greer?"

Greer was silent and stared in defiance at the scientist.

"For the official record, the subject has declined to comment. With the authorisation of Sir Jonathan Longborough, Dr. Alfred Moran and the Signed Warrant of the United Governments, with the grace of God I am about to begin the first ever Longborough

Removal, on this day which will go down in history. September 4th, 2022."

The scientist walked to one of the control panels and set his clipboard down. He took a deep breath and flicked his eyes to his watching superiors.

"With the panel's permission and the permission of the governments and leaders of the world watching live, I will begin the procedure."

The scientist waited, as his superiors behind the bulletproof screen awaited the confirmation of the World's Governments, who were watching via linkup from their various countries. A full minute passed in silence, and then the scientists superior and inventor of the procedure, Sir Jonathan Longborough turned to the window and flicked on the intercom.

"Authority granted. Proceed with the procedure."

The scientist nodded, and then took a deep breath.

"May God be with us." He said, and activated the system.

The huge, intricate machine suspended above the restrained man whirled into life, its multiple arms designed for the most intricate of surgical work. Greer struggled against his restraints but was unable to move as the mask was lowered over his face and the highly potent anaesthetic was pumped into his lungs. He began to lose consciousness as the titanic machine above his head readied to operate. Perhaps sensing the danger, the parasite which was bonded to him tried to force its host to stay awake, but it was no good, and Edwyn Greer was unconscious before the first cut was made.

He awoke in a brightly lit room, and was almost immediately aware of the pain deep in his stomach, followed by the tight, maddening itch of the scar which extended down the full length of his rib cage. His senses were overwhelmed, and he leaned over the side of the bed and vomited a huge gout of blood.

"Just relax, don't try to fight it."

The voice came from a large speaker high in the wall of the windowless room. Before he could examine it further, another wave of nausea swept through him, and he vomited again, adding to the already ejected puddle of claret by his bedside.

"Help me." He moaned, unable to deal with the sensory overload. "What have you done to me?" He shouted as he wiped the blood from his chin. He tried to stand, but the room began to spin, his sense of balance deceiving him as to which way was up or down. He fell from the bed, landing hard on the floor and losing consciousness.

The second time he awoke, he was a little less overwhelmed. It seemed that someone had cleaned up the mess he had made, and he was more aware of his surroundings, and the fact that he was now tied to the bed which he had fallen out of before. His chest and stomach still hurt, and his head throbbed with a painful migraine. He looked around the room, trying to piece together where he was.

White walls, no furniture aside from the bed which he was tied to. In the corner was a security camera which was trained on the bed and below that a round speaker embedded in the wall.

His head felt like a lead weight, and he let it fall back to the single pillow as he closed his eyes. The door opened, and a man walked in. Greer recognised him as one of the scientists who had been watching from behind the window. He was carrying a folding chair, which he set up at the foot of the bed. He sat down and folded his hands over his lap.

"Good morning Mr Greer. My name is Jonathan Longborough."

Greer said nothing and closed his eyes as he tried to ignore the pain which raged through his body.

"Mr Greer, it would be in your interest to listen to what I have to say. I will only say it once."

Greer opened his eyes and lifted his head to look at his visitor.

He was an older man, perhaps in his sixties. His skin was smooth and unlined, and his head bald. He wore a goatee beard which was white apart from a few stubborn black flecks, and he watched Greer with blue eyes which although were serious, were not unkind. There was a palpable air of authority about him, a magnetism which even intrigued Greer enough to listen to what he has to say.

"I'm in pain." Greer said, unable to get used to a feeling that had been absent for so long.

"Of course, you are. Your pain receptors have been dormant for so long, that it's to be expected for you to feel so…delicate. You are actually through the worst if it helps. We had you under heavy sedation to help you to deal with it, but unfortunately, part of the rehabilitation process is in dealing with the senses that you had forgotten."

"What have you done to me, I feel…empty."

"And rightly so. We have cured you, Mr Greer."

"Cured me of what?"

Longborough smiled, and although Greer had a suspicion of what was to come, he couldn't help but ask anyway.

"It's gone, isn't it? You took it."

"Yes, Mr Greer. You are no longer a host."

"Then what am I?"

"You are human again, Mr Greer, just as nature intended."

"That's impossible. It cannot be done."

"It's already done. The things that you think of as pain are just normal, human senses. You feel as we feel. Hot, cold, taste, touch. All are restored and will, I suspect, take some getting used to."

"You took it from me; you took it without my permission." Greer hissed.

"No. We cured you, Mr Greer. For two hundred years you have been plagued, but rest assured, Thanks to my staff here at Longborough Industries, you are a vampire no more."

For the next week, Edwyn Greer learned how to become human again. He was forced to rediscover the taste of foods, and the indignity of performing bodily functions in order to purge the re-introduced products from his system. He received no visitors in that week following his brief conversation with Longborough and was never allowed out of the room which was more of a prison cell than a place conducive to a recovery.

It was on the eighth day when Longborough returned, this time, accompanied by two other men who hid their eyes behind dark sunglasses, even though the room was lit only by a single overhead strip light, and was quite gloomy.

"Mr Greer, I trust you are feeling better?"

Greer didn't answer; instead, he sat on the edge of his bed and stared at Longborough and his two companions.

"I see you aren't in the mood to chat, so I will make this brief."

Longborough motioned to one of the men who were with him, and like a dog obeying its master, the man removed a thick folder of papers from his briefcase and tossed them on the bed. Greer glanced at them and then turned his eyes to Longborough.

"What's this?"

"A legal summons. You are to appear in court for your crimes."

"Really, and what kind of court will hear a case against a former vampire?"

Longborough smiled and folded his arms.

"Because of you, and, more specifically my technique, a lot has changed in the world. Rest assured, you *will* be tried, and you *will* be convicted."

"You seem so certain," Greer said with a smile. "Why bother with a trial at all?"

"We can't all be a law to ourselves, Mr Greer. In the civilised world, there are rules to be followed."

"I get the impression you think that I would be better off beheaded, or hung."

"Either would be a suitable outcome, Mr Greer."

"Then let me ask you why?"

"Why what, Mr Greer?"

"Why did you even bother to separate me from my vampire, when you wish me dead anyway?"

Longborough smiled and checked his watch.

"Why do people climb mountains, or try to break records? Because they can Mr Greer, and besides that, I needed to prove my technique worked. I am responsible for the greatest invention the world has ever seen. Years from now, the Longborough technique will be mentioned in the same breath as Thomas Edison's light bulb, or Alexander Graham Bell's telephone. You were a necessary part of it, unfortunately."

Greer snorted and smiled without humour.

"Then perhaps, since I am the first, it should be called the

Greer-Longborough technique. No?"

Longborough frowned and shook his head.

"I think not. The reward for the hard work is mine alone to reap. You might be wise to consider pleading guilty, and save the world a very long and very expensive legal battle."

"Perhaps I will, or perhaps I will yet live long enough to see you dead, Mr Longborough."

"Please." Longborough snorted. "Your days of eliciting fear are over. You are just a man; a weak thing who I suspect has even now begun to forget the extent of the power he once held."

Greer smiled, and Longborough squirmed where he stood.

"A few weeks ago, if you had spoken to me in such a manner, I would have been feeding you your own entrails by now." Greer slid his eyes from Longborough to the two men flanking him.

"And your colleagues there would be begging for their lives. But as you say, I'm just a human now, and for that, you should be grateful. But I warn you, Mr Longborough, do not make the mistake of thinking me *incapable* of that which my vampire used to *be capable* of."

"Whatever you say," Longborough said with a smile. "Surely you must know you cannot hope to win."

"We shall see, won't we, Mr Longborough?"

"Yes, I suppose we will. Goodbye Mr Greer."

Greer didn't answer, and was content to watch as Longborough and his companions left, and locked him in his room.

Edwyn Greer's preliminary hearing was held six weeks later at the central London County Court. Even though the appearance was only to allow Greer to place his initial plea, the media frenzy was intense, with news crews from all over the world jostling for position in order to get a shot of the world's first humanised vampire. Immense crowds gathered, bringing traffic to a standstill as Greer was ushered from the police vehicle through to the courtroom.

The presiding Judge was ancient and harsh in appearance, and in front of a small team of legal representatives, silence fell and the Judge spoke.

"Please, state your name."

"I am Edwyn Greer." He said, flashing the Judge a sick smile.

"You are charged with the mass murder of over three hundred thousand souls, which, under the Anti-vampirism Act of 2020, signed and verified by the Nations of the World, is punishable by death. How do you plead?"

The room fell into silence, as Greer hesitated. He looked at the Judge and then slid his eyes over to look at Longborough, who was watching from across the room.

"Not Guilty."

The court descended into a frenzy, and the Judge tried to retain order. Eventually, the crowd silenced, and the Judge spoke.

"You will be remanded in the custody of the United Nations Anti Vampire Association until your trial, which will take place three weeks from now on October the Fourteenth, 2022."

Greer remained silent as the Judge motioned to the guards beside him.

"Take him down."

Greer was led by the arms to the cells below the court, where he awaited the trial that the entire world was desperate to watch.

He was given a cell of his own, and there he waited, counting down the days until his trial began. He had been allowed a television and had watched with much amusement of the world's obsession with him. It seemed he had both supporters and those who wished him burned at the stake, which he supposed was a normal human reaction.

He was not expecting his visitor, and for his part, the man who stood outside his cell looked like he didn't want to be there either. He was an obese mountain of a man, who had squeezed himself into a cheap suit which looked to be at least two sizes too small for him. He wore his greasy, thinning hair in a side parting, and his grin was as insincere as it was frozen to his face.

"Good morning, Mr Greer." The man said, clutching his briefcase in front of him tightly enough to turn his knuckles white.

"What do you want?" Greer said, cutting straight past the pleasantries.

"My name is Gustavo Blackman. I am your court appointed

lawyer, I have a few things to go through with you if..."

"No."

Blackman stammered and clutched his briefcase even tighter.

"Excuse me, Mr Greer, I don't think you understand, this is a very, very delicate case and I really think..."

"I said no."

Blackman shuffled, increased the intensity of his grin, and went on as if nothing had been said.

"... Now, I think we might be able to get you a new plea as long as you..."

Greer approached the bars and leaned close to them. From here he could smell Blackman's aftershave and the not quite hidden hint of body odour.

"How old are you, Mr Blackman?"

"Well, I, I think we should..."

"You don't have to be exact, just an approximation will do."

"No, I don't have any reason to hide it, I'm forty three," Blackman said.

"Forty three," Greer repeated as he tapped his index finger on the bars.

"This coming February Mr Blackman, I will reach my two hundred and seventh birthday. I have already forgotten more than you will ever learn. Now you might think that I need a lawyer and that without one my chances of being free are non-existent, but let me clarify, Mr Blackman."

Greer grinned, and lowered his voice to a whisper.

"I don't need or want your consultation, or your services. Furthermore, if you don't leave here right now, I will telepathically communicate with one of my vampire colleagues, and have them feast on your flesh."

The colour faded from Blackmans cheeks, and he stammered, struggled between grimace and smile, then without a word, turned on his heel and left. Greer watched him go, smiling all the while. There was, of course, no such thing as telepathy, but Blackman wasn't to know, and even the prospect of the international television exposure that he would have received as Greer's lawyer, wasn't enough to risk being torn apart by a host of vampires, fictional as they were.

Greer smiled and turned back to his television. There were less than two weeks to go until the trial.

Day one

October the fourteenth was bleak and grey, the wind edged with rain. The hype for the trial had reached fever pitch, and Greer was ready to begin his trial. He was relaxed as he was led from the cells and to the courtroom clad in shackles around his wrists, ankles and neck.

As he had suspected, the courtroom was jammed to capacity with people and television cameras, all trained on him as he stood and waited for proceedings to begin.

"All rise for the Honourable Judge Jeffries." The clerk of the court bellowed, and Greer watched with some interest as the man who would ultimately seal his fate approached his seat.

Judge Jeffries was a slim, sharp faced man, with cold blue eyes and thin lips. He sat with what Greer thought to be deliberate flair, took his reading glasses and perched them on the edge of his nose.

"Be seated." He said with sharp authority.

Greer looked to his right and saw Longborough and his team of expensive lawyers watching him with predatory smiles. They looked to be enjoying the occasion immensely.

Even with the pressure that came with knowing that the eyes of the world were on him, Greer was still filled with a euphoric sense of calm. The Judge went through the preliminary introductions, and then it was time to get down to business and for each party to make their initial statements. Longborough was first up, or more accurately one of his lawyers was. Greer recognised him; he had been hyped up on the news over the last few weeks as something of a big shot. His name was Bernard Winthorpe, and he looked every inch the overpriced, overconfident lawyer that he was. His skin was dark and smooth, and his eyes cold and calculating. He looked at Greer with a half-smile on his face, and then walked past the jury, looking at them wordlessly. Greer looked at them with him, twelve anonymous faces who waited for Winthorpe to begin his case.

"Ladies and gentlemen." He began, making sure to make eye contact with them in turn as he walked back and forth. "Do not be fooled by Edwyn Greer."

He paused for effect and then continued.

"Do not be fooled into thinking that this is about deciding if a man is guilty or not."

He approached Greer and glared at him, then pointed theatrically.

"This man is a monster. This man is guilty of crimes almost beyond the scope of our ability as civilised human beings to comprehend. But, rest assured, those crimes will be paid for, and you, our jury will have the chance to do what is right and see this monster given the punishment that he duly deserves."

He stared at Greer, who looked back, meeting his gaze fearlessly. Realising that he wasn't going to intimidate, Winthorpe walked back towards the jury and stood with his hands behind his back.

"Three hundred thousand. That is the estimated number of deaths that Edwyn Greer is responsible for. Just take a moment to think about that number."

Greer watched as Winthorpe paced in front of the jury. He had to hand it to him, he was good.

"Three hundred thousand." He repeated. "Sons, daughters, brothers, sisters, husbands, wives."

He shook his head as he glanced at Greer, and then back to the jury.

"Three hundred thousand dead. That's more than the New York World Trade Centre attacks in two thousand and one. It's more than the California earthquake of 2015. It's more than the tragic nuclear reactor explosion in Japan in 2019. Three hundred thousand."

He paced, hands clasped behind his back.

"Three hundred thousand." He said, shaking his head. "And remember this isn't a team or terrorists, or a freak accident or even Mother Nature. This is just one man. One man. This man." He said, pointing at Greer.

"Innocent he may look, but don't be fooled. Edwyn Greer is a monster, a criminal on a scale so immense, it is difficult to comprehend, but a criminal he is. And as with any criminal, it is up to you, ladies and gentlemen of the jury, to ensure that this monster, like any other criminal, is punished for his crimes.

Failure to do so means that next time, it could be your children, or husbands, or wives or friends who are the victim. Please, I appeal to you to do the right thing and keep our society safe. Thank you."

Winthorpe walked back to Longborough and his legal team, flicking a smug, oozing smile at Greer as he passed and sat back with his team.

The court and the watching world held its breath. It was the former vampire's turn to speak.

Greer stood, and approached the jury.

"In 1707, a young man was infected with a parasite which would change his life forever. He didn't ask for this, nor did he have any way to escape. But the man became host to the organism which you refer to as vampire, and the man did as the vampire willed, because he was powerless to resist."

Greer paused and folded his hands in front of him.

"He didn't ask for this, nor did he do anything to deserve such a burden, but bonded they did become, and the man was cursed to live under its thrall forever more. Mr Winthorpe talked about husbands, and wives and friends. I once had these things, and my punishment was to watch them die as they grew old and I did not The three hundred thousand deaths that Mr Winthorpe spoke of are true. They happened. But that in itself is not the question that is being asked today. The question that is being asked is this."

He paused for effect, and continued.

"Is Edwyn Greer, the man, responsible for his actions?"

He looked at Longborough and was pleased to see him squirm in his seat.

"Or, was he the innocent victim of the needs and desires of his parasite? That, ladies and gentlemen is the real question. And one which Mr Longborough and his team will try to muddy with his phalanx of experts. I, as you see, stand alone. And I ask you this. Before the cure was found, would you convict a man because he contracted cancer? Would you condemn an alcoholic or an anorexic to death because they were a slave to their disease?"

He looked at the jury.

"I think the answer is obvious. Like me, they are a victim of the thing that controls from within. The vampire that lived within me was responsible for things that I am in no way proud of, but now, as a free man without such burden, the only question that matters is this. Can you condemn a man to death whose only crime was being unfortunate enough to be contaminated by a vicious, dangerous disease? That, ladies and gentlemen, is the question that you would need to keep at the forefront of your mind for the duration of these proceedings. Thank you."

Greer returned to his seat and waited for the first of Longborough's witnesses to be called forward.

The trial format had changed somewhat since the early years of the twenty first century. Gone were the expensive, multi week processes of years gone by. Instead, they were replaced with a new format in early 2017. Now, all trials lasted up to a maximum of three, eight hour days, at the end of which the jury would vote and give their recommendation to the presiding Judge, who would then hand down sentencing. The three day format put an end to the never ending procession of witnesses brought in on any given case to try and sway the jury. Instead, witnesses were to be chosen carefully, and the questioning kept streamlined by the relevant legal teams. Although initially frowned upon, the new rules meant that more cases could be heard more quickly, and more convictions made.

Greer was grateful that his fate would be settled in days rather than months, and watched with great interest as Longborough's first witness was called. The man was sworn in, and looked about nervously, uncomfortable with the high profile nature of the case.

"Please state your name for the court." The clerk said as the man placed his hand on a dog eared copy of the bible and was sworn in. The man's name was Dietrich Barl, a German zoologist, and microbiologist, who looked around the room. He was wearing a musty, tweed suit which looked at least thirty years old, and he wore ridiculous, oversized glasses which made his eyes appear huge as he peered through them. Winthorpe approached the witness, smiling and not quite hiding the predatory edge that was buried beneath it.

"Mr Barl." He began, his voice sharp and crisp and reaching every corner of the large courtroom. "Please tell the court what you do for a living."

"I'm a zoologist and microbiologist." He stammered, pulling at his collar.

"And could you tell the court what you have been doing for the last year?"

"I have been working with Sir Longborough and his team with regards to the parasite known as Longboroughvampirosis."

"And for the court, please explain what Longboroughvampirosis is."

"It's a very aggressive parasite. It has only recently been discovered, but we think it has been active on earth since the early Jurassic period."

"And how might somebody contract this parasite?"

"Well, it starts microscopic and is very resilient. We have so far found it present in undercooked meats and water, so contracting it would have been easy."

"You say would have been!" Winthorpe said, leading the questioning. "Why isn't it now?"

"Well, general sanitation and hygiene awareness makes infection rare, but I think in Mr Greer's time, Longboroughvampirosis would be fairly common."

"And in your examination of this parasite, what were your findings, of its nature specifically?"

"Well," Barl said, unable to hide his excitement. "It's unlike anything we have ever seen before. It's aggressive, and territorial, and resistant to every other virus or disease we have tried to combat it with."

"I see."

Winthorpe walked to the jury.

"Aggressive and territorial." He turned back towards Barl. "Are these traits that would transfer from parasite to its chosen host?"

"Yes."

"Could you tell the court a little of the process of infection?"

"Upon ingestion, the parasite would enter the bloodstream, and make its way to a position underneath the heart. From there it would begin to feed."

"And what would it feed on Mr Barl?"

"Blood."

"And then what happens?"

"The parasite grows and connects to the central nervous system of its host. It then separates, and a secondary parasite attaches itself to the base of the brain, effectively taking control of the host."

"I see," Bernard said, watching the jury with sincerity. "And what traits would this parasite bestow on its chosen host?"

"Well, it's actually quite remarkable. The host and its immune system don't detect the parasite; it somehow remains invisible, mimicking red blood cells until it grows large enough to complete its bond. Once it is attached, the host will begin to change. The ageing process stops completely, and their immune system is boosted by three thousand per cent. Essentially the parasite grants its host immortality and immunity from infection."

"I see. And what else?"

"Well, along with the immunity, the host gains great physical strength and speed, a direct consequence of the parasite's attachment to the central nervous system."

Winthorpe nodded and turned to the jury.

"So, if I understand you correctly, this parasite is actually beneficial to the chosen host?"

"Actually, no," Barl said. Winthorpe knew this of course, but acted surprised for the benefit of the panel of jurors.

"Oh? Please, do explain."

"Well, the parasite has inherent traits burned into its DNA which have allowed it to survive for millions of years."

"And could you tell the court what those traits are, Mr Barl?"

"Well, Longboroughvampirosis is a very aggressive parasite, and this is passed onto the host. Also, its desire to feed is never ending. It is always looking for sustenance."

"And what would one feed such a parasite, Mr Barl?"

"The parasite feeds on blood."

"So presumably, one could feed it animal blood in order to sustain its desire?"

"No."

"Mr Barl, for the benefit of the court, could you clarify the kind of blood that this incredibly potent and aggressive parasite requires to sustain its existence?

"Human blood."

A murmur rose in the court, which Winthorpe left to peter out naturally. Greer watched and had to hand it to the lawyer. He was every bit as good as the newspapers and television had said.

"Human blood." He said as the courtroom fell into silence. " So, just to clarify that I understand you correctly Mr Barl, you are saying that this parasite, once attached to the host renders it immune to age, immune to disease, but also incredibly aggressive, violent and with a lust and need for constant sustenance of human blood?"

"Yes."

Bernard was watching the jury now, and they were looking back, captivated by his charisma.

"Ladies and gentlemen, Edwyn Greer is such a host. These traits, these qualities passed down from the Longboroughvampirosis live within Edwyn Greer, and despite Mr Greer's plea to question if he is victim or protagonist, remember the facts. Edwyn Greer is a monster, Edwyn Greer is a mass murderer on an almost unfathomable scale, and Edwyn Greer is guilty."

He looked at Greer, then to the jury.

"Ladies and gentleman, Edwyn Greer deserves to pay for his crimes."

Winthorpe looked to the Judge.

"No further questions." He said, as he returned to his seat.

"Your witness Mr Greer." Judge Jeffries said.

Greer stood and approached Barl, composing his thoughts.

"Mr Barl, you say the parasite which bonded with me is highly aggressive."

"Yes."

"Would it compare to any other known parasitic or viral infection?"

"I'm sorry; I don't understand what you are asking me."

"I mean, it's potency or aggression. Does it compare to cancer or Ebola for instance?"

"Oh, this is much more aggressive. The Longboroughvampirosis is a highly intelligent organism. It's part virus, part parasite. Not only does it bond to the host, but it assumes full control. It's quite unlike anything that has ever been seen before."

"So assuming this parasite is contracted, could the host do anything to stop the bond? For example by seeking medical attention?"

"Yes, but you would have to know you had it, and because there are no initial symptoms, that in itself is difficult."

"And what about after symptoms begin to be felt?"

"Well, you would have around forty eight hours to seek medical attention, and even then, our treatments are still experimental. Survival rates are only at sixty five percent."

"I see, and could you tell us what those symptoms might be, Mr Barl?"

"Well, you would feel loss of appetite, inability to sleep. You would also become tired and sensitive to harsh light."

"Would these symptoms be incapacitating?"

"No, that's the problem. They would be at worst, an inconvenience."

"And the treatment you speak of, when was it deemed safe to administer?"

"Just last year."

"So if, for example, you or anyone else present in this courtroom today were to contract Longboroughvampirosis, would it be possible for them to guarantee treatment to fully cure them?"

"Yes, but only if they sought immediate medical assistance."

"And after the forty eight hour period, if it isn't reported, what then?"

"Then it's too late. The organism will already be in place and bonded to the heart and has already made the initial symptoms fade."

"So the victim, or host, feels well again?"

"Yes, until at least the traits of the parasite take hold, and by then, the host has no desire to seek help."

"So, just to clarify, physical stature or mental capacity of the host is irrelevant? By that I mean a stronger or more intelligent person isn't less susceptible to the organism than someone smaller of less intelligent?"

"Oh no. it makes no difference at all."

"My final question to you, Mr Barl is this. You say a person contracting this disease would need to seek medical attention for treatment immediately, to be given a sixty percent chance of being cured?"

"Correct?"

"So, if a person was to have contracted this parasite in 1707, would I be right to suggest that any hope of treatment or cure would be impossible?"

"Yes, absolutely."

A murmur rose in the crowd, and Greer slid his gaze to look at Longborough and Winthorpe, then back to Barl.

"Thank you, Mr Barl. I have no further questions."

The day's proceedings came to a close following Edwyn Greer's questions. He was led away back to his holding cells below the court, as Winthorpe and Longborough left the court, barely able to hide the way in which Greer had expertly questioned their witness. Outside the court was a frenzy of media and public, all vying for a look at the players in the case which had captured the imagination of the world. The two pushed past the symphony of photographers and the strobe flashes of hundreds of cameras and ignored the questions of the crowd. It seemed there was an even mix of those in support of Greer, who were calling for his freedom, and those who were calling for his execution, complete with hand painted slogans and burning effigies drawn up to look like Dracula.

Longborough and Winthorpe pushed through to their waiting limousine, and closed out the frenzied chaos outside. The car set off, inching through the crowd who reluctantly parted in front of them.

"What the hell happened in there, Bernard?" Longborough asked, pouring himself a large scotch from the on-board bar.

"Relax Jonathan; this is all part of the game."

"How the hell did he manage to turn our own witness? Hell, even I started to feel sorry for him."

"Did you really expect him to go down without a fight? He turned down his appointed legal counsel, you know."

"I know that, but my point is that he was good. Why isn't he flustered? Why isn't he worried?"

"Come on Jonathan," Bernard said, flashing a wry smile. "He's been around for a long time. One thing he won't lack is knowledge and experience."

"And that's why I hired you. I was told you were the best."

"I *am* the best." Bernard snapped, the flicker of anger in his face quickly dissolving. "But I need you to relax and let me do my job. Tomorrow is a new day, and our next witness will cast more than reasonable doubt on Mr Greer."

"Knowing our luck so far, the girl will break down and forgive him."

"I doubt it," Bernard said with a smile. "He almost tore her face off. She only survived because he was disturbed. Don't worry Jonathan, tomorrow we will show the court the level of brutality that this man possessed. Tomorrow will be our day."

"It's good to know you have a plan, but I still worry. We have to win this case Bernard; otherwise, years of research and money are going down the toilet."

"I still don't understand why it's so important to win, or why you even started proceedings."

Longborough poured another drink, this time filling a glass for Bernard too. He took a long drink and then turned towards the lawyer.

"If the courts decide that Greer is a victim, they will force the cure to be made available for free the world over. Do you know how much money we will lose if that happens?"

"Ten million, maybe twenty."

Longborough smiled, and Bernard shuddered at its oozing quality. "Try three trillion."

Bernard looked at Longborough with raised eyebrows as the scientist took a long drink of his whisky.

"That sounds like an improbably high figure."

"The world is a big place Bernard, and our cure is the only one. We patented it. Everybody is waiting to buy it from us, but until we can prove that these things are monsters that need to be dealt with, we can't distribute it. If we don't win this, my company will go under, I will lose everything."

"You really have gone all or nothing, haven't you?"

"It's how I do things. Just make sure we win. There's a hefty bonus in it for you if you do."

Bernard sipped his scotch and offered a sly smile.

"With a three trillion potential income, there better be."

Longborough said nothing as the car finally broke free of the crowds surrounding the court, and was lost in the citywide traffic.

Day two

Due to the televised events of the previous day, the court and surroundings were in even more of a frenzy than the day before. More television crew were on site, as were the number of supporters and protesters who were either for or against Greer. The courtroom doors were closed, and the crowds settled to watch the proceedings. Today, both Greer and Longborough would call one witness which they would have an opportunity to question. The court called the first witness, one chosen by Greer.

Jonas Hellier appeared live via camera from an undisclosed location. Along with his name, his voice had been altered, and his face was pixelated and blurred to mask his identity. He was dressed immaculately in a charcoal suit which looked every bit as expensive as the ones sported by Longborough's lawyers. He was a picture of calm as he was sworn in, and Edwyn Greer began his questioning.

"Mr Hellier, can you tell the court what you do for a living?"

"I'm an executive director of a well-known global business."

"Which is an import and export business, correct?"

"Yes."

"How much does your company turn over, yearly?"

"Approximately seventeen million."

"Would you consider yourself a high profile member of the community?"

"Yes."

"Could you tell the court some of the people you regard as close personal friends?"

"I'd rather not state names, but I count several politicians, TV and movie stars and musicians amongst my friends, as well as world leaders from a dozen or more countries.

"I see," Greer said, turning towards the jury to ensure they were paying attention to the video feed.

"Could you tell the court why you were called as a witness here today?"

"I have Longboroughvampirosis."

The crowd murmured and order was restored.

"Mr Hellier, how long have you had Longboroughvampirosis?"

"Almost a hundred and twenty years."

"And has it stopped you from becoming a valuable addition to society?"

"No."

"Mr Winthorpe yesterday suggested that those contracted with the parasite would become mindless, blood thirsty animals. Would you say that is correct?"

"Absolutely not."

"Could you explain for us how you managed to deal with the disease?"

"It's like anything, it's about control, discipline. I taught myself to deal with the anger and the aggression, and to make sure I contributed to the world."

"But surely, if what Mr Bahl and Mr Winthorpe said yesterday, we have an urge for blood, a desire that only human blood would satisfy."

"They were wrong."

A murmur rose, and Winthorpe glared at Greer just as Longborough was glaring at him.

"Could you explain in more detail what you mean?"

"Animal blood will suffice. In fact, it actually makes the infection easier to manage, decreases its potency."

"So, in essence, would I be correct in saying that the highly invasive, experimental and not to mention expensive cure may actually be an unnecessary expense?"

"That's not for me to say, but all I can say is that this isn't a death sentence. With some effort, it can be lived with."

Greer turned to Longborough with raised eyebrows.

"Thank you, Mr Hellier, I have no further questions."

Greer sat as Winthorpe stood and approached the television screen.

"Mr Hellier, you say you are able to live with your condition, that it allows you to live a normal life, just like the rest of us."

"Yes."

"Then, may I ask, why you chose not to appear here in court, but to remain hidden?"

"It could have an impact on my business."

"I put it to you that the reason you remain hidden is because the people close to you will be afraid if they knew what you really are. You said yourself, it's possible to control, but it must be a struggle to fight the desires of what is proved to be an incredibly powerful parasite."

"It's difficult, of that there is no doubt, but we are not monsters."

"Then, Mr Hellier, turn on the lights! Let us hear your voice, let us see your face, and let us know who you are. If you are so certain that you have control of this disease, and then show us!"

"Mr Winthorpe, do not badger the witness." Warned Judge Jeffries.

"My apologies, your honour. I was just trying to illustrate that the witnesses' words contradict his appearance."

"Then do it more carefully. Mr Greer is the one on trial here, not Mr Hellier."

"Again, my apologies."

Winthorpe paused to compose his thoughts and then spoke quietly.

"Mr Hellier, apologies for my outburst. I was merely trying to establish why somebody of obvious social stature would prefer to remain hidden, when you state that you are fully in control of your disease."

"I didn't say I was fully in control. I said it's manageable."

"So, although you can feed on animals, you still have the desire for human blood. Is that correct?"

"I don't see how that is relevant."

"Please answer the question, Mr Hellier."

"Yes, it's always there, but the desire is manageable. We don't have to feed on humans."

Bernard grinned, it was a confident smile, and he turned his attention back to the jury.

"Thank you, Mr Hellier, I have no further questions."

Winthorpe returned to Longborough, who also looked smug. Greer grimaced, because although his witness had tried as best he could, his evasiveness had made him look weak. The court broke for lunch, and again, after everyone settled in, the next witness was prepared. Greer recognised her, and his stomach rolled slightly as he saw the way the jury looked at her as she sat down. Unlike his witness who was shrouded in secrecy, the girl was there for all to see. She looked to be in her early twenties, with long golden hair and blue eyes which would surely be seductive if not for the permanent fear which showed in them as she looked around the courtroom at everything but him.

She would have been one of those naturally beautiful girls — the ones who didn't need to wear a ton of make-up or go overboard with the hair styling — if not for the scar tissue which covered her neck, shoulder and the most of her right cheek. The skin was uneven and rugged, and although the surgeons had done an admirable job, the savagery of her wounds was plain to see. Greer looked towards Longborough, who was watching him with a thin smile on his face. Winthorpe stood and approached the frightened girl, as the courtroom fell silent.

"Please state your name," Winthorpe said with sincerity that Greer could just about see through, and that was for the benefit of the jury.

"It's... Clara. Clara Wood."

"Thank you, Clara."

Winthorpe turned towards the jury and then spoke to them in his usual, booming court voice.

"Ladies and gentlemen, Clara Wood was on her way home from a friend's house three years ago when she was attacked from behind. Miss Wood suffered flesh wounds which resulted in her needing three hundred and eleven stitches to her face, neck and shoulders. She was in such a poor condition when paramedics arrived and had lost so much blood, that she wasn't expected to live. In fact, on her way to the hospital, Miss Wood stopped breathing on four separate occasions, only to be revived by the excellent medical staff in attendance."

Winthorpe paused, and the immense room was silent apart from Clara's sniffles as she wept. Bernard handed her a box of tissues, which she took gratefully.

"This woman." He said as he pointed to her. "Has shown incredible bravery by coming here today. She isn't hidden behind a television screen. Her name hasn't been changed, nor her voice altered. She is here today to show you, ladies and gentlemen of the jury, the true face of the Longboroughvampirosis parasite."

Greer was listening to Winthorpe, but watching the jury. They were staring at him coldly.

"Miss Wood was saved from certain death only because her assailant was interrupted."

He paused again for effect, waiting just long enough for the information to sink in with those watching.

"Miss Wood, is your assailant here in this courtroom today?"

She nodded, wiping her eyes with the tissue.

"I'm sorry Miss Wood, I know this is difficult for you, could you verbally answer the question?"

"Yes, yes he is." She said, lowering her head. Bernard nodded and then turned to the jury.

"Could you point him out to the jury please?"

She was shaking, and with some effort lifted her head and pointed a shaking hand at Greer.

"Him. He did it."

Greer sat and stared straight ahead, feeling the pressure of countless pairs of eyes trained on him. He felt a tear of his own roll down his cheek and was surprised. It was something that he hadn't experienced for over two hundred years. Bernard walked towards Greer, a predatory smile on his face as he neared.

"Miss Wood was pleading for her life. But this man showed no sympathy. Miss Wood begged for her freedom, but this man showed no sympathy."

Winthorpe paused and leaned on the desk, his face inches away from Greer's. Winthorpe glared, and said his next words quietly, the microphone on his jacket making sure everyone in attendance and watching the world over, heard it all the same.

"Miss Wood was pregnant at the time of her attack, but this man showed no sympathy."

This time, the court descended into chaos, people shouted and pointed, and the Judge tried his best to regain order. Only Winthorpe and Greer were silent, staring at each other with neither willing to break eye contact first. As the din subsided, Winthorpe stood and walked back towards the jury.

"Look at the injuries sustained by Miss Wood. Look at them and consider that she is just one of the lucky ones. Think of the others, the three hundred thousand other souls who Edwyn Greer took in order to satisfy his urge to kill. In closing, let me ask you this, ladies and gentlemen."

He looked at them in turn and then delivered his closing statement.

"If indeed, Mr Greer's kind are able to sustain themselves on the blood of animals, then why did he feel the need to do this to poor Miss Wood and his countless other victims?"

Bernard straightened and looked at the Judge, nodding curtly.

"No further questions, Your Honour."

Bernard sat back with his team, and Greer felt the definite shift in atmosphere. The Judge told him it was his witness, and as he looked at the poor girl, he couldn't think of a single thing to say. He had already subjected her to a harrowing experience, and couldn't bear to even look at her, meaning that questioning was a non-starter.

"No questions," Greer said.

Across the table, Winthorpe and Longborough smiled

Day Three

The atmosphere in court for the final day of proceedings was tense and heavy. Outside, the police presence had been increased tenfold, due to the increasing number of clashes between both supporters and detractors of Greer. The last day was the one which those who were watching had been waiting for. It would be Greer's turn to be questioned, and he, in turn would have the opportunity to question Longborough. After that, there was nothing more that could be done, and it was down to the jury to decide.

Greer was transported to the witness box, still shackled at his feet and hands. Winthorpe stood and approached him, the swagger in his step fitting perfectly with the arrogant grin as he prepared to begin his questioning.

"Mr Greer! Do you consider yourself to be a good man?"

"In what way?"

"I mean. Do you believe in justice? Right and wrong? Crime and punishment?"

"I do, although, in some instances, the system is flawed."

"I see. And are you a remorseful man? Do you feel sorry for the crimes which, I don't think are unfair to call, a reign of terror?"

"That's a very dramatic way to ask me, councillor."

"Nevertheless, it is a question I would like you to answer."

"Of course, I do."

"Then why did you continue?"

"Mr Winthorpe, it's easy for you to stand there and judge me, but unless you have experienced it for yourself, it's hard to make you understand."

"Oh, please," Winthorpe said, flashing a wide smile. "Enlighten us."

"You are a smoker, aren't you Mr Winthorpe?" Greer asked.

"Not that it matters, but yes, yes I am."

"Even though you know that every drag you take is killing you, I would bet my life you will be lighting up a new one the second you are outside. You know it's bad, and you know you should stop, but you just can't. Now imagine that feeling and multiply it by a hundred thousand, and you still don't come close. I hated what I had become, but I was powerless to stop it."

"But you have done it now for over two hundred years, surely if you were so unhappy; there were other ways to stop."

Greer smiled. "You mean suicide?"

"Well, was it never an option Mr Greer? Not that I advocate such a thing, but I think the question has some validity."

"You really don't understand, do you Mr Winthorpe?"

"No, I don't think I do. So please, explain to us all why you chose to continue to kill instead of doing what some might deem the honourable thing and take your own life."

Greer smiled, and then grew serious. Everyone was looking at him, and taking a leaf out of Winthorpe's book, he spoke softly, yet clearly.

"In the winter of eighteen eighty eight, I was in London. The Jack the Ripper murders were still fresh on the minds of the community in Whitechapel, but I have to admit that I wasn't one of them who cared. My body by then was alien to me. You call me a monster, but the conscience is the thing that seems to last the longest. The terrible things that my parasite had forced me to do weighed heavy, and I tried to blot out all thoughts of it with drink. Whitechapel then was a violent, dark place Mr Winthorpe. The poverty was a physical thing that you could smell in the air, buried beneath the stench of the slaughterhouses and the human waste which flowed through the streets.

I would get into fights, and even though I would let them kick me, and stab at me, my parasite kept me alive. That didn't make me feel any better, so one night; I walked down to the docks. I filled my pockets with heavy stones and jumped into the Thames. I hoped that it would be enough, but the vampire is a clever one, Mr Winthorpe. Especially when it comes to its own self-preservation. Even though I fought it, my body emptied the stones from my pockets, and I pulled myself out of the filthy water gasping and furious that I had failed.

I tried again in nineteen twenty. Hung myself from a tree. I didn't die. I just hung there, unable to breathe. Of course, my parasite could have freed me, but it was angry, it wanted to show me that it was in control. So it let me hang there, feeling the pain, lost in the limbo between life and death.

For five days I swung from that tree, just waiting for my vampire to free me. Eventually, a young hunter came across me and cut me down. My vampire pounced on him seconds after I hit the ground. It had a point to prove you see. And it proved it well."

Greer looked around the court. Everyone, even Winthorpe was watching him as he continued.

"Lesson learned, I went on until early sixty eight. I was in America then, my wanderings taking me from one continent to the next, trying to find a place where I belonged.

I encountered a man in Texas. He tried to rob me, and my vampire took control and split him from chest to pubic bone in the blink of an eye. As my vampire feasted on the spoils of its victory, my eyes fell upon the man's gun. It was a pistol, and I thought that if I did it quick, then it would be done before my vampire could stop me."

Greer smiled, and the expression melted away just as quickly as it had come.

"Well, I tried for it. I scooped up the gun, whirled it around and jammed it into my mouth, but the vampire knew. It had known all along. I stood there with that hot, oil tasting steel pressing onto my tongue, and yet I couldn't pull the trigger. I tried, tried with all the will I could muster, but the vampire wouldn't let me. My punishment was that it forced me to cut off my own genitals."

He looked at the shocked faces and licked his lips.

"I stopped trying to fight it then. It was already too strong. I tried to kill myself Mr Winthorpe, more than once. But the vampire inside me just wouldn't allow me to do it."

Greer looked at Winthorpe and watched as the lawyers smile faltered a little. He composed himself, and then looked to the crowd.

"A moving tale, Mr Greer. One told expertly by a man who is obviously intelligent. Told by a man who knows that his only chance to become free is to make this jury feel sorry for you. And perhaps they do. But I implore them to consider the facts as they stand, and not to take into account the moving and well told story that you have just relayed to us all."

"You call it a story, Mr Winthorpe; I call it answering the question that you have asked."

"Really? Well, I put it to you, Mr Greer that this humble, remorseful persona is just that. An act, a way to try and sway the minds of these good people of the jury in your favour. I put to you that not only did you learn to live with the Longboroughvampirosis, but you embraced it, you thrived on it. And for two hundred years you pillaged and murdered at will.

"You are wrong."

"I also put to you, that given the chance, you would take back the parasite, and once again feast on those who our legal system serves to protect. People like Clara Wood, a young girl who had a promising future cut short by a foul beast whose only desire was to maim, murder and feast. She is a self-confessed shell of the bubbly, outgoing person that she used to be, and we, as a society, call her one of the lucky ones because she happened to survive?"

Winthorpe glanced to the jury and shook his head.

"No, Mr Greer, I don't think we have the right to call Miss Wood lucky. I think a ruined life, is a ruined life however you try to spin it. She was lucky to survive, that much is true. But what about the others? What about the ones who didn't survive? What about the countless innocents who have their blood on your hands, Mr Greer? What about them?"

Greer glared at Winthorpe and spoke softly.

"I'm not hearing a question, councillor."

Winthorpe flashed a false, elastic smile at Greer, and turned to the Judge.

"No further questions." He said as he returned to his seat.

The tension was heavy in the air, and with everyone in apparent need of a break, the court broke for an early lunch, and when they returned, it was Longborough who was in the witness box, and Greer who was preparing to question him. Those in attendance waited with bated breath, as Greer approached the man who had, for better or worse, changed the direction of his life forever.

He was still shaken, stirred by the powerful words of Winthorpe, and for as much as he didn't particularly care for him; he had to acknowledge a certain professional respect for the lawyer, who had delivered a masterful performance. Greer composed his thoughts and approached Longborough. He looked at him carefully and then spoke.

"Do you believe in the law, Mr Longborough?"

"Of course, I do." Longborough snapped.

"Do you abide by it? Do you follow its rules?"

"Yes."

"And would you consider me as a law abiding man?"

"Of course not."

"But a man all the same."

"Yes."

"Would you please tell the court how the parasite is removed from someone unfortunate enough to be infected?"

"Objection." Bellowed Winthorpe. "This is hardly relevant."

The Judge looked at Winthorpe, then at Greer.

"The line of questioning is valid. Answer the question please, Mr Longborough."

Longborough took a deep breath as Bernard watched carefully.

"The process is complex, I'm not sure I could explain fully."

"Oh, I appreciate your need to keep the specifics private. Your company stands to make a lot of money if this trial goes the way you expect it to."

"That's irrelevant I..."

"Its fine." Greer said with a thin smile. "Just a general

description of the procedure for the court will suffice."

Longborough squirmed in his seat, and seeing no way to get out of the question, reluctantly answered.

"We put the host under a local anesthetic, then using specialised laser equipment, we open the ribcage. Then, our teams carefully locate the parasite by moving the heart aside. From there, we carefully cut the parasite free."

"And what about the part that you said attaches to the brain?"

"That isn't removed. Without the main body of the host, it cannot survive. They are in separate locations, but part of the same organism."

"Is the process a complex one?"

"Very," Longborough said, straightening in his seat. "There are very few people alive that could perform it in the world."

"And you are one of them, correct?"

"You know I am. I performed it on you, and here you stand."

"So for those of us who do not understand the complexity. Would it be at the same level as, say a heart transplant, for example?"

"Yes, I'd say it was in the same ball park."

"So," Greer said as he turned back towards the jury. "What we have here is a very dangerous, invasive surgery, correct?"

"Yes, but if it's done by someone like myself, who knows how to perform the procedure safely, the survival rate is almost seventy percent."

"I see." Greer said, taking another leaf out of Winthorpe's book and pausing for a few seconds.

"With such an invasive procedure, I presume that release forms would have to be signed?"

"Longborough locked eyes with Greer and again fidgeted in his chair. He glanced at Winthorpe, who looked back blankly.

"Yes of course, but this was experimental."

"So, you are saying that you performed a dangerous, invasive, potentially lethal surgery on me without my consent?"

"Yes... no! You are different!"

"True, I'm different, but I'm still a man. A man who has the same rights as anyone in this world, and yet, you snatched me off the streets, and performed a very dangerous procedure on me without my permission."

“You are a beast, a creature!” Stammered Longborough.

“Am I? But your own witnesses and your own council have said on numerous occasions that this is a parasite, something that attaches to the host and controls it. It doesn’t change the man into beast; it alters its behaviour. Isn’t that correct?”

“I refuse to answer anymore,” Longborough said, a light sweat forming on his brow.

“You will answer the question, Mr Longborough.” The Judge ordered.

Greer waited. The public watched. Longborough squirmed.

“Maybe it doesn’t change the person in so many words, but the advances in science are worth the risk.”

“You call me a monster, but yet you are the one who brought me against my will and performed surgery on me that wasn't permitted.”

Greer lifted up his shirt, showing the huge scar to the jury.

“You did this without my authority. You took another man’s life in your own hands, and even though you say it’s for science, we both know that it’s for financial greed. Isn’t it Mr Longborough?”

“No, it’s not like that!” He raged.

“How much does your company stand to earn from this procedure? How many people will you have rushing to your clinics, sure that they are infected and paying your extortionate fees just to be examined?”

Longborough stammered, and couldn’t formulate an answer.

“You paint me as a monster, and it’s true that there are crimes that I am guilty of, but you are worse because you can’t admit to yours.”

Silence.

Greer looked at the jury. They were looking at him in wonder and at Longborough with contempt. Winthorpe had his head in his hands and had seemingly lost interest in proceedings.

“No further questions.” Greer snapped, and returned to his seat.

“Okay.” Judge Jeffries said. “We will take a brief thirty minute break, then reconvene for the final statements from both parties before we hand over to the jury."

Court was dismissed, and the various television crews hyped up the final statements. Public opinion was strictly divided, and the consensus was that the result could go either way.

The court reconvened, and the final statements were ready to be made. Winthorpe stood, having recovered from his head in hands dejection from before lunch. He approached the jury, smiling confidently, then paused, basking in the silence.

"Ladies and gentlemen." He began. "You have heard the information. You have heard the testimony of experts and also of those directly involved. You have also heard the words of Mr Greer, a man who delivered a very convincing, heartfelt speech. But don't be fooled. Here is a man that for two hundred years has maimed, killed and murdered all for his own self-gratification. Look at him now, ladies and gentlemen."

Winthorpe paused and looked at Greer with a smug half smile.

"Look at him. What looks to be an innocent man on the surface, is actually a cold blooded monster. And yes, perhaps mistakes were made by my client in his manner of treating Mr Greer, but nevertheless, his intentions were sincere. And rest assured, his reasons for the manner of removing the Longboroughvampirosis from Mr Greer were genuine."

Winthorpe turned back to the jury, making sure to make eye contact with each of them.

"My client has devoted his life in the pursuit of a cure for what is, without a doubt, the biggest single threat to humanity, bar none."

Winthorpe smiled and inserted one of his trademark pauses.

"Just think about that for a moment. On one hand, you have a man who has devoted himself, his life, and his own personal fortunes and that of his company to devise this cure, and then on the other side, you have Edwyn Greer. A murdering, violent monster that has terrorised this planet for over two hundred years. Make no mistake. Edwyn Greer is guilty. And Edwyn Greer deserves to be punished if only to show others of his kind that wanton murder of innocent people is unacceptable, and will be punished.

Make no mistake, ladies and gentlemen. Ensure that whatever decision you make is the correct one, because to make an incorrect choice, could lead to more deaths, murder and more suffering for countless innocents the world over."

He stood straight and clasped his hands in front of him.

"Edwyn Greer is guilty, ladies and gentlemen. And it's up to you to see that he is punished. Thank you."

Winthorpe returned to his seat, and the Judge motioned to Greer. He hesitated, his mouth suddenly dry. He wasn't even sure if his legs would hold him, but he stood up smoothly, his restraints rattling as he shuffled towards the jury. He wasn't even sure how he was going to begin, or what he intended to say until it happened and he found the words ejecting themselves from his mouth.

"I won't try to dazzle you like Mr Winthorpe over there. I won't even try to sway your opinion. I'm sure by now you already know what you are going to decide. All I will say is that I didn't ask for this. On that day many years ago, I was in the wrong place at the wrong time. And because of that, and the control that my parasite held over me, yes I did terrible things. Things which, now that I am free of it, I deeply regret. Truth be known, I don't blame Dr Longborough for what he did. Although he performed his procedure on me without permission, I don't blame him. In fact, I want to thank him. Because he freed me. And yet, it seems that he also wants to see me put to death, which begs the question why? Why would a man who was referred to by his own representative as a man who had devoted himself to curing this disease, then be so determined to see me put to death?"

Greer walked towards Longborough and watched him carefully.

"Greed? Personal gain? Fame? All valid reasons. I wonder if this is the fate that befalls everyone cured of the parasite he has given his own name to. What if one of you, here in this court contracts it and do not seek help in time? Perhaps you too would be put on trial and put to death. Freed of your curse, only to be punished at the very first scent of a freedom which is then taken from you."

Greer walked back towards the jury.

"Perhaps, this entire procedure is worthless if those cured are put to death. Some might even say a waste of time and money. In closing, ladies and gentlemen, let me ask you this. If the parasite is responsible for my actions, and then removed, why punish the man? Surely I am as innocent as any of you here in this room? Either way, for better or worse, I have lived for a very long time and think I have seen enough of human nature to know that we are a flawed species. The real battle is already won, and with Dr. Longborough's cure, nobody need suffer as I have suffered. So please, ladies and gentlemen. Do not punish the man for his misfortune of contracting a disease that was neither understood nor curable. Perhaps I am wrong, and the flaws that I have seen in our species over the years are not quite so clearly cut. That is for you to decide. And whatever the outcome, I thank you."

Greer returned to his seat and sat as Judge Jeffries organised his papers.

"The jury will now recess to formulate their findings. We will reconvene as soon a decision has been made."

Greer was led away to the holding cells, as the jury filed away to discuss the evidence before presenting it to the Judge. He assumed the jury would take a lot of time to go through the evidence that had been presented, and thought there was a good chance that the trial could yet stretch into a fourth day. He was wrong, however, and less than three hours later, a verdict had been reached.

For what would be the last time, no matter the outcome, Greer was led back into the courtroom which was already full, as nobody wanted to miss the verdict.

Greer glanced over at Longborough and Winthorpe, but both were intently watching the Judge.

"Has the jury reached a verdict?"

The head juror, a middle aged woman with short hair stood and responded.

"Yes, Your Honour. In the case of Greer versus Longborough, we find the defendant. Not guilty."

The courtroom became a symphony of whispered chatter and excited murmur. Greer sat for a moment, not quite able to comprehend what had happened. He glanced at Longborough, who was glaring at him.

"You got it wrong." He bellowed standing and staring at the Judge with wide eyes. "He's a murderer, a mass murderer."

"Sit down, Mr Longborough." Judge Jeffries warned as Winthorpe tried, and eventually succeeded in calming his employer.

Judge Jeffries took a deep breath and addressed the court.

"The decision of the jury is, for the record, one which I am in full agreement with. The actions of Mr Greer were conducted under the influence of what has been confirmed to be a very violent, very potent parasite. One which is now cured. I urge everyone here in this courtroom, and everyone watching around the world to acknowledge this fact. And also to allow Mr Greer to live his life now in peace as he should have done many years ago. Even though many have suffered, Mr Greer cannot be blamed. He was as much a victim as anyone, and although I won't go into it here, I suspect that the main reason for this trial taking place was, as suggested, financially motivated.

Mr Greer, you strike me as a man who has lived through years of things which most of us cannot begin to imagine. You also come across as a very sincere man who, despite your years on this earth, has not yet had a chance to experience life as it should be lived. I urge you to go forth from this courtroom and live that life to the full, and try as best you can, to put the events of this trial and the events of your life, which have led to this moment, behind you."

Greer nodded, and the Judge turned to Longborough.

" As for you, Mr Longborough, for as much as your procedure is appreciated, and its brilliance cannot be denied, I sense that you are a man who will do anything to achieve whatever he wants to in life, and will stop at nothing to do so. Your treatment of Mr Greer was nothing short of barbaric, and Mr Greer would be well within his rights to take legal action of his own if he so desired, although I would hope that he would take my advice and not waste any more time with disputes in this or any other courtroom.

I give you this warning, Mr Longborough, knowing that the eyes of the world are upon you. Pursue this no further. Leave Mr Greer to enjoy his life and you in turn go back to the brilliant work that you are conducting in the advancement of science."

The Judge stood, and looked at Greer with a small smile.

"You are free to go, Mr Greer."

The armed guards that had been with Greer since the trial began released his shackles, freeing him at last. He rubbed his wrists and looked around the courtroom, unsure what to do. He hadn't planned for winning, or what he would do with himself if he did. He supposed it was possible that some fanatic might try to kill him, or make an example of him, but he decided that it wasn't something that was worth worrying about too much. The world, for better or worse, stretched out in front of him, and finally free of the thing that had consumed him; he couldn't begin to even imagine the possibilities. With everyone watching him in silence, Edwyn Greer stood, and walked out of the courtroom as a free man.

CANDYLAND

Bill Norton was almost out of gas. The Arizona Desert rolled by his blue Cadillac as he enjoyed the peace of the road, which for the best part of the day had pretty much belonged to him alone. It had been blisteringly hot, the kind of day where just standing out in the open would leave a man covered in sweat within minutes, but Bill was kept cool by the constant rush of air as the car raced on.

He had decided to drive from Los Angeles to San Antonio because he was deathly afraid of flying. The entire notion of being inside an aircraft of any form horrified him to the point where he suffered severe anxiety attacks, and so the only option had been to hit the road. He only wished that the reason for his trip had been something positive. His sister had called to tell him that their mother had suffered a stroke and that he really ought to get down there as soon as he could. Without her having to say it, he could read between the lines well enough. It wasn't a get well visit as such, but more than likely a farewell.

As he imagined happened with most people in similar situations, he wished he had made more of an effort to see her, made time to go visit, or even just to call more often to ask if she was okay. He could give many reasons why he didn't, the job that demanded so many of his hours, the family who he was trying his best to nurture and protect, or even the fact that there never seemed to be enough time. However, he knew, deep down, that they were all just bullshit excuses.

He never went, because he was selfish.

His attention was drawn back to the road by the sign which rolled out of the heat haze as he continued down the pencil line of blacktop.

REST STOP/ SERVICES!
Last chance for gas for the next 100 MILES!
Take next slip road!

He smiled to himself at the urgent nature of the faded green sign and the way in which its message was composed. There was a demanding quality to it. Why so many exclamation marks? He imagined the words being said by some backwater preacher, each line read in such a way as to give importance to what should otherwise be a standard message for a driver looking to take a break. It read like a demand, which served to further pique his curiosity.

Take next slip road!

"Whatever you say pal." He said to the relentless desert, smiling as the sign flashed past him. Even though he very much doubted that the aforementioned rest stop *was* the last chance for gas, he didn't want to take the risk and be left out in the middle of nowhere after dark with no fuel and a car which had no roof.

He could see the slip road ahead, snaking off out of sight around a brushy hillock, and if he wasn't curious enough, the next sign ensured that he would definitely be stopping to check this place out.

Like its demanding counterpart, this sign was also green and aged by the elements, but if the first sign was demanding, this one was written with some sense of finality, a statement of fact. The chipped and faded white letters, this time, carried no bullshit, no false information about how limited fuel supplies may be. It stated where in the world Bill Norton was going.

ENTERING
Candyland
Pop. 122

As far as place names went, it was pretty cool, and Bill didn't think twice as he slowed and peeled off the main highway and down the bumpy slip road.

Candyland, he thought to himself as he jostled the car along. *What a fantastic name.*

The car bustled and jolted on its suspension, as Bill Norton made his way into the unknown.

Candyland was barely a town. Bill cruised down what he presumed was the main street, taking in the ambiance of the place. The stores - those which weren't closed and boarded over - were tired and jaded, and looked to be showing signs of giving up the fight against the constant abuse of the elements.

There was an eerie silence, and Bill immediately noticed that the streets were empty. Nothing moved, and he was aware of just how loud the Cadillac's engine sounded in the hot July air. Despite the heat, he felt a chill brush down his spine.

There was another sign ahead; penned in much the same way as the one he referred to as the 'shouty' sign. It was tied across the length of the street between two lamp poles and was no less subtle than its predecessor.

This is CANDYLAND!
Do NOT mis the fete in the town square!
Hot Food! Cheap Gas! Frendly welcum!

Not only was this also an exclamation point overload but was also badly spelt. He didn't like it and was so overcome with the feeling of being watched, that he almost turned around and headed back the way he came.

You can't do that, He reminded himself.

And why not?

Because you need gas and this is the last chance to get it for the next 100 miles. The sign said so.

He thought about telling his inner monologue to go screw itself, and that an exclamation mark did not mean something should be taken as gospel. Besides, surely to god in today's modern world, somebody, other than in a shithole like Candyland, would have decided to set up shop and supply gas for weary travellers like him.

But you can't be sure…

Again, his inner voice was correct. The facts were that he needed gas, and if he had to stop in Candyland (Population 122) to get some, then so be it. He tried to ignore the ramshackle storefronts and sagging roofs as he proceeded down the street, which although devoid of people, did have some life.

A skinny, runt of a dog with patchy, matted fur limped

across the street ahead, and he also saw a couple of alley cats pawing through a mound of garbage bags piled at the side of a bakery that last looked to have done business in the fifties. But of human life, however, there was no sign. The road turned right ahead, and he hoped that somewhere beyond there would be some signs of civilisation. He drove around the corner, and suddenly, the world of Candyland was alive.

The town square was filled with people. Stalls were set up around the perimeter, leaving ample room for people to mingle and chat. The explosion of chatter and the mouth-watering smell of barbecue instantly dispelled Norton's fear, and he noted that even his inner monologue had retreated back to its hiding place. Norton brought the car to a halt, instantly feeling the burning heat of the sun. He looked at the on-going fete which had been advertised by the sign on Main Street. There would be ice cream, maybe even deliciously cool lemonade, and of course, that wonderful smelling barbecue, which was making Norton's taste buds come alive with desire. Part of him knew time was of the essence, and that he couldn't afford to stop, but on the other hand, he *had* been driving all day and was a good couple of hours ahead of schedule.

"Hell with it." He muttered to himself as he shut off the engine and climbed out of the car.

He walked towards the village square, his shadow thin and stretched ahead of him. One of the locals saw him and veered to meet him.

"Good afternoon to ya' good sir! Welcome to Candyland." The man said.

He had some kind of speech issue, and pronunciation of the letter's' came out as a 'ttth' instead.

He was short and overweight and somehow squeezed into an ill-fitting cheap blue suit which looked straight out of the '70's. Rivulets of sweat ran down his balding head and over his face. The man whipped out a handkerchief and wiped himself dry, and then rolling his eyes he looked at Norton and flashed a yellow toothed grin.

"It's so hot the god-damn birds are layin' their eggs sunny side up."

Norton nodded, as the man stuffed the handkerchief back into his breast pocket, then held out a pudgy hand.

"My name's Clayton Candy, it's a pleasure to meet you."

Norton shook the man's hand. It was soft and sweaty, and Norton couldn't wait to have his grip released.

"Pleased to meet you, Mr Candy, I'm Bill Norton."

"So, what brings you to Candyland today?"

"I uh, need some gas. Almost out."

"Oh, we can certainly help you out there. No problem at all. Won't you stay and enjoy the fete with us? It's quite the event here."

"I would, but I'm a little pushed for time."

"Oh come on Bill, surely a few minutes rest won't harm? Anyway, our gas station attendant is right here at the fete. I'll show you around and introduce you so you can be on your way."

Clayton slapped Norton on the shoulder and steered him towards the fete, taking all arguments out of the equation. Norton didn't fight too hard, he was, after all, pretty peckish.

"So, Mr Candy, is this your town?"

"Oh no, not at all. I'm just the Mayor. My great, great granddaddy founded Candyland way back. I'm just the latest in a long line of Candy's running the show here."

The two walked past stalls selling various brick a brac. For every local that greeted Mayor Candy with a nod of the head, a wary eye was cast towards Norton. There was something unusual about the people, something he couldn't quite put his finger on. Clayton went on.

"We're a small town Bill, and between you and me, I like it that way. We keep ourselves to ourselves and let the world go on without knowin' about us. Oh, you gotta try this."

Clayton waddled over to the barbecue, which was immense and filled with sausages, burgers, steaks and chicken legs. It looked beautiful and smelled even better.

"Franklin, this 'ere is Mr Norton, he's new in town. Why don't ya give him one o' your special burgers?"

Franklin looked older than time itself, a withered shell with leathery brown skin and a distinct sprinkling of liver spots. But ancient or not, Norton appreciated the old man's cooking skills, and gratefully accepted the giant burger offered to him.

"Ketchup?" The old man asked, holding the bottle towards Norton.

"Yes, thanks." He said as the old man squirted a generous amount of sauce on the burger before replacing the top half of the bun. The burger was almost as wide as the span of his hand. It wasn't some shitty processed McDonalds fare either, but a real, homemade burger in an actual bread bun.

"How much do I owe you?" Norton asked as he started to fish for his wallet.

"Oh, don't ya worry about that. Take it as a welcome as our guest today." Clayton said, once again pulling out his handkerchief to wipe away his sweat.

"Thank you, that's very generous."

"Go ahead and try it, boy." The old man said as he flashed a gummy grin.

Norton obliged, taking a large bite.

It was heaven.

The meat was succulent and juicy, the char grilled taste giving it a kick that was out of this world. Even though he had been fortunate to eat in some high class restaurants, Norton didn't think any of them came anywhere close to the fare served up by the old man.

"My god, that's amazing," Norton said between mouthfuls as he wiped his chin with the back of his hand.

"Glad you like it son, it's an old family recipe."

"It's delicious," Norton said as he took another bite.

Clayton clapped Norton on the back and steered him away from the barbecue and further into the crowd.

"You married, Bill?"

"Divorced." He said as he finished off his burger. "I had a wife for three years and she has been my ex for two."

"I'm sorry to hear that."

"It's okay, she was a bitch."

Norton laughed, and then saw that Clayton looked quite offended, so he morphed his laugh into a cough and hoped it went unnoticed.

They passed a stall filled with handmade wind chimes.

"Oh, Mr Norton, there's someone 'ere I would like ya to meet."

"Actually, I really have to be going, if you could just point me to somewhere I can fill up I'll..."

"Oh, this will just take a minute, then I'll personally take ya to Herb who will refuel you. Okay?"

Norton wanted to refuse, but Clayton seemed quite insistent, and a little put out by Norton wanting to be on his way. There was a glimmer of something in his eye, and just for an instant, Norton was afraid.

"Okay, but then I really must be getting going." He said, wishing he wasn't so easily influenced.

"Wonderful, right this way!" Clayton said, flashing an uneven yellow grin as he pushed his way through the crowd.

"Christine, oh Christine where are you precious?"

Norton followed, watching in amusement as the sweaty Mayor pushed his way through the crowd. He knew the instant she turned around who Christine was. She was obviously Candy's daughter, and the two were almost dead ringers. Norton had to fight not to grimace as Candy's 'precious' waddled towards them. She was aged somewhere between twenty and forty, and at least three hundred pounds, if not more. Like her father, she was sweating, and although she had tried to comb it across to hide it, her greasy black hair was thinning, receding from the front and making her forehead appear huge. Her features were almost exactly the same as her fathers, although they seemed somehow compressed into the middle of her flabby face. He didn't like to ridicule people for their weight but the only description he could find for her that would fit was piggish.

"Mr Norton, I would like to introduce my daughter, Christine. When I retire, she will become Mayor of Candyland." Clayton said, beaming with pride.

"Pleased to meet you," Norton replied as politely as he could, trying not to stare at just how huge she was.

"Hello." She mumbled, not making eye contact with Norton and instead looking at her own immense shadow on the grass.

"Mr Norton 'ere is new in town. You go ahead and get him a drink now."

"No, really Mr Candy, it's fine, I really do have to be going, and if you could just show me where I can get that gas…"

Clayton glared at Norton, and actually looked angry. His cheek twitched once, and then the moment had gone, and he smiled.

"Of course, my apologies." He said, wringing his hands together. "If ya wouldn't mind keeping ma daughter here company for a few minutes, I'll go and find Herb an' have him fill up that gorgeous caddy of yours and get you on ya way. Good enough?"

"Yes, thank you," Norton replied as Clayton moved off into the crowd.

He didn't want to stay in Candyland any longer. He was starting to feel more than a little uncomfortable with the place. He noticed that although they were trying as best they could to hide it, everyone was watching him, taking secretive glances. And he had started to notice other things. How not only did Candy's daughter look almost exactly like him, but most of the other townsfolk bore a resemblance to him too. He felt his stomach begin to tighten as he started to wonder if he might be in danger.

"Help me."

Norton flicked his eyes towards Christine, and she was now looking at him, her narrow, blue eyes filled with hope and fear.

"Say again?"

"Help, me, please." She whispered.

"Help you how? What do you mean?"

"Take me with you when you go. Please."

"I'm sorry I don't understand…"

"I'm a prisoner here. We all are."

Norton's already unsettled stomach rolled as he looked into Christine's piggish face. She could almost have been beautiful in a way, had nature treated her differently. Norton had always considered himself a good judge of character and was always sure he could read when someone was lying, which made the fact that he believed every word she said immensely disturbing.

"What do you mean, trapped?" He whispered.

"My daddy, he's not a nice man."

Despite the heat, Norton went cold as she spoke, wringing her tiny hands in the same way her father had earlier.

"Why don't you leave, he can't make you stay here if you don't want to."

She shook her head and lowered her voice even further.

"He does bad things if you upset him."

"What kind of bad things? And why don't you go to the police?"

"Shh, he's coming back." She said, licking her lips as she continued to wring her hands. "Look at Herb. That's what happens if you upset him!"

Numb and unable to take in everything that had been said to him, Norton joined Christine in watching as Clayton approached.

He was pushing a skinny wretch of a man in a wheelchair. He had a dirty, salt and pepper beard, and his skin seemed to be wafer thin and stretched over his skull, exposing pale blue veins with stark clarity.

Look at Herb. That's what happens if you upset him!

Christine's words echoed in Norton's mind, yet somehow he managed to find a smile as Clayton approached.

"''Ere we are," Clayton said as he pushed the skeletal man to a halt in front of the pair.

"Mr Norton, this 'ere is Herb."

Norton held out his hand. "Pleased to meet you."

Herb didn't move, he stared at Norton, his yellowed eyes betraying no hint of emotion.

"Now come on Herb." Clayton said, laying a podgy hand on Herb's shoulder. "That's no way to treat our guest."

Norton was sure he wouldn't have noticed it, had Christine not told him about her father, but sure enough, he was certain Clayton had squeezed Herbs shoulder just a little too hard, his fingers digging a little too deep into his collar bone. Herb even registered a half grimace, and then like a well-trained animal, he held out a shaking hand.

"Welcome to Candyland Mr Norton."

Norton shook the old man's hand, which was dry and leathery. He just wanted to be on his way, to leave the residents of Candyland to whatever it is they did out here in the middle of nowhere.

"I uh, I was hoping to get some gas for my car."

Norton was running on autopilot, his voice seeming to come from someone else.

"Pumps are down, but I got ya a couple of jerry cans to get ya on your way," Herb said, jabbing a grubby thumb over his shoulder.

Norton could have reached out and kissed the wrinkled old man when he saw the cans hanging over the handles of the wheelchair but kept calm even despite the way his heart pounded in his chest.

"Thank you. How much do I owe you?"

"Oh no charge Mr Norton. Think of it as a courtesy gift from the people of Candyland." Clayton said smoothly, unleashing that grin which now, to Norton, had a more sinister undertone as his impression of the man changed.

"That's really very generous. I don't mind paying my way, really." He was going through the motions, saying what he knew he should say.

Does he know? Does he suspect you are on to him?

Norton asked himself the same thing and took a moment to really *look* at Clayton. If he knew, he was hiding it well.

Screw it. Just get the gas and get the hell out of here.

For once, he didn't try to ignore his inner voice. In fact, he thought it was a damn good idea.

"Are ya okay Mr Norton?" Clayton asked, watching him with sharp eyes.

"Fine, I'm just… Not used to such generosity, that's all."

The lie wasn't great, but he thought it would suffice.

"Well," Clayton said, clapping his hands together. "Let's walk ya to ya car an' get ya back on the road."

It was the best idea Norton had heard for a long time, and he had to force himself not to rush. The trio left Christine behind, Clayton pushing Herb and the precious gas as Norton walked alongside.

"So, what ya think of Candyland?" Clayton asked.

"It's different to what I'm used to."

"You from the city?"

"Yeah. L.A."

"We manage to avoid all the troubles of the wider world here in Candyland. Nobody really notices us out 'ere on our slice of the world."

"You must have some kind of trade, though, right?"

Clayton glared, and again, Norton saw that little flicker of pure rage bubbling beneath the surface.

"Actually, ma family have worked 'ard to make sure Candyland remains entirely self-sufficient. We look after our own, and are quite happy for the world to go on without knowing we exist."

Nobody knows I'm here.

It was the first time such a thought had entered Norton's head, and the reason for it was simple.

Clayton Candy scared him.

As a physical presence, he wasn't in the least bit intimidated, but there was *something* about him that was making the hairs on the back of Norton's neck stand up as they picked their way through the crowd. He no longer wanted to speak to Clayton, and with Christine's words still fresh, he turned to Herb.

"Mind if I ask what happened?"

Herb opened his mouth, but before he could speak, Clayton interjected.

"Ol' Herb 'ere had a nasty fall around twenty years back. Broke his spine in three places."

Norton looked at Clayton, searching his face for any hint of a lie.

"Can't Herb speak for himself?"

"Oh he can, but he doesn't like to say much these days. Do ya Herb?"

"No, Mr Candy sir," Herb said, looking at Norton with such desperation, that he decided not to push the subject.

The trio walked back past the barbecue, which despite everything still smelled as good as ever. Norton could see the blue paintwork of the caddy, glittering in the sunlight, and his mood lifted at the thought of leaving such a backwards little town behind.

"Oh, my…"

Norton's Cadillac was exactly where he had left it, except now it was without wheels. They had all been removed, and the car was propped up on bricks.

“God damn it! God damn kids!” Clayton raged, looking into the throng of people at the fete.

“Messin’ with our guests like this, wait till I get my hands on the little bastards…”

For all of Clayton’s flapping and making a show of his dissatisfaction, Norton was more interested in Herb’s reaction.

Unlike Clayton, he didn’t seem in the least bit surprised.

For the next few hours, Clayton made a song and dance about trying to find out who had removed Norton’s wheels. He stalked around the fete, asking questions, and demanding answers. Norton was certain that the entire performance was for his benefit. He leaned against his car, watching Clayton stalk around the fete, and keeping a watchful eye on the sun as it started to get lower in the sky.

“Mr Norton?”

He looked at Herb.

“Yeah?”

At first, he didn’t respond. He sat in his wheelchair, chewing at his filthy, overgrown thumbnail. Just when Norton thought tha he had only imagined Herb speak, the old man looked at him, his eyes wide and frightened.

“This is how it always goes.”

“How what goes?”

“'Ere in Candyland. It always works like this.”

“What is it Herb? Tell me what to do and I can help you.”

The old man smiled without humour and shook his head.

“Ain’t nobody 'ere who can help you, me or anyone else.”

“As soon as I get back on the road, I’ll come back. I’ll bring help.”

“You don’t get it do ya son?” Herb said as he held Norton’s gaze. “You ain’t never getting outta Candyland now.”

Clayton walked back towards Norton, shaking his head.

“I really do apologise for this, I promise ya I'll find the culprit and they will suffer the consequences.”

“It’s okay. Does Candyland have a garage? Someone who can fit me some new wheels?”

Clayton squirmed, and Herbs words returned to the forefront of Norton’s mind. “Actually, we don’t, nearest garage is in Shadowlands, and that’s a good thirty miles back in the direction ya came from."

Norton checked his mobile, hoping against hope that there would be a signal, but he hadn't had one for the last hundred miles, and sure enough, out here in the middle of nowhere, he had no service.

"Damn it." He said as he shoved the phone back into his jeans pocket.

"Tell ya what," Clayton said. "Since it's getting late in the day, how about you stay the night 'ere in Candyland? Then first thing in the morning I'll get someone out 'ere to repair this beautiful caddy of yours, and ya can be on ya way."

You ain't never getting out of Candyland now.

"I appreciate the offer, I really do, but I really have to be on my way. Perhaps there's a phone I can use?"

"As ya saw from your own mobile, we don't get much of a reception 'ere in Candyland. We only 'ave one phone, but unfortunately, my cousin Jacob has taken it with him outta town with him. He won't be back 'til late I'm afraid."

"I can wait, I don't mind hanging around until he gets back with the phone."

"Look, there ain't no phone and there ain't no garage." Clayton spat, his face twisting into a furious sneer.

Norton couldn't hide his shock this time, and thought that this was perhaps his first look at the *real* Clayton Candy. Candy, for his part, recovered quickly, and reverted to a wide, fixed grin, as he wiped at his sweaty face.

"What I mean to say is, we are just a small town, and we can't do much until morning. As soon as Jacob comes back, we can get ya on ya way."

Norton was growing angry, and the oppressive heat seemed to be fuelling his frustration.

"Are you sure you aren't trying to keep me here Mr Candy?"

Clayton's cheek twitched and he slid his eyes towards Herb, then back to Norton.

"Course not. Ya free to do whatever ya want to Mr Norton. As I said, if ya want to walk, Shadowlands is thirty miles back the way ya came. Next town in the opposite direction is Freeborough, but that's a good eighty miles. If ya do decide to walk, then I ave to advise ya to be careful after dark. Some of the local critters 'ere wouldn't think twice about setting upon a person if he was out there at night."

"Then it looks like I'm staying the night. Is there a motel here in Candyland?"

Clayton's mood changed instantly, and he reverted to grinning widely. "Excellent! I'm afraid we 'ave no motel 'ere, but you can spend the night at ma home. I'll 'ave ma daughter make up the guest bedroom for ya."

"Thank you," Norton said, his uneasy feeling growing by the second.

He glanced at Herb, who was staring at him, his eyes pleading a mixture of fear and horror. Clayton saw it too.

"Well, Mr Norton, why don't cha go ahead and enjoy the fete as best ya can. When it's all finished, we'll show ya to our 'ome. In the meantime, as soon as Jacob gets back, I'll have Herb 'ere get in touch with a mechanic from Shadowlands and get him out here first thing to fix up ya car. Ya should be outta here after breakfast."

Clayton moved to Herb's wheelchair and readied to push him away.

"Come on Herb, I'll take ya back to ya stall. Mr Norton, please enjoy the rest of the day."

Clayton left, taking Herb with him. Norton still couldn't shake the jittery feeling in his stomach, the feeling that told him that something was wrong with the entire situation. Like it or not, he was stranded there, and decided that although Clayton Candy was something of an oddball, he would still try as best he could to fit in, at least until he could put Candyland behind him.

For the rest of the afternoon, Norton grew more and more uneasy with Candyland. Outwardly, he made a show of enjoying himself, but inwardly he was ever desperate to leave. He started to notice little things, things that he probably wouldn't have without the warning words of both Herb and Christine, who were both nowhere to be found, despite him trying to seek them out to get more answers. He had touched on it earlier, but now as he looked closer, he noticed that pretty much everyone in Candyland looked freakishly similar. Not all of them of course, but most of those he had seen certainly resembled Clayton Candy to a disturbing degree.

Maybe that's why they keep staring. Because I look different.

Norton was starting to wonder just how much power Clayton had over the tiny town. Everyone he looked at had the same haunted eyes, the same sense of spirits being broken.

Although the fete was in full swing, Norton got the distinct impression that the townsfolk involved were just going through the motions. He half considered running for it, just getting out of town and taking his chances on the road, but he wasn't ready for that yet. There was every chance that the knot in his stomach could just be his own overactive imagination making more out of the situation than necessary.

One thing was for sure. He wasn't looking forward to staying at Clayton Candy's house. In fact, the idea filled him with dread. Either way, there was nothing he could do, and as the day drew to a close and the townsfolk started to head home, Clayton returned, along with his giant of a daughter and together the three of them made their way towards Candy's house.

Norton took a longing glance at his disabled car, wishing for the umpteenth time that he had never made the decision to stop at Candyland.

Clayton's house was on the far edge of town. It looked old and tired, its paintwork cracked, faded and in need of repair. The grass out front was sick and yellow. As far as Candyland homes went, it actually looked luxurious, but Norton saw it for what it was, a rundown ugly looking house.

"Come on in Mr Norton," Clayton said as he walked up the creaking porch steps. Norton followed and waited as Clayton opened the door.

"Come on in," Clayton said over his shoulder.

Even though every instinct screamed at him not to, Norton followed, waiting just over the threshold as his eyes adjusted to the gloom.

The inside of the house was quite unremarkable. Old fashioned for sure, but still clean and tidy, which was a pleasant surprise to Norton, who had expected worse. The house was set up for simple living. There was no television. In fact, He hadn't seen a single modern convenience at all during the tour of the house. The layout was simple, a modest kitchen and sitting room downstairs. Bathroom and three bedrooms upstairs. As he was shown around, Norton tried to gauge some kind of picture of who Clayton Candy was, but the house gave away no secrets. Everything was tidy, and even though the house had a dry, musty smell and showed some signs of age, the yellowed wallpaper and frayed carpets gave no indication of anything sinister.

Norton's guest room looked out over a vast expanse of open desert, and in the very distance, he could see the faint pencil line of the road, which was tantalisingly close. Clayton had told Norton to get some rest, and that supper would be ready at eight.

Alone for the first time, Norton had lay down on his bed, which creaked under protest, and closed his eyes, hoping to get a few hours' sleep.

He woke to the sound of hushed voices outside his room. The sun had sunk low in the sky, and it had elongated the shadows in Norton's room. As quietly as he could, he got up and crept to the door, placing an ear to the wood to try and better hear the heated conversation.

He could tell it was Clayton and his daughter, but what they were saying was inaudible. They were speaking in a near whisper themselves, and apart from the odd snatch of a word, he couldn't make it out. All he knew was that they were in a disagreement over something. Clayton's tone was sharp and demanding, Christine's was pleading and afraid. He half considered opening the door and making himself known, but wasn't afraid to admit that he was more than happy to go along with things as anonymously as possible as long as it meant he could save his own skin and get out of Candyland in one piece.

He was about to go back to his bed, content to let the Candy family argue it out amongst themselves when he heard something which changed the entire complexion of his stay. It was Clayton, and the three words he said to his daughter were clear and sharp, and no doubt a little louder than planned. Norton heard well enough, though, and that feeling of unease which had been niggling at him, became a full blown fear.

The three words hissed by Clayton to his daughter were a simple enough instruction, but one which raised even more questions about Clayton Candy and the town which bore his name, and it was then that Norton knew that if he wanted to leave Candyland again, then he would have to escape to do it.

Numb and unsure exactly what to do, Norton went to dinner at eight as instructed. Clayton sat at the head of the table, his chair oversized and higher than the others, probably to make up for his physical shortcomings. Norton didn't think he would be able to eat, but the meal served up by Christine was spectacular, to say the least. A delicious roast with all the trimmings. There was enough to feed a family of eight, and he piled his plate high, topping it off with delicious, thick gravy. The three of them ate in silence for a while, Norton very aware that Clayton was watching him with some amusement from the opposite end of the table.

"So, Mr Norton, whatcha think of Candyland?"

Norton took a moment to swallow his food and take a sip of water, ensuring he said the words in exactly the right way.

"It's a nice place. Quieter than I'm used to, but the hospitality shown to me is second to none. Thank you again."

"Ah, no need for thanks, that's what the people of Candyland do. We are a very close community, just one big family working together."

"Do you get many visitors from outside of town?"

"Not really. As I said earlier, we keep to ourselves pretty much. We don't bother the outside world and they don't bother us. We like it that way don't we precious?" He said, looking at Christine and smiling.

She didn't answer and looked down at her plate, which was piled high with enough food for two people.

"You'll have to forgive ma daughter Mr Norton, it seems she's taken something of a shine to ya."

He didn't know what to say to that, or to the hopeful glance thrown at him by both father and daughter Candy. As before he took a mouthful of potato, chewing slowly and sipped his drink, giving himself time to compose his thoughts.

"I'm flattered, really. But I'm not looking to get into any kind of a relationship right now."

He saw the hurt in Christine's eyes and felt bad. Clayton's expression remained neutral as he watched Norton eat.

"How old are ya Mr Norton, if ya don't mind me asking?" Clayton said, his piercing gaze doing a fine job of raising goosebumps on Norton's skin.

"I'm thirty six. Thirty seven next month."

"I see. I see no ring so I presume ya still unmarried following ya divorce. Do ya have anyone in ya life right now?"

Norton hesitated, not liking where the line of questioning was going.

"No, as I said, I'm happy enough to be single for the time being."

"But surely, ya ain't getting any younger. Don't ya feel the urge to settle down, find a good woman to live out the rest of ya days with?"

He didn't like this. Clayton was becoming pushy, and even at the best of times, Norton wasn't comfortable discussing his personal life with anyone.

"Not really, I have a busy life. I work hard, and don't feel ready to settle down."

He allowed his irritation to show, just enough to give Clayton the hint that he was uncomfortable, but Clayton went on regardless.

"Now I don't know about that, but ya seem to me like a man who would benefit from settling down with a good woman and maybe having a few kids whilst your seed is still good."

Although he was still afraid, his anger took control.

"Look, Mr Candy, I appreciate you putting me up and all, but I'm uncomfortable with this."

"With what?" Clayton said, feigning surprise.

"With this entire matchmaking thing. I'm happy as I am, and as much as she seems like a lovely person, I have no interest in settling down here in Candyland with your daughter or anyone else."

Christine's lip began to tremble, and she stood and hurried across the room, ornaments shaking as she hurried out of the room and upstairs. Norton knew he had gone too far, and he looked at Clayton, who was gritting his teeth and glaring at Norton with the purest and uncompromising fury he had ever seen. In fact, Clayton Candy looked about ready to explode.

"Excuse me a moment." He hissed, tossing his napkin down on his plate and following his daughter out of the room. He heard Clayton ascend the steps and attend to Christine, who was wailing loudly.

He made his decision then to leave. The entire situation was all wrong. And besides, he had heard those three words hissed by Candy to his daughter, and he didn't intend to stay around long enough for it to happen. He glanced to the kitchen door, knowing that beyond was the back door and freedom. He could get to the road if he went straight across the desert, and he was sure that neither of the Candy's was in any sort of physical shape to give chase. He got to his feet and hurried to the kitchen, pushing through the door.

His intention was to head straight outside, but what he saw froze him in his tracks.

Herb was in the kitchen. Or more accurately, what was left of Herb. His upper torso was on the counter, the lower half absent. The oven tray was on the kitchen table containing one of his legs, a huge chunk of the thigh missing which although he hated to acknowledge it, matched the joint that had just been served for dinner. He vomited, just managing to get his hand up to his mouth, but his recently consumed meal still spattered on the kitchen floor. He realised then what Clayton had meant when he said the people of Candyland were entirely self-sufficient.

They were cannibals.

He staggered across the room, those three words he had overheard earlier made him even more afraid than he already was.

Just kill him.

That's what Clayton had said, but whether it was meant to have been applied to him or a precursor of what happened to poor Herb, Norton wasn't about to stick around to find out. He charged across the room, almost slipping over in his own vomit, yanked open the door and charged down the porch steps. It was cooler now, and he ran, the exhilaration of feeling the air against his skin reminding him of being back on the road before Candyland even existed. He was moving across open land now, making for the road which was looming on the horizon. He looked behind, half expecting to see Clayton giving chase, but he was standing at his kitchen door, watching Norton run. He turned back to the task in hand. Keeping his eyes on the road and enjoying the physical exertion of running when his leg exploded in pain. He fell, screaming in agony, his calf feeling as if it were on fire.

The bear trap was locked in tight, its steel teeth embedded deeply into Norton's flesh. Blood welled up and then spilled over, turning the sandy earth dark as it flowed. He had never known pain like it, and with shaking hands he tried to pry the jaws open, but even just to touch it sent waves of hot agony racing through him. He couldn't move, and as he looked about him, he could see more of them. A minefield of bear traps set between Candy's house and the safety of the road, all hidden and partially buried under the loose earth.

You ain't never getting out of Candyland now.

Herb had been right. It seemed he knew well enough what happened in Candyland. Perhaps that's why he was in a wheelchair; perhaps he had tried to escape from Clayton and had paid for it with a broken back, and eventually his life. Norton gritted his teeth and tried to drag himself across the desert, but movement of any kind reignited the fire in his lower leg, and he was forced to give up, lying there helplessly and watching as Candy strolled across the desert towards him. He was whistling and smiling, sidestepping on occasion to avoid one of his hidden traps. His shadow fell across Norton, and he was grinning that same lion's grin, hands on hips as he breathed hard from the exertion.

"It didn't have to be this way, Mr Norton. I just wanted to make ma daughter happy. I know ya suspect what is happening here, but it ain't like that. I love ma children, all of them. And you will learn to love ma daughter Mr Norton. I can guarantee ya that."

"I just want to go home," Norton said, feeling light headed from the agonising pain in his leg.

"You are home," Clayton said with a sympathetic smile. "Ya will learn that eventually. They all do."

Norton blinked, the memories of that day still fresh in his head. His leathery hands worked the grill, making sure the meat was cooked. He had long ago stopped questioning where it came from and tried not to think about it when he ate it. His eldest son, Jed, walked over to him, asking if he needed any help. He shook his head, watching as the fifteen year old returned to looking after his brothers. Norton's other seven children frolicked and played. He wasn't convinced that they were all his. At least two of them looked like their grandfather, Clayton. But that was how things worked here in Candyland, and he had learned the hard way not to question it. He stood and stretched, watching as his wife, Christine waddled towards him, her weight now over four hundred pounds, and the years doing nothing to help her looks. Norton's youngest son was held against her flabby stomach, clinging to her dress and watching Norton with eyes which looked remarkably like Claytons. She was in charge now, and although Clayton was still alive, he was on his way out, and when that happened, he would return to the group. There were no funerals in Candyland because nothing went to waste.

He glanced down at his one good leg, then at the other, which was absent above the knee. That one was his own fault, he had tried to escape again, and that time when they caught him, they made sure he would never be able to try again. He set down his tongs, picked up his crutches and limped out of the green, moving towards the rusted shell of his Cadillac, as he always did on the anniversary of his arrival in Candyland, he then stared at the road, which cut across the horizon and looked open and full of possibilities for those who were free. Every time he saw a shimmer, a flash of metal reflected by sunlight, he prayed that whoever was driving paid no heed to the signs or the demanding way in which they were written, and drove past Candyland and onto wherever they were heading. Christine stood beside him, and linked her flabby arm through his thin one, and helped him back to the barbecue, back to his life in Candyland, which was now all that Bill Norton would ever know.

AUTHOR NOTES

I always used to like reading author notes in short story collections. I used to enjoy hearing a little bit about the thought process behind the stories and gain a little insight into the mind of the author. I wasn't sure if I was even going to include notes of my own. They had been in and out of the book in various forms during the editing process, which actually took a hell of a lot longer to do than I initially expected.

Even when I was young, I loved writing short stories. There is something about being able to leap straight into the meat of the story without waiting for two hundred pages for things to get going. Even though my first book, *Dark Corners* was a collection of short stories, they were interconnected, which meant that I wasn't afforded the kind of freedom to pretty much go and do what I wanted to in the same way as a regular collection of stories.

It was during the process of working on my first (and only at the time of this writing) feature length novel, *Whisper*, that I started to think about putting a new collection of shorts together. I had plenty of them kicking around in the archives, stories which I thought people might like to read. During the early stages of editing *Whisper*, I took a closer look at what I had.

Some stories had aged well, others, not so much. I put together a rough manuscript containing eighteen stories and gave it a name – Destination Nowhere. As edits to *Whisper* dragged on, I put it aside with every intention of coming back to it. Long story short, Whisper became a pain to edit, and I duly didn't come back to Destination Nowhere until February of 2013. With eyes well rested and fresh, I looked over the manuscript which I couldn't wait to get out to my readers…

And I hated it.

The problem was that, although the stories, which had seemed fine at the time of putting that first manuscript together, now looked less good in light of the fact that I had grown as a writer. Although it would have been easier (and, in hindsight, a lot less stressful) to just release it, I didn't want to do that. Firstly, because I didn't want to send out substandard work just for the hell of it, and second, because I wanted my reader to enjoy my work the way I enjoyed the short stories of my peers.

With much grumbling, I started to edit. Then cut out huge chunks of the various stories, then, inevitably, delete then in full. I trimmed the initial eighteen stories down to twelve, and the new edit became what I naively thought to be the final version of Funhouse. I set it aside again and dived into working on a new novel. It was sometime in May or June that I next looked at the manuscript, and found to my dismay that I still wasn't happy with it. The simple fact was that some of the older works, even after a thorough edit, just didn't hold up. I did what any self-respecting and slightly insane author would.

I started again.

I wrote new stories from scratch. Incidentally, one story and one alone has survived from that initial Destination Nowhere manuscript, and that one is Cabin Fever. Although it could be a bit long for a short story collection, there is something in there that I like, and like an underdog Sylvester Stallone in the Rocky movies, it always managed to avoid that knockout punch. Eventually, after what felt like an eternity of adding, removing, editing, deleting and rewriting, the book you have just read was pretty much in shape. Of course, by now you will know if you enjoyed it or not, and I sincerely hope you have. In the vein of those who came before me, I would like to take this opportunity to leave a few notes on each of the included stories for those interested in a little background info. For those who couldn't care less, I invite you to close the book here, and will say thanks again for reading. For those who share my nerdy desire to peek behind the curtain as it were, here are my own personal notes on the included tales.

Mr Ghoul's Quaint Little Ghost Train

I have to confess to not being the greatest fan of funfairs. I find them a little bit creepy. I like clowns even less, so decided in my infinite wisdom to write about them. I always saw Mr Ghoul a little bit like Captain Spaulding from Rob Zombie's, The Devils Rejects, and the idea that this timeless travelling circus moving from place to place and showing people their hidden past was a strong one which made for pretty interesting subject matter. At its most basic level, this story is about consequences of actions, and how one day they might just come back to bite you.

99.9am

Whenever a famous musician dies, I find it odd how the media always bring out the line about how they are now 'playing music in heaven'. That got me thinking about how this would play out if not only was this true, but if we could somehow tune into these heavenly broadcasts and listen in. That was literally all I had idea wise when I started writing the story, and just really let it take me where it wanted to go. I thought it came out as a pretty good story in the end, even if it might have all been a figment of poor Doyle's imagination.

The Eye

I like the idea that sometimes things can just happen for no real rhyme or reason. There are no real secrets in the world anymore, no surprises, and I'm not entirely sure that's a good thing or not. 'The Eye' is a story about a world that just may have a few secrets left to share.

Scarecrows

I have a friend who lives on the English coast. On the way to visit him in the summer of 2012, I happened to look out of the window as we drove past rolling fields and farmland, and saw what can best be described as scarecrow overkill. There must have been seven or eight scarecrows, an average of one per field of crops, and although we were past the bizarre scene in seconds, the imagery stuck with me. It wasn't until I was writing the new stuff for this collection that I dug that image out of my head and used it for the basis of Dwayne & Randy's story. This is actually one of my favorite stories in this collection.

H_NG__N

I was playing the game hangman with my daughter when I started to ask myself what it would be like to play the game for real with an actual person in the noose. So strong was that image, that I couldn't wait to write the story, and did it pretty much straight away, just going with the flow and letting the story shape itself and drag me along for the ride. I was pleased with the end result, and apart from a few minor changes, it has barely changed from its initial draft.

The Boy Who Saw Spiders

I will be the first to admit that I am deathly afraid of spiders. Even to see one skittering across the carpet freaks me out, and in the Bray household, it is my wife who is responsible for all spider based removals whilst I cower as far away as possible. I wanted to see if I could write a story that would make everyone as uncomfortable with arachnids as I was, and after some time thinking about what would be the absolute worst thing that could happen to a spider hater like me, the idea for 'The boy Who Saw Spiders' was born.

The Man In The Alley

I sometimes think about how the world has changed over the years. When I was younger, it seemed to be a much safer place to be. I had the idea that it would be interesting if people were born either inherently good or bad, and that in turn got me thinking about what sort of responsibility might fall upon someone who could see this in those people and how he might react. The idea for this story started to grow in my head and was written in a single sitting. I was really happy with the finished piece, and count it as one of my favorite stories.

Sick Day

I have often been intrigued by how little we actually know those people who we are close to in our lives. I explored it a little in 'That Gnawing Feeling' from Dark Corners, but I wanted to explore it further, particularly in regards to marriage. It's a strange commitment to make to someone, to promise yourself to them through sickness and health, rich or poor, until death etc. I asked myself what might happen if one half of such a union had a darkness in them which might render those values as moot, and how their spouse might react.

Jasper

This story was initially one never intended for publication. I was asked by a friend if I was able to write on spec about any specific subject matter given. I suggested that I felt confident that anything can be turned into a good story within reason, and was given the brief of composing something containing a mind reading bird. Undaunted, I started to write, and found that not only was the subject matter workable, it made for what I thought was a pretty good story. As with most of my work, there was no happy ending, although in the first draft there was – Jasper made it to the outside world. I always found that ending to be a little bit 'Hollywood' though, and so replaced it in the second draft with the bleaker finale you have here.

Tilly

It's surprising how many people think this story is a supernatural tale about haunted dolls. Although on the surface, it looks that way, this one is actually about the advances in technology as far as toys go. Even kids as young as four are pretty proficient at navigating touch screen tablets and phones etc, and that itself is pretty disturbing. I wanted to look at what might happen if some of this super advanced technology went wrong, and if the super advanced artificial intelligence suddenly became less than artificial and actually started to go into business for itself. You could argue that it's more sci fi than horror, but I like to think it strikes a happy medium between the two.

Long Tall Coffin

I have wanted to approach the subject of bullying for some time. There were a couple of stories in Dark Corners which touched on it, but I never had a story to really tackle the subject as head on as I would have liked, until *Long Tall Coffin.* Having been on the receiving end of the schoolyard bully on more than one occasion during my youth, this is a subject that is close to me, and I am happy to finally have the story out on paper.

50/50

As is often the case when I think about random things, the subject of freedom of choice came up. I asked myself what would happen if that freedom of choice to control your own destiny was taken from you, and how you might, given the circumstances, choose to give life one last try.

Cabin Fever

As I touched on earlier, *Cabin Fever* is both the oldest story in this collection, and also the only story to survive the very first draft of the book when it was called *Destination Nowhere*. The initial draft of the story was written in 2007, and was significantly longer than this edit. Although some might say that this version is still lengthy for a short story, I don't think it's too long, or at least I hope not. This is one of those stories that questions the difference between right and wrong, and when faced with a seemingly impossible decision, would you know what to do for the best?

The Langton Effect

This story was initially written for submission to a flash fiction anthology which had a strict 999 word limit. The story was rejected, and in hindsight it was with good reason, as I had to sacrifice much of the intended storyline to meet the word count. Here it is now restored to its original pre-chopped state, and is my tribute to the superb Rod Serling's Twilight zone type of story which were a great influence on me growing up.

The Trial Of Edwyn Greer

The literary world has become over-saturated with vampire stories. Most of them following the same rehashed plots. I wanted to approach the subject from a completely different angle and asked myself what might happen if a vampire, after years of murder and maiming, was somehow re-humanised. *The Trial Of Edwyn Greer* is my idea of how such a thing could possibly play out.

Candyland

I was watching a documentary about a Congo tribe that had lived undiscovered by modern man until they were stumbled upon by accident. The idea of a community with no knowledge or form of interaction with the outside world was incredibly intriguing, and I tried to figure out a way to bring that same kind of situation a little closer to home. I was speaking to a fellow author friend of mine from across the pond who told me that the Arizona desert was a pretty isolated place, and with that nugget of information, *Candyland* was born. Of all the stories included here, I think this is my favorite. I like it a lot, and hope you do too.

www.ingramcontent.com/pod-product-compliance
Lightning Source LLC
LaVergne TN
LVHW021047100526
838202LV00079B/4590
* 9 7 8 8 0 9 2 6 5 5 7 0 4 *